NEXT

Christine Brooke-Rose

VP Festschrift Series:

Volume 1: Christine Brooke-Rose
Volume 2: Gilbert Adair
Volume 3: The Syllabus
(Edited by G.N. Forester and M.J. Nicholls)

Reprint Titles:

The Languages of Love
The Sycamore Tree
The Dear Deceit
The Middlemen
Go When You See the Green Man Walking
Next
Xorandor/Verbivore
by Christine Brooke-Rose

Three Novels — Rosalyn Drexler
Knut — Tom Mallin
Erowina — Tom Mallin

other Verbivoracious titles @

www.verbivoraciouspress.org

NEXT

Christine Brooke-Rose

Verbivoracious Press

Glentrees, 13 Mt Sinai Lane, Singapore

This edition published in Great Britain & Singapore

by Verbivoracious Press

www.verbivoraciouspress.org

ISBN: 978-981-09-2168-2

Printed and bound in Great Britain & Singapore

First published in Great Britain by Carcanet (1998).

Wandering Rocks: An Introduction

BRIAN McHALE

Christine Brooke-Rose once wrote to set me straight about James Joyce. I had claimed in print that her novel *Such* parodied the "Circe" chapter of Joyce's *Ulysses*. No, Brooke-Rose informed me, that couldn't be the case, because at the time of writing *Such* (published in 1966) she had not yet read *Ulysses*. She was in those days, she explained, a Poundian, not a Joycean, and loyalty to one master (in the avant-garde sectarian politics of that era) precluded taking an interest in rival masters. But then she acknowledged generously that maybe I was right after all, since one can "read" a precursor without having actually read him. She says the same thing in an interview with Lorna Sage from around 1999: she resents being saddled with Joyce as a precursor "because I've never managed to read him through." But then she goes on to say, "influence is mysterious, and perhaps it's as Butor said somewhere, 'we're all influenced by Joyce, even if we've never read him.'"

Evidently she did finally get through Joyce, but too late for him to have influenced *Next* (1998) except, of course, in the "mysterious" way of which Butor speaks. Nevertheless, I'm going to claim here that *Next* is Brooke-Rose's version or rewrite of *Ulysses*. On the face of it, this is manifestly absurd. *Next* is a slight book, relatively modest in scope and ambition (though not in accomplishment, in my view), while *Ulysses* unmistakably aspires to be what it in fact became, *the* canonical modernist masterpiece. But *Next* is also, like *Ulysses*, a novel of (post)modern urban life in which characters circulate on foot and by public transport around the city (London here instead of Dublin), intersecting with each other, then parting, reacting continuously to the urban pleasures and perils that press in upon them. In particular, *Next* seems to me a version of Joyce's tenth chapter, which we know from authorized sources is called "Wandering Rocks," where Dubliners pursue their individual itineraries around the city, running across (and sometimes avoiding) each other, while the viceroy's cavalcade processes through their midst. "Wandering Rocks" has long been viewed as *Ulysses* in miniature, a sort of *mise-en-abyme* of the whole, so when I say that *Next* rewrites it, that's as much as saying that it rewrites the whole novel.

Granted, *Next* encompasses, not "a day in the life" (like *Ulysses*), let alone an hour in the life (like "Wandering Rocks"), but a week in the life—and not of two Dubliners, Bloom and Stephen, but of ten Londoners, all homeless, sleeping on the street when they can't doss for the night at a homeless shelter. Nevertheless, these characters, like Joyce's, are in constant motion, ambulatory ("We're all ambulant," says one of them). Their routes through London's districts and across its parks are frequently traced, with close (Joycean) attention to urban landmarks encountered en route: along the Edgeware Road toward Cricklewood first the Beacon Bingo Hall, then a Total petrol station, then Courts the furniture factory, a complex of cinemas, Peugeot, a Benetton hoarding, a Discount House, Blockbuster Video, an off-license, a Burger King, and so on. We move restlessly in the characters' company, piggybacking on one's consciousness and then lurching into another's, segueing without announcement from mind to mind. This is one of the connotations of the title: now one character, *next* a different one. It's sometimes hard to be sure whose mind we're in, and sometimes these minds themselves are hard to follow, wandering as they do from moment to moment, from here to there, from present to past. "I do stray a bit," says one character, "that's what wandering the street does to you." "Straying" and "wandering" here have a double sense: wandering the streets, wandering mentally. The character who says this, incidentally, is named Ulysses.

Like the Dublin of *Ulysses*, the London of *Next* is saturated with mass-mediated noise. Bloom in Joyce's Dublin is constantly repeating to himself and mulling over the language of signage, posters, advertisements, headlines, throwaway handbills—all the degraded verbal commercial detritus of a modernist-era city. The commercial noise pollution in *Next* streams from televisions, which are ubiquitous – "Telly on as usual," someone reflects, and that's true here of pubs, shelters, canteens. As in Don DeLillo's *White Noise*, tv language keeps leaking into the world of *Next*, forcing us from time to time to do a double-take when an utterance that we thought belonged to a here-and-now conversation proves actually to have come from the telly over in the corner. Two kinds of programming dominate: either news and current-events interview programs, where an anchor or interviewer imperiously declares, "Stay with us" for the segment coming up on the other side of the commercial break; or soap operas, supplemented by the "tv mags" that float through this novel, bringing us up-to-date with "The Story So Far" in the glamorous world of Derica and Brad and Doug and Cindy. Both types of program hinge on the experience of raw *nextness*—the next segment, the next talking head, the next plot-twist, *wait for it*—another connotation of the title. "**Next: Problem Talk-Out,** with Bernie Driscoll. But first we'll take a break. Stay with us." "NEXT! The End of the World Coming Up! But first, we'll take a Break. Stay With Us." "Where's the zapper?" somebody asks, impatient with all this aggressive *nextness*. Where indeed.

As with *Ulysses*, the realistic surface texture of *Next* is sustained by a formal armature of generative procedures and constraints, some of them more or less perceptible, others invisible—"structural secrets," as Fredric Jameson once called the Language poets' procedures. The structural secrets of *Ulysses* include crucially the system of analogues between the day in the life of Bloom and Stephen and the adventures of Odysseus, augmented by a whole ancillary schema of times of day, bodily organs, key symbols, arts or sciences, techniques, etc. ("Wandering Rocks," as it happens, is the only chapter of Joyce's novel that lacks a Homeric analogue.) The structural secrets of *Next* include various more or less submerged formal constraints like the lipograms that Brooke-Rose used in earlier novels since at least *Between* (1968), where the constraint she observed was, "Use no versions of the verb *to be*," appropriate for a novel whose protagonist *is* no-one and nowhere in particular but always *between* identities and places. In *Next* the constraint is, "Use no versions of the verb *to have*," appropriate for characters who possess nothing—literally *have-nots*. A supplemental constraint bars the pronoun *I* when characters are on their own (as they regularly are); they can think *I* only when they are in company with others.

These constraints are nearly imperceptible to the reader, I find, even when that reader is on the lookout for them, though they no doubt subliminally color our reading. More visible, however, is a generative procedure that the novel wears openly, even brazen, right on its face. The ten homeless characters in the novel correspond to the ten letters of the top line of a keyboard: QWERTYUIOP. They are named Quentin (called Croaky, for his hoarseness); Wally, the ex-butcher; Elsie; Ricky; Tek (short for Wojtek); Yuppy (nickname for a character with the unlikely given name of Jesse James); Ulysses (surnamed Grant); Ivy; Oliver; and Paula (called Pavlova, because she is an ex-dancer). The name-games extend to nicknames: Wally, Yuppy, Ully, Ivy, Olly. (Other characters—the ones with homes to go to—evidently correspond to the other sixteen letters of the alphabet, though I can't fully confirm this aspect of the system; my inventory of the characters seems to fall a couple of letters shy of a complete alphabet.) In case you don't notice the alphabetical system of naming right away, various characters play variations of an alphabet game, foregrounding the system. Elsie recites a "Cockney alphabet": "A fer 'orses, B fer mutton, C fer yerself . . . D fer lution E fer lution F fer vesce . . . L for leather, M for sis, N for lope," and so on. (Read it out loud.) Tek, gloomy and apocalyptic, counters with "the century's alphabête," a list of twentieth-century atrocities in alphabetical order: "A for Auschwitz. B for Belsen. C for Cambodia. D for Dresden . . . E for . . . Ethnic Cleansing"—obviously, he won't run out of possibilities. Humoring Elsie, Tek at one point collaborates with her on a alphabetical list of dances—A for allemande, B for bourrée, bellydance, boggie woogie, bolero, C for Charleston, chaconne, contredanse, courante, cakewalk—but can't stay on task and slips back into his atrocity alphabet: "D for Dance of Death." "We don't seem to speak the same language," says upbeat Elsie. "Not surprising," replies Tek. "The alphabets are different."

Ulysses, as everyone knows, entailed a massive labor of research and reconstruction. Joyce drew on his memories, but also on informants back home in Dublin—and, in the case of "Wandering Rocks," on street-maps and a stopwatch—to construct a simulacrum of Dublin in 1904, from the distance of Zürich-Trieste-Paris and the period 1914-1920. The resulting document, he liked to boast, could be used as a blueprint for rebuilding Dublin from scratch if it were ever destroyed. *Next,* too, gives a similar sense of in-depth street-level knowledge of *its* city, London, and the lives of those who use its threadbare social services and sleep rough when the latter fail them. In particular, *Next* seems deeply knowledgeable about the *languages,* the multiple Englishes, spoken on the streets of that city in the 1990s. Brooke-Rose is attuned to the *registers* of London English, its professional and occupational varieties, especially those newly emergent or undergoing transformation in that decade: stockmarket English, hightech and hacker English, admin English. "All institutions develop their own jargon against the public they're supposed to serve," observes Ulysses (Ully), who then goes on to cite medicine, law, insurance and architecture as prime offenders.

More impressive than her ear for professional jargons, however, is Brooke-Rose's astonishingly fine-grained representation here of the degrees and varieties of "Estuary" English, the London vernacular—what used to be called, disparagingly, "Cockney," but which has by the '90s (if *Next* is to be believed) emerged as the standard local dialect of the city. Some of her characters (Ully, Olly) still preserve the Received Pronunciation they acquired at school and university; others (Elsie) can shift freely between RP and Estuary English. ("Silly," Elsie scolds Croaky, "there's two Englishes, dinn yer knaow, wahn fer beyin yerself an wahn fer work.") Londoners who once belonged to the managerial class, but lost their economic footing in the high-tech transformation of the workplace—there are several in *Next* who fit this description—speak generally standard English with only occasional Estuary diphthongs. Working-class Londoners like Ivy, however, speak wall-to-wall Estuarian:

> Yer neeydn be galant, Croakey. Ah'm wie paas tha'. Sixty-fahve laas birthdie. Aonly son killed in Belfast iyteeyn years agao, fahv years widaowed with much relieyf but nao provision. Aonly the meeysley aold-ige pension. Aow Ah did work for a bi', servin at Tom the grocer's, an then cleeynin jobs on the QT bu' thn i' cudn last, an the pension waon pie the rent will i', le' alaone the lah' an 'eayt an the foowd. Streey's rent-freey an lah'-freey, there's aonley the caold's a problem at nah', specialley in winter. (p118)

One of the pleasures of *Next* is puzzling out passages like this one. I find that reading them out loud helps, but even then they playfully resist complete translation. The passage above, normalized, would read something like "You needn't be gallant, Croaky. I'm way past that. Sixty-five last birthday. Only son killed in Belfast eighteen years ago," and so on; I leave the rest to you. One of the payoffs of this somewhat impeded reading is belatedly getting the jokes—another form of double-take: "Five years widowed with much relief but no provision." Funny!

The plausibility of Brooke-Rose's realism here—not just at the linguistic level, but at the level of her image of the material city, its streets and parks and businesses and amenities—prompts me to wonder, how did she do it? We know how Joyce "did" Dublin—with informants and street-maps and stopwatches and vivid memories—but how did Brooke-Rose "do" London of the *fin-de-millennium*? She once knew the city well, but I wonder when she had visited it last. By the time of writing *Next* she hadn't lived there for decades, and was surely in no condition, in her infirm seventies, living in the south of France, to undertake the kind of participant-observer research that her novel seems to demand. She certainly wasn't immersing herself in the experience of people like the characters in her novel by sleeping rough with them. The insider's knowledge of that kind of life—or the appearance of it—can't have been achieved in the way that, say, Orwell achieved it in *Down and Out in Paris and London*, by actually *living* that way. How did she produce the astonishing illusion of knowing the city and its people, especially its down-and-outers, so intimately, at that geographical and experiential distance?

A novelist's imagination, it goes without saying. But apart from that, my best guess is that she exploited the same channels of information that saturate her novel and bombard its characters: electronic media, television and radio, the internet. This novel, every bit as much as its predecessors, the "Intercom Quartet" of *Amalgamemon* (1984), *Xorandor* (1986), *Verbivore* (1990) and *Textermination* (1991), is both a product of and a reflection on the experience of electronic interconnectedness. The world that sluiced through the airwaves and cable to her house in Provence is both the source of *Next* and an object of its representation and reflection. It's there, I suppose—on the air, onscreen and online—that she observed "Estuarian" and learned to distinguish its varieties, and there that she reacquired her expertise in the (post)modern London cityscape. I don't know whether one could use *Next* as a blueprint for reconstructing London, as Joyce claimed you could use *Ulysses* to reconstruct Dublin, but you could surely use it to reconstruct the *mediascape* where the novel's story-world and Brooke-Rose's everyday reality overlapped and coincided.

Karen Lawrence, who wrote the book on Brooke-Rose (literally), finds almost nothing to say about *Next*. Her authority for neglecting it is Brooke-Rose herself, who went on record as dismissing the book: it was, she said, her "least original in terms of subject matter" and her most off-putting because of its Cockney transcriptions. With respect, and with some trepidation, I beg to differ with both her and Karen Lawrence. I think *Next* marks a distinct revival of Brooke-Rose's somewhat flagging imagination, which had become (to my taste) a little attenuated in the last two novels of the Intercom Quartet. Or, put it another way: *Next* forms a necessary bridge between Brooke-Rose's fine and moving autobiographical narrative, *Remake* (1996), and her last two novels, *Subscript* (1999) and

Life, End of (2006). *Next's* place in this sequence allows us to think of Brooke-Rose's last four novels as constituting yet another quartet, a final one, complementing her earlier quartet of *Out, Such, Between* and *Thru* and her mid-career Intercom novels—a quartet of beginnings and endings, for herself as a person and a writer and for all of us as a species, with *Next* as an indispensable, load-bearing middle.

Would Brooke-Rose herself agree, if she were still with us? Maybe not. I regret that she cannot write to set me straight again.

Brian McHale, The Ohio State University

The Story So Far: Derica, long married to oilman Brad, ran his ranch for years and reared the twins Rex and Regina, but could not ever conceal her strong love for Trix, born of an old affair with Jesse, business rival to ried to Tina, but Doug, a new friend who now fascinates strongly attracts Brad and later mar- now pursuing Gina. of Rex, brings Cindy, Brad, while Gina Doug, but is herself too powerfully involved with Rick who now helps Derica manage the estate. After a violent scene with Sal, Derica asks Dan to intervene with Bradley.

The square arch under the descending motorway, growing like a tree inside a fenced circle of tired grass, was nevertheless too high, and let the night rain slant down seeping across the carton slept on, save for a nar- row strip down the middle and a round spot on the TV mag containing The Story So Far used as a pillow over the plastic bag, forming an ima- gined dry man, a stick and a spot. But the woolly damp of the red balaclava chills the cranium, as when a child wakes to a wet warm bed that rapidly cools to iciness. Un- der closed eyelids floats the dim awareness of the washtub-drubbing trucks overhead that grunged the short night's sleep. Stiffened as a coffin lid, one live corpse rising from granite, sitting up against the concrete column peering at the pinkish grey drizzle which turns the square arches in the ac- cess-complex of the motor- way into an ancient film dazed across with the constant white beams, and the over- headtrucks into a loud mech- anical projector, somewhere behind the brain. A crisis of horns and brakescreams from above scatters the mental furniture what was it, the happy rich unhappy in their high bourgeois tizzies.

The garbage mag now freed from headweight soggily flaps, feebly ges-

ticulating like
   a slave
         too vlase to run away
   a refugee
         too guferee to go back
   a citizen
         too zenitic to protest

MEN BORN EQUAL. *Natus sum*, giving rise to *natio*, but the Declaration forgot that a slave is not a national, that a refugee, like a dropout, ceases to be a citizen.

The infra-orange rectangles of highpressure sodium splay their flow-charts in fuzzy logic upwards and away like the internet nexus of a giant brain in open surgery, or stepstone straight off in diminishing pink icons up the Edgware Road.

It used to be ultra-orange, lowpressure sodium, that morphed faces into cadaverous grey-green clams. Presumably people complained, unable to accept themselves as they would become. If you wait long enough, without bothering to march or write furious letters to the papers, horrors do go away. But only with trivia.

The trucklights throng white through the drizzle, dazzle, then slant off, then more.

The alienated cold wet fingers unclip one plastic button in the closure-bar of the plastic bag to make the smallest opening against the rain, thrust through it fumbling among the disconnected pieces of a dry second self inside it, the rough synthetic of a dirt-stiff sweater, the thick rigidity of rolled-up jeans, the creased teeshirt, the acrylic socks and the strangled sneakers, the Montaigne unread for months, at last finding the plastic-wrapped piece of bread and the tin with the two cigarettes and the lighter. The plastic bag is snapped shut again. Then, munching the papery meal, the best moment of the day,

   breakfast

     in

       BED

with no wife to bring it and cheerily talk

reading

 the morning paper

watching

 the telefilm drizzle

 though it isn't morning yet and the paper is an old TV mag

 of vertiginous virtual.

Then the first puff

 that tickles alive

  that itchy throat

  gravelling to a cough

  tearing the lungs

Where's Croaky for petessake?

After a violent scene with Sal, Derika turns to Dan, asking him to intervene with Brad, who is blackmailing Rick to kill Doug. Dan complies but Rex overhears their conversation and accuses Derika of scheming in favour of Trix and Cab. Cindy discovers she is pregnant.

No lumpish proles only lumpen bourgeoisie, a dream and

by a sleep to say we knit up another worldwideweb, another

half-hour maybe?

  The century's alphabête, that usually does it despite

  traffic.

A for Auschwitz. B for Belsen. C for Cambodia.

 D for Dresden. For Deportation. E for Ethiopia, for

 Ethnic Cleansing . . . F for, What's F?

Famine . . . Mao's Great Leap into, 1959. Stalin's ditto,

Ukraine 1933.

 Fundamentalism. There's usually more than one horror

for each letter.

F for Fire! Cease! Fire! Cease! Fire! Peace! Process! Peace! Protest!

Ello ello ello what's this? Pack up that trash and

move along now.

But the old film bobby's dead, now called fuzz or filth or

crap,

though trash it all is,

get up and go before the modern ones drive up

in their clean white cars streaked blood red

and blue.

Funny how peace-brokers of broken peaces are all failed

politicians.

As are Eurocommissioners and Euromps.

The muscle-aches restructure upwards and trudge off,

combat boots squelch through the grass inside the fenced off

circle, leaving the TV mag at the foot of the motorway-tree as a

polluting tourist would, then squelch back to pick it up,

leaving the wet carton, and away again to clamber over a

concrete stake in the round fence, tip of boot on a hole in the

wire,

jayshuffling

through the

thundering trucks into

the Edgware Road towards Cricklewood and the mileoff public

lavatory for a bit of a wash and shave and a change into dry

clothes at least below the scratched bomber jacket of brown

leatherlook that kept the uppers dry, the combat boots slurping through sewery puddles.

The road goes up a bit, over a railway bridge, then down.

The Beacon Bingo Hall so garish red and blue last night

now extinct. A Total petrol station, lit up, as is

Courts the furniture factory below the road on the left,

among a complex of cinemas.

Peugeot to the right. And an old horrorcore ad from

Benetton, and now

low dark brick housing, a Discount House,

Blockbuster Video, an off-licence, a Burger King,

The champions of reengineering, its workers paid only

according to threshold-crossing customers though who eats

beef nowadays serves them right;

such is the empty orangey cityscape to walk through at dawn.

Originally villages, Kilburn, Cricklewood, Brent,

Stonegrove, Edgware.

Then the Council Estates, with their curtained or

uncurtained pink-glinting windows,

crossword buildings at odd angles

like statistical graphics.

The Cricklewood Lodge Hotel, who stays there

in this dingy district 7

This is an Indian area.

And now low dark rowhouses again, above low

shops, estate agents, sweetshops, wineshops, why?

The Wishing Well, tiny pub for tiny wishes,

McDonald's for soggier desires,

then downwards again towards the rounded black arch of

the railway bridge like an ancient citygate, Kilburn

Underground Station.

Ah, a tall plastic brown garbage bin, return the soaked

TV mag to its origins.

Recently emptied.

At the bottom, a huge soggy headline

JAP APOLOGY AT LAST!

Several silly seasons ago, the paper lying there ever since.

That heavy heatwave, nothing to interest anyone

except peace processes

and the weather

so they zoomed it up, is it an official apol or merely

a personal

remorse, regret, recognition?

How the world insisted. Here's the public waterloo. Down the steps.

As if those responsible for human miseries ever admitted

past wrongs.

Then each bit of world would apologize, for the Slave

Trade, the Boer War, the Black Hole of Calcutta, the Great Trek,

the Armenian Genocide, the Napoleonic Wars, the Norman

Conquest, the Conquest of Ireland, the Islamic Invasion, the

Saxon Invasions, the Inquisition, the plundering of Peru, the

Indian genocide, the Gulag, Greater Portugal, Greater Britain,

Greater Holland, Greater France, Greater Russia, Greater
America, Greater Japan, Greater Germany, Greater Israel, Syria,
Serbia and all the rest.

Suppose the Nazis lost that election? The century's whole
history would be different.

And no example given to Japan to go beyond the
Chinese War into South East Asia. Though it did hasten
decolonisation.

Or imagine the infant State of Israel turning to the
inhabitants of Palestine and saying The Turks are long gone
and now the British. We too suffered. Help us build a land
of milk and honey out of the desert, we'll share it with you,
the water, the power, the shrines, the spirit of God.

Or the Europeans to the native Americans and
Australians.

Suppose no empires and their violent legacies, Africa left
African, India Indian, the Americas wholly Aztec, Mayan, Inca,
Apache, Iroquois, Navajo, Huron and the rest, discovered long
after the late discovery of humanitarianism as virtual substitute
for politics.

No nukes, no pollution of land sea air, no planned
planetary death.

Oh but the ifs of history.

One phrase common to non-European histories,

Asia, Australasia, America, Africa:

'Then the Europeans came'.

The worst predators they ever knew.

The wet corduroys and the soppy socks are stuffed into the

plastic bag

   like unresolved problems to steam dry.

  One last grey-eyed look at a haggard, scumblond reflection

  then up the steps

and out on the long trudge along the endless Edgware Road

  become Kilburn High Street, an Irish area,

    low black houses, junk shops, sweetshops again,

    Safeway, Bank of Ireland,

    Granada, State Kilburn Bingo,

      McGoverns Free House, fish and chips,

     another railway bridge, Elf, Sunrise Food Mart,

and, in the distance, the Drop-Out Centre.

      Centre for marginals. As if periphs could be in a centre.

      Like Homeless Persons Unit, HPU.

    And why are the excluded said to live in inner cities?

Maybe Croaky'll be there.

The streetlight is still sodium pink, spore-swirling with rain.

      Human bundles in doorways

    blissed-out junkies or rough sleepers, in foetus position,

      one or two in lucky brown blankets, young mostly,

      very young.

  This is new. Most of them crowd the Embankment

    or WC2 theatreland, bright lights, people, Shaftesbury,

    the Strand.

Or Waterloo, where the mentally ill forgather, turned out of

homes closed in favour of

A Return to Community Care.

Were they deported, expelled? Or did they choose this as a

quieter, crime-free area?

But it suits the government to leave them there, as a

warning.

For Self-Reliance.

Virtue is the business of the Universe. Said Emerson.

In fact they're slowly training us to avoid the

Millennium Festival area.

Drop-outs mustn't be visible.

Street strewn with soaked papers, fag packets, beercans,

broken glass.

More glinting metal cars now as well as trucks, though it's

only five-thirty on some jeweller's clock, taking advantage

to move fast with long sniffs and blurps.

A few Indians early opening up their shops, food,

clothes, or whatever.

There'll already be a queue at the Drop-Out Centre. Not for

sleeping of course, those are the other end of town and run by

thugs for thugs, those in charge become thugs.

Just hot tea and bangers and bread, the charity's equiv of

Big Macs, still stuck in the Second World War

and long tables

and in the back the recess with the loos and washstands,

three washing-machines and three drying cupboards.

Sharing, instead of ejections and state terrorism against terrorism and double standards of development and illegal settlements against the peace process peace protest cease! fire! cease!

And on, feet aching already and legs painfully destiffening.

Queue not bad, first batch all gone in. Q for T. High up on the dividing wall a dead television, which flickers up suddenly for ads before Daybreak News. Shabby jackets and coats already cling to three coathangers like preying mantles, or to the one radiator along the sidewall. Most drop-outs don't change clothes and hope to dry out by just staying a while, so the room's already getting steamy, ah, there's Croaky.

Small and lean and swarthy and smiling, under the backworn baseball cap that pudding-basins off the auburn hair, with the wide black elastic bar across the brow, eating sausages in a purple teeshirt logoed **HARVARD UNIVERSITY** as a yellow arch, the green and cyclamen anorak hanging on the back of the chair at the head of a long table.

Hi Croaky.

Hi Tek. G for a drink.

T for two. Where were you?

Caosy pad up the raoad, deeyp doorway with a porch. Slept well?

No.

Grumpy aole Tek, as usual.

I sit on the end of the bench beside him, the other dropouts shuffling down snuffily. The tea scalds that scolding mood to silence and sausages and more, the mood melts and finds me, Tek, half a name down from an older generation elsewhere.

A West Indian girl in a wet black rabbity fur and wet black hair stands next to Croaky mie Ah? Not much of that may I around these days. And a lanky one-earringed one-nostril-beaded boy crouched over food, in a once swanky now blackened sheepskin jacket as if he didn't want to leave it around but open on a shiny black shell-suit, with putty-coloured face and hair, shoves everyone along too.

Cheers mi'e.

She discards her wet fur onto the edge of the bench, emerging in a malesize teeshirt labelled **Innocent Bystander** in black on a splashed red and white design like blood on flesh, offwhite really and stained, over blue jeans darkwet from the knees down that disappear under the table as she sits. The fur crumples its edges on the floor and oozes puddles.

Craowded inni, can' even ear the telley.

No response above the environmental clatter.

No' tha' there's ever anythink on the telley, stiuw, ah lahk ter watch the world ah doow, can' see i' reely in the streey'.

Wha' fooar? the sheepskin asks. Putty hair bristles like a Simpson.

Ah lahk the ads, thy's ever sao machao.

No take-up, no demand for examples.

No' tha' thy knaows i', or cares if thy doow.

No feedback.

The putty boy says. Ah aonly watch the business neuws.

An every tahm i' says NEXT, an wha' bi' of world's camin ap, yer ge's Bu' first wey'll tike a brike. An the brike's ever so long, the ads, then the praomaoclips, then more ads, then an infomercial, then more praomao-clips. Jes lahk lahf inni? But ah can' ear from ere, there's too much baow-mond in the wie. Wha' was yer before?

Croaky coughs. I sip tea. The putty boy says Ah lahk i' when Footsie come on and Nikkei and Hang Seng and Dax an Cac an Daow.

Wha' are thaose then, Jap videaonasteys fer kids?

The boy looks offended.

Nime's Euwsey. Ah was a workin mum, then thy was tiken from mey, then ah loss me work. Ere, this was mey.

She takes a crumpled coloured photomat from the tum slitpocket of her jeans and thrusts it at me to pass round. A pretty half-caste with dark curly hair but a popeyed criminal look from the flash. Now the brown face is grey with fatigue, like a black-and-white.

Ah lahk ter carrey i' on tum, ter remahnd mey of aow Ah useter bey.

Croaky stares in disbelief at the small square of nostalgic need for past identity. The putty boy barely glances at it before handing it back.

Ah was in aitek yer knaow, wiv a cumpyew'ah. Bu' there was toow many of us thassa fac'.

Aow, says the putty boy.

The shrinking repugnance rarifies behind that berlinwall that crumbles. Croaky warns me off with a frowning glare or is it a glaring frown but do you really mean hitech or just typing?

Well, thass coowl Ah musseye. Yer can't tahpe a' a screyn withou' yer knaows somethink abou' wha' gaoes on beyahnd.

But

She stares,

Oh yer meeyn the grammar.

Well.

The putty boy giggles.

Yer meeyn Ah daon' talk proper lahk yoow.

I only said But and Well.

Weuw bu' Ah c'n teuw. Silley, there's two Englishes, dinn yer knaow, wahn fer beyin yerselfan wahn fer work. Bu' anywise it was maossly fig-ures in raows and raows, nao grammar in figures, yer knaow nothink abou' i' mister. Whass the nime?

Tek.

Thass no' a nime.

It is. I was in Hitech too.

Yer meeyn? Lumme they're droppin us orf lahk dogshi'.

This is Croaky by the way.

Pleeysed to meey' yer Craoakey.

Hi Elsie. We'd better gao Tek.

Wha' doow thy cauwyer, li"e boay?

Oow yer cauwlin li"e boay? He sits up and suddenly looks tall not just lanky. Ah was in the Ci'y.

A heron boy?

Nao! A star-trider! Ah mide a fuckin forchoown, then Ah fuckin baounced.

Aow! A yuppey! A gaolden boy. Pleeysed to meey' yer Yuppey, never me' wahn o' tha' lo' before. Sao yer was rich? Ear tha' Tek? Ee was rich. So wah couldn' yer ge' i' back?

Sno' sao eeysy lahk. Ah mide mistikes and loss truss.

I made a mistake too, I join in, friendly at last.

Yer meeyn talkin ter mey?

No, a technical error.

C'mon Tek.

Yer never! Ah did tha', many tahms. Couldn't ge' back inter the praogram seey, i' kept ge"in locked in beyahnd a herrorwinder, nao access i' says, shared herror i' says, an lo's of figures an bars an le"ers, shared with oo ah'd lahk ter knaow. Mide the technicians cam. An after threey tahms thy faound thir'ey ai' elements damaged, bu' Ah go' blimed jus the sime. The world's stiuw a stag-party inni', sor' of stagflaition.

She doesn't mention race. I was a soldier, I join in.

Yuppy giggles again.

Cmon Tek, wey can't stay here for ever look at the queue.

I must go and dry the night's wet things.

Shit, why didn' you do that earlier? I did it while I ayt.

Forgot. The welcome sight of you Croaky. What's the hurry anyway? No office hours you know.

Elsie cackles as the soaked stuff comes out of the plastic bag.

Bring back those in the corner cupboard, will you.

How'll I know them?

Cmon Tek, you knaow them, greeyn UCLA windcheeyter, orange pants black jeeyns yellaow sweater and socks, white nikes, well, grey with red laces.

I follow him eyewise as he sneakers off up the room between the long tables, holding the wet bundle up high and leaving the plastic bag on the bench.

Cor, wha' didee doow?

Complicated

Aow gaowon.

You mussn' encourage him Elsie, he should forget it.

From the sublimated to the meticulous.

I look over the cup then put it down. She's suddenly talking proper as she called it, as everyone still calls it, and being quite witty with it. But a bit too pat, as if used to bringing it out. I don't know what to say. I roll a cigarette and light up.

Yuppy's embarrassed too, or flummoxed, out of it.

Yeah, weuw, Ah'll bey shovin orf, tara.

I nod, he's immensely tall now and drifts away, she nods, but quickly looks back at me, curling on the bench like a question mark.

Friendly fire.

Saounds nahce and caowsey.

Nao. He was detached to the Americans in the Gulf War, to learn their super-instruments. But thaose are naow more sophisticated than their operators, and they shot down several British planes by mistake.

Cor. Lahk aown-gaolin.

Called friendly fire. Cauwsed an embarrassment at the time, but we're always caowed by the Yanks. Nao explanations to families, top brass just disciplines and disaowns.

Accountable but not guilty.

Surprised again, I stare into her small dark eyes, pouched with fatigue.

Oh I know you lot. You think because I like to relapse into native speech I'm an idiot. But how else can I talk in a place like

Nao, nao, I was just taken aback at the double game. I aonly talk middling proper meself. But what dyer meeyn, native, you're West Indian aren't you?

Dad was, but married ere.

Anyway, all that's changed, long agao, dinn' you hear, we're a classless society naow, look, even the weathergirl's quacking out her troughs of laow pressure in the broadest Cockney. Aow daon bristle, Elsie, it was ajaoke, you look like her toyclouds with little lines packing out of them just like a hedgehog.

Or very like a weasel. But whassee go' ter doow wiv i'? Tha' friendley fahyer Ah meeyn.

Nothing. He just happened to be there, watching, learning.

Or sao ee says.

Nao. I was there with him. The Americans wouldn't — well anyway, he somehaow identified with it afterwards and got convinced he was at the controls.

And 'e was chacked ou' for tha'?

Nao, not eyven. Naobody knew. But he got out. We baoth got out, well, deserted, you can' get out of the army just like that. Then it was tough. We couldn't present anteceydents, as they say, and eyven if we could they daon't like saoldiers off the daole queue for life coming back on.

Oree was upse' an couldn't things the wie thy are naow?

It wasn't, well, but in a way you're right, Elsie, infotech was all the thing and too many youngsters like you were encouraged to rush into it, when the whaole point of it is to economise peoyple. It's not aonly the manual workers naow it's everyone, middle managers, even managers and directors, with firms gaoing bust or swallowed up in mergers and multinationals, big is beautiful sao slim daown, and cheeyp labour the other side of the world, and naow it's the other way raound, firms daon pay saocial charges on temps an laow wages seey, sao make everyone temp an laow, nao minimum wage naow, and with saocial protection gone at that level we're the world's sweatshop naow and the big bosses from Japan and Taiwan all come here for cheeyp labour. An eeyven educated students, they're recruited as unpayed gaofers in glam enterprises to save on

Whass the m"er Craoaky?

Shit, you got me into useless talk. You knaow, when there were still frantiers inside Europe the wife used to examine the customs official and if he waved us through with his hand she'd say ah, he's a manual, and if he nodded us through sideways with his head she'd say ah, he's an intellectual. Made the kids screeym with laughter.

And mey! Brill. Sao you're married?

Here he comes, keep quiet on all I've said Elsie pleeyse.

Hi Tek.

The joke is stale, but from her, sounds new.

Here you are, Croaky, better check it.

Cheers. Is it all dry?

Yes. Cupboards nice and hot today. I'm going to get another cup of tea.

Nao, cmon Tek, we muss gao.

Anyone wanna cuppa? Elsie? It's free.

Daon mahnd if Ah doow. Ah'll come up withyer and brink one for Craokey.

Who croaks into a cough and stubs the cigarette in the tea mug.

Is ee ill? Whah's ee wanna leeyve? Thy daon' thraow us ou' doow thy?

Well later, to clean up before lunch, or in the dead of winter when it gets very crowded. November's wet, but mild usually.

Cauw i' moild! Ah was proper fraoze.

Where did you sleep?

In the tyuwbe.

But

Aow Ah ahdes in a bi' o' mergency stairs at claosin tahm. But thy faound mey a' fahve and threuw mey ou' so Ah sa' in a doorwie.

Three teas please. I'm sorry if I sounded

Aow never yoow mahnd, daon' tike on saow.

Yes I do a bit. I get so angry.

It's ard Tek, but Ah lahks the freeydom, daon' yoow after the army?

The? Was Croaky talking?

Yer said yer was a soldier.

Oh, yes. Regular databank you are.

She snorts, takes two of the mugs. We sit down with Croaky who accepts a mug from her with a muttered Cheers mate and lights up again.

Yer ough'er seey to tha' corf, Craoakey, daon i' keeyp yer awike a' nah's?

Out comes the little tin from the trouser-pocket. Can't offer you one Elsie, it's the last one.

Aow Ah daon' thanks, Ah stopped. On zoowbs.

Mind if I do?

Cor, goa'ead. When Ah can' sleeyp Ah teuw meself an aole alphabe' mum taugh' mey.

An alphabet? Why —

A fer 'orses, B fer mutton, C fer yerself. But Ah loss some ere an there, can' remember haitch. Haige fer the yang? Doan' saound rah' do i'? Dyer appen to knaow i'? D fer lution E fer lution F fer vesce ah lahk tha' one.

G for a drink.

Srah', Craoakey, so yer knaow i'?

G for Genocide, H for Hiroshima.

Ey, whass tha', anather wahn? Bu' i' ain' fanny.

No, a private alphabestial bestiary.

Stop it, Tek.

Can yer fill the aoles, Craoakey? Ah loss J toow, an R. Did yer mum teeych i' yer?

Nao to baoth questions. Cmon, Tek.

Half a mo, I

R fer mao! Thass i'!

want to talk to Elsie. Why don't you move on if you're so keen and I'll find you somewhere? Or here tomorrow?

Whatever next!

NEXT! The End of the World Coming Up! But first, we'll take a Break. Stay With Us.

Astonished at her sudden Received Pronunciation. Just another dialect but Received, by whom, by the receivers and deceivers ever, the dialect that won. Eyes meet. Her black stragglers are dry now and curling round her thin avid face, more like the photograph. Croaky intercepts, okay see you. After the break.

Why I do believe he's jealous of me. Yes Tek, I told you, two Englishes. Picked up the posh stuff at college. But I like to relapse. Especially now. And here.

College?

Three A-Levels including English so there, then Business School and more English but mostly computer science. Fat lot of use. And you?

Oh, much the same, Reading University, History. End of.

And then?

Let's not exchange life-stories Elsie, let's just walk. Er, the rain's letting up. Why didn't you dry the coat?

Oh it dried enough. Might get gypped you know. It 's a protection, an aparthide.

Where do you want to walk, Elsie? Gladstone Park's the nearest.

No. I like Hyde Park best. I know it's far but we're used to it aren't we? Oh look, there's a discussion coming up with worlds twirling as glass globes, shall we stay and watch?

Globes empty as the discussing heads. In-depth coverage they call it.

Oh, it's only a promoclip, what did I tell you.

Well, it's getting very steamy here.

With lumpish proles?

Eh?

A funfair of strumpets, hobbledehoy polloi. Even I know you mustn't say *the* hoi polloi since hoi's already *the*. Don't you like wordgames Tek? I can do them for ever, cheers me up, and what's there left when language becomes meaningless? Liberty Equality Fraternity Democracy Socialism Liberalism. Six Words in Search of a Referent.

Oh Elsie, I think we're going to get on.

But we'll take a break.

And then an infomercial.

And then another promoclip.

And then more ads.

Just as she said.

Unisex
creature
mullet haircut
jewelled dark eyewear
mouthing
black
bald
mike
finger-hugged
like a penis
NEXT WEEK
man rubbing hair with lotion
towelling it
throwing the towel down to be picked up by elegant lady in
evening dress gliding through opera foyer to Tosca music
reaching rich laden table with huge well sharpened knife sli-
cing skinthin strips of luscious Parma ham in Italian and as
luxury car hugs the road
so very
well along
dangerous
mountain bends
caressing a
baby's bottom for pampers or
chocolate icecream
slimfast on
exquisite nude stretched out onekneeup against sky
ALWAYS
understands
the mystery
of
WOMAN

Funny, she used Yuppy, like it was true.

And like the Citymates.

Nice bit of minge for the place and time.

Well, not like it used to be but can't be choosy.

Face like she peeled off the Ole topskin every night with
AHA to look younger.

Like Debbey did. Nikkei and Footsie and Dax as Manga-heroes!
Whizz! Bang! Sploosh!

Good tits under that Innocent Bystander. But she needs
proper dressing like.

And she'll get that fur coat sploshed with paint by the
animal lovers.

Still, keeps her warm I spose
like this sheepskin relic.

Gonna wait till she comes out and stalk her,

Wanna know her she's bright and brill in the sad circs.

Wanna tell her it's not Yuppy it's Jesse.

Why the lie? Why always protect him? Covering the lie he
perhaps told by saying we were together in the Gulf.

Up the Edgware Road that's called Kilburn High here then
Maida Vale past the highrise yellow tenements haphazard
among bits of yellow grass,

that become the posher dark redbrick blocks
conventionally aligned
with their large but lit up doorways
till it all becomes the Edgware Road again at the

Grosvenor Victoria Casino and the foodmarts and

exchange shops

towards Marble Arch.

Bet he persuades her to walk all the way to Hyde Park at

least an hour's trudge.

He haunts the West End for some reason

fancies himself as a Westender

Well, better cut across towards Finchley and walk across the

Heath towards Kentish Town. No, not that.

Or be a Westender too, spend a quid on a bus

to Marble Arch

and look at the shops

and maybe call at that Jobcentre off

Oxford Street.

Here's one. Crowded. Go upstairs. Crowded

too, one seat.

Why so many Exchange shops, every ten yards?

And get lost in the still sparse bits of humanity soon

multiplying to crowds shopping already for Christmas. WE got

out, WE deserted what the hell.

Dad once said there used to be cheap News cinemas

everywhere, just newsreels and cartoons round and round for

sixpence, you could go in any time just to keep warm or rest or

wait for a friend, but there weren't so many tramps, and the

telly killed them and now the cinemas are like theatres, grand

productions at fixed hours and pricy. Marble Arch, we get out here. Who's we?

    WE couldn't give antecendents to the

        tall red buses already crawling fart to fart glutted in a

        bog of low cars and black taxis

            a roller-blader weaves in and out nearly knocks

            a dame down

a lie to conceal a lie only half told

        disgorging craps of happy workers salesgirls floor

        managers credit accountants

    umbrellas opening in all colours, street a herbaceous border

        HEY LOOK WHERE YOU'RE GOING

        as the shops glare with golden trumpets and silver

        angels and Christmas trees toys party clothes on blank

        dummies in angular attitudes.

            Old shelltoed sneakers full of marbles

            already.

The Military Look red or
navy blue with gold braid
over sexhigh skirts and

he remembers every bloody thing and

            The Aristocratic Look,
            flowery waistcoats and
            flourishing neckfrills

While here there are only brain-holes.

            The Cowboy Look.

Where's the sidestreet to the Jobcentre? To Q or not to Q for O

for the Wings of a Dove

        or spend the last bit of cash on a tube to Kentish Town

so come up in the world

and stare at the little old terrace house in Andover Way

years and years ago.

The American Heritage Look
long skirts and puritan collars
among glistening mixers and
percolators and cream computers.

Oh Hilary coped all right she always did. Why protect him when he can't even be bothered to come here and at least try? He merely collects misery Benefits so he says, they'll stop them if he can't show he tried.

The drizzle evaporates and a pale sun peers round a bloated grey weasel. Rum girl that. Maybe read Hamlet at school who didn't. Of all the unskilled and unschooled unemployed in that place she picks on us, as if the skilled and schooled sought each other out by instinct.

Three queues and the still hopeful young black brown beige and pale pink examining the walls lined with offers and taking notes. Funny how Shakespeare seeps through the language like an English drizzle. Feeling mentally at times like sixty-five, reading a paper all day in a public library and forgetting every item, picking up that thick Penguin off the pavement last summer, Martin Chuzzlewit by Charles Dickens it was, reading it right through on park benches in the Drop-Out Centre in doorways for days, couldn't put it down, the low life the middle life the slightly higher life, no essential change since then bar the outer garments of things. And now, all gone, not a single scene, not a single event, not a single character remains except the old man of the title well there's the younger Martin but he's a wet and the fat hypocrite what's his name. Oh chuzzle the wit well what's the matter mister you deaf or dreeyming?

Aow, sorrey.

I called NEXT laoud enough.

The maternal blond behind the counter looks forgiving what are you looking for?

Anything.

Naow you knaow that's unhelpful. You all say that, but I can't call up a file called Anything can I?

Nao, but you could call up maybe, gentleman's gentleman, ostler, footman, scribe in Chancery, hackney caoachman.

Daon be sao cheeyky naow.

But she says it unsnootily and even smiles. Name and socsec number. It's a melancholy smile as if there but for the grace of God I saw you before didn't I?

Nao daoubt many times, but you wouldn' remember mey as I remember you, obviously, you seey sao many. I see aonly you. Or one other or two, this added to neutralise the last sentence, which flatters her a bit all the same as she examines the screen slanted away invisible to him.

Aoh yes. You never give qualifications and experience, although you're thirty-eight. Very unhelpful. Suicidal I should say. Any reeyson?

Nao. I really will do anything. I'm still young. I'm small but strong.

Sao's everyone. I can hardly help if you daon't help yourself as if she were God. You afraid of not being up to scratch? Longterm unemployment does that she adds kindly but you must start somewhere.

That's what I meeyn, I want to start somewhere but not where I was even if there was anything at that level.

What level would that beey?

Aow. Well mam since you insist. I was a young dynamic middle manager out of business school with a nice job in a small dynamic firm that made electronic gates that went bust.

The gates? Sorry. Why? You'd think with all the crime they'd sell like hot videos. Did you manage it badly?

You tell me, I wasn't the boss. I tried to start up independent like, something more diversified seey, but I couldn't find the backing, so I left haome, pretending a business trip. Married with two kids. That was seven years agao.

So why didn't you put all that down? We do get, occasionally

Nao I'm sorry, but seven years in the streeyt without using the aol' brain except for day to day survival, well, even a small-firm manager neeyds memory for detail, in spite of computers, and they're scleraosing all memory anyway, and presence of mind, you seey I can't even sell myself any more, but you did ask.

Seven years. So you've long run out of Unemployment Benefit.

Daon't I knaow it, see p.12 of Pamphlet FB2, **Income Support**, if you are this if you are that and finally or if there is no money at all coming in. Just that last little phrase. There are so many ifs in that pamphlet, all apparently applying to peoyple with haomes from which to write hundreds of applications in six copies at fifty pee a time who are sick or invalid or pregnant or can't pay their rent, it took me weeyks to find out where I belonged, but I knaow it by heart.

And you didn't look under a family to support?

Nao.

Hmm. Well that's none of my business. But I'm glad you taold me. There's nothing in that line at the present time but

And I wouldn't want it if there was, I'm much more modest.

Sao's everyone. You're placing yourself among the millions. What I was gaoing to say was that naow I knaow I can bear you in mind, and that doesn't meayn forget, but bear you in mind actively for anything that may turn up to suit. She types slantwise into her slantwise computer. A slantwise tree of knowledge appears, she clicks a rectangular leaf, slotting me into it presumably. Thank you.

But you should give an address you knaow, I can't keeyp such an opportunity for days until you choose to present yourself.

Nao address nao job, nao job nao address.

Well you must call regularly. Goodbye. Next.

Past the queue with its weary unexpectant faces one crewcut head flat at the top as if sliced off, another twigged with dreadlocks. Perpetually disappointed and perpetually hopeful.

Damn her the moment you look like a cut above she gives you

pref treatment

and false hope. Where next?

Kentish Town? Means Oxford Circus

change at Euston.

Or Tottenham Court Road, further to walk but direct and save

twenty pee for relief damn that girl either way Holborn

direction through crowds cramming a worldender sandwich
man. Like Tek. That's the one element common to all these
hundreds of millennium-brewing sects, with them as sole
solution. Perhaps he was enticed once, and kept only that,
rejecting the sole solution. Brainwashed. Cos brainy he is, but
shrunk with strong detergent.

     Besides, no return fare anyway Q for Benefits tomorrow

  so walk back or sleep somewhere there

     or cut the angle now and walk all the way.

  Just for a stare. Alibi baby on a treetop. Or bottom.

      But they're in their teens by now.

Pish.

Excuse-me, can you spare a minute?
What for?
Slim black girl with a clipboard.
Just to answer a few questions sir.

Oh, a sugger, a data-frugger. I used to belong to class B1 or B2, or
maybe A3, the class that never buys bottled mayonnaise and reeyds the
Financial Times. But I'm on the streeyts naow lady, and never buy anything, sorry.

  And on.

  A window of long dark green gowns and stoles.

  The madonna in green, shying away, Uffizi Gallery, with

  Hilary.

  Very arty she was.

     The endless steep stairs and long galleries and

      countless rooms

    but nothing to the present trudging.

All those nudes and virgins well virgins clothed

with their creamy heavylidded lashless eyes

pale or clipped eyebrows

tucked off creamy hair and

curly sulky mouths,

one of them in a long green gown against massive gold,

shrinking away and making such a face at the angel's

announcement, her mouth curved down, almost an upside

down U (for me) why me? she seemed to say and Hilary laughed

in delight. I just love the Quattrocento she said.

Not surprising, with her Q face.

But the kids came, whatever **look where you're going!**

Sorry. But she wasn't looking either, stepping back

from staring at a garish ski outfit skis an'all in

scintillating snow under electric sun.

But then, why anyone?

Who is Tek anyway?

So Holborn it is, the decision made itself. The library is brown gothic and up stone stairs. Odd mixed smell of polish and dust and unwashed sweaters. Talk proper now.

Would there by any chance be an illustrated catalogue of the Uffizi Gallery?

The what Gallery?

Uffizi. Italian for offices. You know, Florence.

The Computer Catalogue is over there. D'you know how to use it? Okay I'll show you. Superiority restored, then lost again with What was it again?

Uffizi. U, f, f, i, z, i.

Ah, you're in luck

Am I?

Here's the reference. Row Q on the left. You must learn to use the computer yourself next time. Come with me to the desk will you please. You can take it out and look at it at that table and you must hand it in here when you leave. Now, name and address?

Quentin Stockwell, 14 Andover Way, Kentish Town.

Post code?

Er, sorry, I forget.

Rows and rows. U for Uffizi. Art for Art's sake. Won't walk off with it after all so what does giving the address matter?

The Old Bridge, the River Arno and the Hills around Florence, seen from the window of the second corridor.

Unnaturally blue river blue sky pale gold houses, bridge reflected gold in blue. Just like a painting inside. Opens at Room 7. Gold blue and red people; one green, heads like potatoes around a hanging basket with two people in blue and pink inside it. **Coronation of the Virgin, by Fra Angelico. Madonna and Child.** More potato heads on paler robes but Christ in blue crowning Virgin in White someone called Monaco. Must be earlier.

The man opposite is reading the paper in a raincoat with a huge bib of black dirt from along greasy beard. Next to him a thin woman in glasses taking feverish notes and every few seconds turning her head and wrinkling her nose at the smell.

Gold, gold. **Deposition by Giotto,** this is Room 4, ah, there it is. All gold again, five delicate arches, the middle one taller, and under the left one a blond boy in faded pink. Under the right one a woman in faded blue, peculiar inversion, blue for a little boy pink for a girl. Another man on the other side of the thin woman in glasses leaves and she moves all her books and papers into his place, the unwashed black-bibbed man oblivious. In the three central arches the angel on the left in goldish white holds out a branch and kneels before the Virgin who's sitting on a golden chest (why?), shrinking away and making that U-turn face. But her dress is blue-green, not green.

Annunciation, between Saints Ansano and Giulitta, by Simone Mar-

tini and Lippo Memmi.

No wonder those names vanished. Who were Ansano and Giulitta? Let alone Martini and Memmi? Did anyone except experts remember them among the milling potato heads in the gallery? We come, we reproduce, we struggle, we go, what's a human life? The West creating cliff-hangers if a couple of foolhardy tourists are taken hostage in a world trouble-spot but switching on conventionally solemn horror at foreign massacres. That woman on the box yesterday, a tourist in Jerusalem, unable to control her smiling ecstasy as she tells the mike just walking along you know I'm from North Carolina and suddenly I heard an almighty bang behind me so I turned and saw the bus with my own eyes in flames, throwing bits of clothes and seats and baggage and human body all over the place it was awful, thoroughly enjoying it.

Slowly through the gold, the red and blue, the ochre, the brown and yellow, the green, Flora, Madonna of the Long Neck, Death of Adonis (by Piombo! what a name), Medusa, Bacchante, Portrait of Isabella Brandt who's she when she's at home, all the way to Room 45, Portrait of the Countess of Chinchon's Mother on Horseback. By Goya. Ah, he's famous. The Horrors of War. But not her. Or her mother. Or her horse.
Goodbye Mrs Pyeombo.
Goodbye. Oh there you are Leonardao. Pyeombao! Did you hear that? Can't they learn to pronaounce a foreign name properly, it's only polite.
Aoh Ah'm used to it after forty-fahve years graowin ap ere.
I think they do it on purpose. Just because I'm aonly on halftime.
Nao, Stella mia, it's aonly for reassurance lahk tha' Britain's still on top. The French doow the sime yer knaow, baoth ex-empires. But mah mites learnt the nime. Sime me dad as Peey Aow Dabbleyoow. Yer jes neeyd ter beey friendley and tell'em nahcely.
Here's the bus-stop. So many peoyple! Pushing, pressing.
Besahdes, it's aonly 'abit tha' mikes us call i' alftahme yer kanow Stella-Bella, it's auwmaos' the norm naow.
Not at the Jobcentre it isn't, trust governments not to observe their aown laws. All morning, Leo, man after man, and women too, queuing for

jobs that daon' exist. There was a funny little feller, scrawny and dark ginger, quoting nineteenth-century jobs at mey, I forget what they were. Just to shaow that whaole trades and professions disappeared before, maybe to kid himself new ones'll get invented again, just for him.

Ey, ere's aour bus. Less gao apstairs.

Pushing, pressing. On.

Full up too. AOW nao, two seeyts up there on the left.

Thass lackey. Yoow si' bah the winder. Go' enaff roowm? Ah guess thy didn cauw i' alftahme when workin aours kime daown slaowly from six-teeyn to aigh'.

Smelly. Trundling through the traffic monsters like a tortoise, through teeming humanity.

Wha' didyer sie?

Nothing, it's the noise, I was aonly thinking. Funny how when the telly wants to shaow teeyming humanity say in Taokyo or Calcutta or London they claose craowds advancing in streeyts, gaoing to work. But thaose are the lucky ones. There's all the others, tramping, begging, sitting on park benches, sleeyping in doorways.

Piano piano Bella. It's nao uwse crahying aover the world auw the tahm.

I'm not crying I'm thinking.

But tahring yerself. Aokay I'll reeyd the tellymag.

> Sally is still in shock: after surprising Jack, her future hus-band, kissing Gina at the Japanese café only a few hours be-fore their marriage, she annuls the wedding, much to Jack's bewilderment, who tries to get an explanation but meets with total silence. Gina is delightied. Meanwhile Karen tries to reassure Hank about their future together, deeply to Helen's anguish, who haughtily refuses Hank's offer of ten million dollars for her business, which Brad refused to buy.

Whass on?

Aow nothing. Film called Fornicator 3 on the ads. None too deeycent. Didn't eyven knaow there was One and Two. And nothing but crime stories and sport.

Prahm tahm crahm ey?

It's wicked haow all governments everywhere are failing with the problem, thaough you could see it coming thirty years agao, I remember reeyding prophetic warnings about technology as a girl.

Weuw, technologey's feeymile, in Italian anywise.

What are you talking about?

Thy sie iss camin daown, the Unemployment Ah meeyn.

That's just the official statistics, I knaow better. The rich get richer and the poor get poorer that's what I say.

Yer daon' sie!

I do say! Naobody can caope. Same with the world. A few bits of it stay rich and the rest of it gets poorer. Charity used to be claose to haome and naow it's glaobal.

It alwies was Sao, Stella mia, i' ain' spread, wey jes kanow more abaou' i' . . .

There was a time when I was little, when personal charity all bu' vanished, except for Red Cross Tins and that, cos the State was at last taxing the rich reel high to help the poor. But that's aonly a pretence naow, a minimal gesture, like Lady Bountiful's soup. Same in the world with governments sending aid, but more and more the biggest is done by NGO's and it's us that contributes, appealed to aover and aover through telly marathons, even thaough we pay taxes too. There's something wrong.

Samthink auwwyse is. Ere, greeynery a' lahss, the park. Took us twenty minu'es to crauw ou' of tha' jam.

There's one of 'em, sitting on a bench, seey, huddled in a braown leather jacket and red woolly hat in the drizzle and feeybly gesticulating. Talking to himself I guess.

A' leayst yer can tauwk ter mey.

It isn't my funny little man thaough, he wore a pink and green anorak and a black baseball cap worn backwards, you knaow, with the elastic in front, what was the name, Quentin Something.

Forge' im cara mia, tauwk ter mey.

I am talking to you, who else?

> Hank relieves his feelings in a lively discussion with Sheila. A violent pain tears across his chest. Sheila, alarmed,

A' lahs we're turning Naorth raoun Marble Arch, i' should speeyd up a bi' naow.

Sometimes I think they should all link hands and revolt. You remember that trailer on the telly where an actor, I forget his name, was shaking hands with President Kennedy?

Nao.

Well it was a long time agao and we never saw the film. Anyway they shaowed how it was done, Special Effects it's called. Against a blank blue screeyn first, the actor shaking hands with naobody, like the weather map.

Wha' weather map?

You knaow, the girl stands in front of a blue screeyn, pointing to claouds that aren't there, the map's projected separately. I guess she's really looking at herself and the projected map offscreeyn, off aour screeyn I meeyn.

Wha' are yer on abou', woman, yer tauwk toow mach.

You said to talk to you.

Yer tauwk a' mey.

What's the difference? You're there, and I talk.

Zappin mey. Aokey aokey. Ere's Kiwb'n comin ap.

Naow I lost the thread. Aow yes. I meeyn that, well, if that man instead of feeybly gesticulating, if he could shake hands with the tens of thaousands sitting on volcanic rock say in Africa like tons of potatoes save for bright stuffs wrapping a baby on a back or tugging violently at an empty breast but from the air it's a maowsaic of misery. Or with thaousands of other hands in other maowsaics, in Harlem slums, in shanty towns and what are they called, favelas and bidongvilles, or squatters in empty office blocks, or with oodles of humanity on raoads pushing prams and wheelbarrows and handcarts full of bundles piled araound infants or grandmothers, or eyven back in time like Kennedy, thickpacked in cattlewagons to Siberia or to the deathcamps, or with the Disappeared in Saouth America or further back with refugee Europeans deeyp in Steerage to the Land of the Freey and Brother Can Yer Spare a Dime, and they'd all rise up and

Yer nuts, Stella. Le' mey teuw yer bou' mah mornink.

There you are, a nice caosy family in Brussels, Berlin, Budapest, Buenozair, Bang-cock or a cool mud hut in Sudan then suddenly you're a saoldier off to get killed for you daon't knaow what or if you're lucky queueing in rags for thin soup or stripped naked for shaowers of lethal gas and ovens for drying in.

There's the buiwdin sah' camin ap, aour stop next, c'mon

And down the curving steps of the bus and zigzag through the monsters to a grey block patch-worked with flat metal-edged windows and up drab concrete stairs home at last to a superview over the abandoned building site, huge, half a complex of quarter-built offices and shopping-malls and supermarkets waiting desolate for a take-over, not even a dinosaur yellow crane left on guard like, the low walls spray-painted up and down in the universal style unchanged since the Sixties, sinister as a ruined city in the desert, except for a leaden sky above the roofless walls. Meantime it offers great concrete spaces hidden from the street in huge basements down concrete steps for local rockers and knockers, rappers and crackers, ADHDies and baddies and skateboarders to anarchise in during the long summer nights, very noisy, though empty right now on a November afternoon oh no it isn't.

Wha' are yer m"erin? Wocher lookin a'?

The site for sore eyes. There's a group of boys spraypainting a pink maoped black.

Aow Stella, doow concentri'e on dahyly lahf wiuw yer, ge' mey me lanch a' leeys if yer can' tauwk ter mey iss past toow.

Yes, sorry Leo. It's all ready anyway, just needs popping in the oven, why didn't you do it while I relaxed and watched. If there's one thing I can't stand it's moralising. Like Western governments, impaosing sanctions for segregation policies they were still practising aonly a decade earlier and still do unofficially like or insisting on democracy they aonly reeyched this centurey and very imperfekley too, or human rights they daon't observe themselves.

Whass tha' suppaosed to meeyn? Ah doow mah share daon' Ah? Eeyven with the kids Ah did. Whah daon' yer gao an work fer an Enn Geey Aow stead of rantin on bou' the misreys of the world?

I couldn' leeyve you Leonardao, you knaow that.

Whah no'? Yer'd be drahvin senza piombo.

Very funny. You're not withaout a sense of humour anyway.

An a lo' euwse, if yer'd aonly learn ter listen a bi' an jabber less.

There you are Signor. Canellaoni, aow gratteng.

Ou' of the freeyzer. Ah ope they're dan.

Why do they serve them up if nobody cares?

You needn't watch, Tek, you didn't this morning.

And the little old woman bent at right angles supported by two young-er ones on a Vietnam road, wringing her hands at the camera. The naked little girl in flight from Napalm bombing. The Chinese boy in front of the tank. Er, the skeletal black baby in Ethiopia. Pictures that go round the world, Elsie, causing erm a reassuring shudder as the sociologists say. In this televorous, posthuman age.

He hums and haws, all on one tone, a litany. Must jolt him again.

You're walking in the park now. Didn't you notice Marble Arch? It's big enough.

They're old pictures. But haunting.

Isn't the morning weirdo? Look at the mist hanging round the trees like other trees, but paler green, and the concrete path slanting off like a shining ribbon in the damp sunlight. Why posthuman anyway? We're still here.

Humans seem to be the only animals that do everything to die out as a race, er, you know, in full consciousness. Even, if you like, I mean here and there, stepping back several centuries, and not out of nostalgia for simplicity either. Four fifths of them over-reproduce so under-consume, the tiny remnant under-reproduce, overproduce, over-consume, over-presume.

Rhymes and all, you hoarded that one for ages.

These people. We know nothing about them Elsie.

Can't know everybody's life. It's hard enough to know even neighbours, or fellow rough-sleepers.

And those pictures don't go round the world.

Listen Tek, I tried to cheer you but there's just no response, on the con-trary, you do nothing but depress me. Ever since we started out. You're monotonous.

Monday morning blues. No, erm, days are all alike to us. But it's only headline depression Elsie, you know, like headline inflation versus underlying inflation.

Whatever that means. So I should rise above it? Why should I if you can't? And it's the underlying depression that gets me. If you're going to gloom all day I'm not walking with you.

Let's sit then, here's a bench. Still wet through.

Good, the old feet are killing me as ladies in high heels used to say at cocktails.

You chose Hyde Park.

Yeah, I love it. I was brought up in the slummy West Indian part of Notting Hill. Queen of the Carnival one year, at seventeen. And here I am, between integration and segregation. I integrated so well I'm on the streets, like you. Anyway I'm seeing a friend there, later.

He sits, but looks straight ahead at the world, never at me.

Don't get me wrong Tek, I did want to walk with you. But we accumulate so much walking in the legs, what with Job Centre here and Benefits there and HPUs and Food queueing elsewhere we don't always realise. I don't sit like patience on emolument.

Faint smile.

So perk up will you. You sarcasted on the way at NGO's being NO-GO but also railed at governments. You can't argue against everyone. All progress from the spinning-jenny on and probably earlier caused miseries galore, now forgotten. It'll all adjust itself in the end.

You don't mean progress you mean technological development. There is no progress, there's only . . . But you're rooted in old ideas. Rootedness, that's the root of all evil. Yes, we're the new nomads, erm, us and all the maimed and the . . . but then at the top there's a new overclass, yes, er, nomadic too but in virtuality. We're cut off from that. In between is the vast middle area of the rooted, and you're one of them, Elsie, one of those thoughtless optimists, no I don't mean selfish, forgetting the fact that you're caught up in the miseries galore. That's er, typically feminine.

Yes Tek. The eternal feminine, not always achieved, is affirmation, not confrontation. It'll save the world in the end. Slower but less destructive.

Is it now! And eternally cheerful no doubt.

What's wrong with that? Here we are near Speakers' Corner, empty of speakers on a Monday morning, and you go on like them obsessively about what's wrong with the world, but unlike them you're flat, passionless. You don't even seem to care. Don't you try for jobs at least? With those qualifications you

I get by. Tell me, er, why did you say you were a working mum if it isn't true?

I like word-play, I told you, and I like harmless fantasies. Do we ever, did you, tell the truth? In a world of lies? Why don't you change that alphabet to, to well, dances say. A for, oh lor, for what?

Allemande.

Is that a dance?

Was.

B for bebop.

Or bourrée.

Or bellydance, or boogie woogie, bolero . . . bossanova. There's always too many B's in this game, look at capitals. C for chachacha, for Charleston.

Chaconne, Contredanse, Courante.

Cakewalk.

D for Dance of Death.

Oh you're hopeless Tek, I wish I could remember aitch and jay. After J there's K for pub, L for leather, M for sis, N for lope, isn't it a scream?

No.

Okay then, F for Foxtrot.

Fandango. Farandole.

Flamenco. G for hell I don't know.

Gavotte, gaillard, gallop.

Those are all dead, historical.

I'm a historian.

Were. And don't dance I bet. H for what? Funny how H always blocks.

Highland Fling?

Good! I for . . . no I.

No I, probably.

It was I for Novello that shows how old it is. J for Jitterbug. Still can't the other J though. J for son? That's pulling it a bit.

In Alabama they put prisoners back on chaingangs and stonebreaking.

Foot-cuffed and hand-fettered. And er, a well-dressed woman approved into a mike saying erm, why should they sit in comfortable cells watching television.

W for quits. Okay Tek I did warn you. We don't to speak the same language.

Not surprising, the alphabets are different.

Right. The cockney one may be old hat but it's still funny, the one you play with is phoenician or something, antiquated, dead. Goodbye.

And off on jingling feet towards Notting Hill.

Leaving him immobile on the bench, near Marble Arch.

Foot-cuffed and brain-fettered.

Not looking back at him though

Nor even to the other side at Tyburn Convent

in Hyde Park Place

with its deep inset porch so often slept in

now left behind and on

along the hard path that crosses the dripping green

cutting across towards the tall red buses that crawl

the Bayswater Road.

Along it a tall lanky boy in a sheepskin jacket is racing to the

little outgate why it's

Yuppey! Fancy mey'ing yoow ere.

He peers down at me from that thin height making me feel immensely small. Face is shredded wheat up there, no, he looks like a loofah.

Yeah, weuw, Ah follered yer, an Euwsey.

Ah seey. Whah, Yuppey?

I' was yoow called mey tha', reel nime's Jesse.

Jessey? Thass a girl's nime.

Ah knaow. Bu' iss Jesse Jimes, a yank crao. From Westerns, seey. Surnime's Jimes.

Yer daon' sie! Ain' parens damb?

Yeah. Stchewpid inni'? Bu' yer wasn' wrong Euwsey, auw the mi'es in the Ci'y fel' tha' an cauw'ed mey Yuppey lahk, sao Ah kime ter lahk i' be"er. Ahther wie thy teyses mey bu' Yuppy 's more wiv i', seey. Aonly Ah wann'ed yer ter knaow mey fer reel lahk. Willyer wauwk wiv mey Euwsey?

For a bi', Yuppy, Ah meeyn Jessey.

Wiv them nimes samtahms Ah daon knoaw oo Ah am. Ah ca' orf lahk, ever seynce Ah baounced.

Was i', sudden lahk? Aover-nah?

Yeah, in a wie. Ah meeyn, the crash was, bu' Ah thouuw' Ah could tahd i' aover for a bi', an bluff i' ou', an Ah jus lived more careful lahk, bu' wance yer ou' i' all gaoes samhaow, Ah saold the swank pad and lived on tha' for threey years, trahin' to ge' back in, bu' i' was nao uwse. Nan of them elped mey, said Ah was ter blime. The girlfriend toow, Debbey, shey skidaddled fast from tha' itek pad, ifi pop, videaos an moowvierahds an auw. Naow Ah can' eyven affoard the cybercayfes le' alaone the pickchyures. Ca'orf, lahk Ah sie.

Sao whay didn' yer watch the telley this mornink Yuppey? Tha' keyps yer in tatch.

Aow, tha' crap. Sauw poli'icuw. Iss no' treuw the bad gahs ge' auw the good lahns, no' when the bad gahs are the poli'icians. Yer larf Euwsey, bu' iss treuw. An Ah lahk yer larfin.

Ah'm no' a replicemen fer Web Euwphoriah, Yuppey.

Nao? Yer look lahk an ypertex on the Web, auw starry wiv subliminuws. Or lahk a bungeeyer, leeypin brively orf a bridge 'n ap agiyne on a lastic. Wiuw yer bey ke'ameeyn for mey?

Bey wha?

Yoow knaow, ki'kat, Vi'amin Kie, kinduv ou'of body freeykou'.

Oh ketamine. I momentarily receive Received English. Ah daon tatch drags, Yuppey.

Saonley a himige Euwsey, lahk a pan on eroin.

Ah unnerstan. But rah' naow Ah'm gaoin to seey an aole friend in Nottinkill.

Aow. Ah seey. Wha kahnuv friend then? A man lahk?

He looks ahead, distress in the voice, and eyes if I could see them.

Daon bey snoopey Yuppey. But nao, a woman friend, married, wiv kids. Ah'm taychin er to reeyd.

Aow, thass nahce. An shey pies yer?

Cauwse no'. Shey feeyds mey samtahms. When er usband's ou', ee don' like mey.

Ah lahk yer Euwsey.

Ah lahk yoow Yuppey. Bu' we're nearly there, sao sam ather tahm ey?

When? Where?

Weuw, seeyer tomorrer a' the Drop-Aou', ey? Then yer can teuw mey auw abou' yerself an aow rich yer was an aow yer dropped ou', ey? Bah fer naow.

Bah Euwsey, tiuw tomorrer then.

He looks crushed. Wet loofah after a bath.

Who do they take women for, round-the-clock dispensers of joy?

Why didn't he stay a historian comfily teaching

in a warm stuffy classroom or researching in a library?

That Gulf story, don't believe a word of it, too

long ago to fit.

But then that working mum story wasn't true either as

he soon wormed out, and even then the drug and detox

straightedge bit dropped out.

He didn't tell nothing in exchange. More likely he

just wasn't good enough for an academic job and invented it

anyway he's sure screwed up

for all that everyhank handsomeness

not worth bothering about.

Unlike Adelina, now she is.

In a damp basement room and a bit, bringing up four kids

and an odd job man as an odd job cleaning lady and trying to learn to read at over forty. But she never went to school in Goa,

forgets the cat sat on the mat as soon as it goes in.

    Choose one word and spell it over and over in your head

while you cook and clean, but she can't.

        Does she think at all as she works?

Nor can she do the copying exercises on her own

so no homework's possible only lessons

and all's forgotten in between.

          Each time there's a progress then bang, start again

from scratch it's amazing. After two years.

Bough cough dough enough rough tough though through

thought's

          way beyond her, not surprisingly,

          and high sky lie hi Adelina it's

mey, Euwsey, down the area steps into a pervasion of slow-cooking curry and a deepscented sari hug of frail bones, orange over a pink sweater, then the dark brown face, almost grey, emerging, with rimmeled eyes and a scarlet spot on the brow, radiantly goddessy.

Euwsey, wha' a surprahse, didn' espectyer todie. Ah'll mike some coffee.

Tha'er bey nahce, Lin, aow's things? Rosario cam back?

No' good. Raosie shey stiuw wiv tha' boy wha' can't ge' work, lectrician says ee is but shey waon come aome an tike er I-levels. Ah'm reel worried. Ah think she mussbe aow yer sie spectink an waon teuw. An Joaquim ee gao with a gang on is scoow'er wha' cost so much to look for work ee says as messenger when ee brings i' aome. Aow Euwsey an Ah brings em up so reglar in the Christian religion, Catolica lahk yer sey, ao Ah knaow yer not bilif bu' iss all Ah go' an Xavier ee so

Tha' saounds lahk a cri-de-coeur.

A creeyd uv wha'?

Aow thass byuwi' fuw, Lin, creedy cur, never thou' of tha'.

Bu'Ah doow lav yoow Lin, Ah would if yer was Moslem or Indoo whass the difference. Cheers, lavley, iss ours since tey a' the Drop- Aou' Centre.

Aow Euwsey. Where yer sleeyp?

Never yoow mahnd. Kids at school? Did yer doow

Nao. Me aomework yer meeyn. Aow Euwsey, iss so ard to fahnd momento.

Weuw, ere's a moment now. C'mon, ou' wi' them books before any of em cam in.

The small primitive kitchen with the slow scent of curry and a loo the other side of it is beyond the great damp room that seems all beds, one large bed in the left corner and four single mattresses piled up as a sofa along the other wall, one wonky armchair by the gas fire and a tressle-table in the area window, covered with a garishly flowered plastic cloth, at which we sit with coffee and a child's reading-book. Ere, whass tha' firs' word?

Y o g

Nao. The **y**'s a' the end. It starts **Gr**. Wey did auw the **BR**s, **CR**s, **DR**s, **PR**s and **TR**s yesterdie. Whass **G R** ?

Jorg

Nao, it's a 'ard **g** afore anather consonant. Trah agine.

G r o g

Good. But tha's no' an **ao** it's an eey.

G r i g

An **ee**, when Ah sie **ee** thass the nime o' the le"er, no' the saound, which is *e* as in leg.

Leggery

Fahn, naow replice that **L** with **GR**.

G l e g

GR, mikes **grr**. Yer said i' when yer said Grig.

G r i g

Go on.

G r i g

Look, when yer reeyd wahn bi' of the word, doan jes gao back, remember the saound an gao forward.

G r i gg y

Auwmaos. There's an **r** jes before the end.

G r i gg e r y. Aow! Gregorey! Thass a nime!

Beuw'ifuw. Naow wha' does Gregorey doow?

Ti ks

Terrific. Naow doow baoth words.

G r e g o r y t i k e s

Lavley. An wha' does ee tike?

h

And then?

is

Pu'm tergether: **haitch** and **is**.

. . . h i s?

Good! Naow the threey words.

G r e g o r y . . . t i k e s i s

Is wha'?

b o g

Nao, look, the tile's on the rah of the curl, so i' can' bey a **b**.

p o g

The tile gaoes up, no' daown.

d o g!

Maarvellous. Naow from the beginnink.

G r e g o r e y t i k e s i s d o g

Fahn. Next? Where does ee tike im?

o u t

Good!

f o r a

Super, lav. Ou' fer a wha?

w a l l

Aow Lin, listen ter wha' yer reeyd, aow can ee tike is dog fer a wauw?

Walk!

Yes!

Bu' whah **al** an no' or lahk **for**?

The black-framed eyes look bewildered.

Diffren' istry. Yeah there's an istry eeyven fer words. But daon yer bother bou' tha'. English spellink stuck in the fourteynth cenchry jes to mike i' arder for schoowkids. **W a l k** and **t a l k** with **a l**, but **f o r** and **f o r k** with **or**. Naow reeyd the aole sentence.

Y o g a r

Yer've forg"en is nime! **GR.**

Gregory!

Good. Next? Gaow on.

t i k e s   i s   g o d

dog

d o g fer-a-walk.

Brill. Naow Ah'll sie the sentence an yoow wrah' i' daown. Readey?

The morning blathers by, me as alphabent as Lin but zapping off during her bending. We did consonant + r last time, but it got lost in the curries. And will again. I never taught before, maybe I'm going about it the wrong way, specially as she seems dyslexic . . . **fr** as in from . . . from. Yet intelligent in other ways I never was. She keeps a family, just about, which I never did. I couldn't even cook proper for Jimmy, not after work, what with the shopping 'n all, and he got fed up and moved out. She shops, **gr** . . . **and**, recognizes cleaning products and packets of rice and spices without reading, and she could always count money. How come? Aow Ah learns money ever sao young, she told me. Of course. No, **br** . . . **ick**, not **prick**. Tail up. What sort of brain is it that takes in sums and sounds but not letters? A traffic jam along one road and fluidity along another? **Tr** . . . **ick**. Why didn't she go to school in Goa? The troubles, she said. When were those?

Then Xavier comes in. Darker than Lin and older, a lined lean face framed in greying black hair. English is almost non-existent. How is it even an illiterate woman learns the language of another country when her husband can't? And he's hard to understand when he speaks at all, but his looks do it for him as he sits in the wonky armchair resentful of me and scornful of his wife's useless efforts, he did all right without reading and writing he seems to be thinking, at least till he lost his job as builder, someone can always be found to fill up forms and he too knows figures, and all the bus numbers and all their routes.

He scolds her silence in Portuguese. A man in a macho-culture exists only by his work, take that away and he ceases, goes to pieces, blames his wife, everything's her fault, the children going wrong, the poverty grind, she brought them up wrong, not him of course, and he won't see his only daughter who's disgraced him, and all the rest. Now that Rosario's left, Lin struggles alone in an all-male family, the boys siding with their father unless he goes too far, then there's just silence as the side crumbles. They never lift a finger to help her, not even if she's sick, oh you make such a fuss, get it for yourself. She goes out cleaning, shopping, she cooks, she waits on them. Disgusting.

Now she's insisting on me staying to share the curry and Xavier at once transmits a not-enough-to-go-round scowl, but I'm hungry, I'm not going to curry flavour with him but I feel I earned a bite and maybe I can bring a moment of peace and cheer to the threesome meal, two women laughing against one man grumping, unless the boys come in. But no, Joaquim's with his gang, Diogo and Vasco are at school. Not that they help their mother with her reading. Aow dyer wrah' **grumpy**, Lin, **grr**? Gaowon, **gr...um...py**. Lin giggles but can't do it. Aow dyer wrah' **brat**? Cmon, **brr...** yer produwced four of em. Laughter, Scowl. **B...R**, yeah, bu' gaowon naow. **B, R...** yes? Now add at. **A, T**. Lavley. Silencio, from Xavier, then one of them enters, Joaquim, short thin and brown, holding a bright pink helmet. Pigs, there's nothink left. Cauwse there is, lav, sidaown. Call tha' a dinner? Yer scripin the dish! Glares at me. Splenty luv an ow am Ah to knaow if yer comin in or no'? Swear word in Portuguese, probably very rude as Lin's dark face darkens.

Wha' yer bin doin, Joaquim, faound a job ye'?

I try hard but get a shrug, not just the shoulders but the whole body it seems, the chest the hips the buttocks the knees if I could see them, a seizure of hate and it's time to go.

An good riddance any coffee?

Aow Joaquim, shey's me friend.

Weuw shey can bey yer friend a' er plice for a chinge.

There ain' nao plice, shey sleeyps ou', yer should

Whass shey doin paokin er naose in ere for? The niggerly bitch. There aint nao roowm ere is there? Where dyer meey' er anywyse?

Wey was cleeynin at Tahburn Conven'. Shey's teeychin mey to reeyd.

Fuck tha'. Ah'm orf.

Where yer gaoin?

Dad's already lying on the big bed, waiting to fuck her as he can't at night with us there, and hardly twitches as I slam the door and leap up the area steps to unlock the pink scooter from the railings and brumph away along the terraced streets of Notting Hill

    joy

        slalomming through

   the motorised clutter of

        the Edgware Road towards

  Kilburn and the gang the lost generation as they say

          might as well be lost for a sheep as they say

      what lost sheep anyway they were sheep

    to leave India for this fucked up stepmother-country

        stupid loreabiders cleaning for the rich or queuing

        for no jobs

or beastly benefits

I'll showem.

    One day I'll be rich oh it'll take a while

        smalltime jobs now, shoplifting and bagsnatching

and a bit of crackpushing here and there

bigger later

  when we get better at it and bolder.

    Any job needs training.

    And Sam's training us.

Stinkin city, pong buses and cars

    well this'll become a car one day and showem

not that it'd be better in Panjin or Bombay but then I never was there was I, born here I am.

Why did they ever come here instead of Portugal in the sun

well she was only eight at the time she says

but he'd be say fifteen or more.

Land of hope and glory they thought not that they knew each
other then.

Fuck it why didn't they stay it all came out okay in
the end.

Instead of belonging nowhere.

Why does she keep the sari an all in this climate
must be hopeless for cleaning.

But I don't belong to THEM I belong here

and there they'll be behind the wooden wall of the building site

Sam and Ken and Shauny and Fred and Blake.

Now THEY accept me besides, Blake's real black. With
dreadlocks

falling all over his face

We're creating the mixsoc not them. There's the broken
door.

Ere's the paki, Sam.
Ooer yer callin paki Blike?
Well ee is ain' ee?
Ah says nao libellin for difference Ah says, gang ruwle, unnerstood?
Yessam.
Aowd yer lahk i' if Ah was ter cauw yer
Okiy okiy Sam. Ah was jes bein friendly lahk, paki was jes friendly.
Well clamp i'. Shauney, the pint.
Yer no' gaoin ter pint im black?
No' im cre'in. Ere ee is. Hi Jaokey, c'mon up.

The scooter pinkly humps and bumps across the vast muddy area into their midst and sputters to a stop. Joaquim proudly dismounts and cranks it up, then unclips the straps of his pink helmet that hang on either side like skimpy locks of greasy hair Ey! Wha' yer doowin?

They each start spraying black paint all over the pink scooter.

Ah taold yer. Tha' think's toow ahdeeyable. Gimme yer elmet.

Bu', bu', aow nao!

Joaquim's full mouth crumples in his still helmeted face that curdles like a teleframed weathermap about to rain.

Aow dyer spect ter work wi' us on tha' candypink veeecle yer damclack. C'mon, gimme yer elmet or Ah'll pint it on yer an yer'll ge' black auw aover yer black fice.

Joaquim removes the helmet and hands it over with a hiccupping sob.

Crahbaybey. Blubberbag.

And the baby cries, the bag blubbers. His paradise pegasus. His ridden girl of gaudy pink buttocks, his rosegold crown. His mitzy-bitchy. Soon a black stallion, a gleaming negress, a stove-black head.

Naow we'll le' i" drah.

Waon drah in this damp Sam, aow'll Ah ge' aome?

Iss quickdrah pint. Lessgao on daown in.

Ah'll stie ere.

C'mon Jaokey, tha' was yer rah'opassige an yer passed, i' di'n ur' did i'? Aow shuv i', warn tha' bad, ere's a bi' o' crack, staoke i' boy an graow ap. Black's byuw'ifuw, inni Blike?

Turning to me with a grin.

But I sit watching Joky.

Ere Jaokey, tauwk te as, yer one of as naow, tell us bou' yerself. Aow cam yer in Bri'ain? When Angola bekime innerpenden' whay didn yer famly

Aow Blike. Mah famly 's from Gaoa.

Where's tha' then?

India.

Aokiy weuw when Gaoa bekime innerpenden'.

I' dinn. India took i'.

Aow. Sao wha couln yer stie? Yer Indian ain' yer?

Ah wasn eyven born. Me mum was aigh'.

Well yer famly then.

Whass this, another rah'opassige?

Nao, Jaokey, jes friendly lahk. Ah'm intrested seey, Ah meeyn, when the wah'es go' ou' of Nahgeriah thy maniged ter recolonise a lo' of us back ere as sabci'izens to doow their dir'y work an Ah was just wonnerin if Porchuwguw

Ah dunnao, i' wasn the sime. Ah'm ere thassall, leeyve mey alaone.

No' too P.R.y are wey?

Whass peeahry?

Silence. I won't tell him. We're all tired out by the afternoon's work.

Ey! Dyer knaows where wey auw kime from?

Shrugs. Origin isn't their thing.

Ah meeyn, there was this pikcher on the telley, bou' fackin ipes an gorillas standin ap on their ind legs in Africa, them finds baones an skeletons wha' fackin proowved i' lahk, an aow thy first stood up ter coowl their eads sao's the brine graows bigger an b''er than animals lahk on four legs. Millions of years i' took bu' shi', civilahzed man was born in Africa.

Sam looks at me, hesitating.

Di' i' spline whah civilahziyshn kime to bey Europeeyan then?

Nao. Guess thy emigri'ed.

Wah?

Dunnao. Clahma' mybeey.

The question kinduv throws me. Oh I know what he means. He means why did Africans then remain at almost ape stage till the Whites arrived? But what did the Whites bring except slavery and scorn and skyscrapers and squalid city sprawls like Lagos looks on telly and traffic jams and exhaust pollution and petrol magnates and bloodshed and black imitations of white corruption in Western uniforms with goosesteps and medals and palaces and huge limousines and deals with world banks to build and build and build up enormous debts and huge drops in the prices of cocoa and coffee and cattle meat and all the rest and the cattle munching up all the bush and the forests murdered and the desert advancing and the shanty-towns and the poverty? Besides, wasn't them bones found in East Africa? Africa's huge. Hell, my head's heating, get up, like a man-ape.

Well, Ah'll bey shovin orf.
    Ere, where yer gaoin?
    Dan me work fer todie, pintjob, remember?
    Stie ere Blike, there's a shopjob ter plan.

    Cacount mey ou' this tahm Sam. Ah'm no' civilahzed lahk yoow, seey?

        And I walk away from them across the concrete basement
        floor
                    and up the concrete steps and out
                        towards the wide rectangular doorway
        past the black scooter
        with damp dust particles all over its gleaming paint
        giving it a granulated surface
            and across the mudrubble of the future carpark
    and out by the broken wooden door in the fence
    feeling all the way the generalised shrug behind me which let
    me go.

    But Ah can shrug back, after all the world's a general shrug,
    No' hug, aow nao, bu' bugger all an Sam's a smalltahm thug.
    An wha' doow Ah ge' ou' of i', yeah Ah'll ge' oul of i'
    An rap me why daown Kiwburn Igh an further Saouth of i',
    No' North ter Shoow' Ap Ill an Cricklewoody Broadwhy.
    Iss all the Edgware Raoad for mahles, an' mahles to Edgware
        Broadwhy
                                nao, bored why
    Ter Staonegraove Igh an Brockley Ill, erm . . .
    Ter Staonegraove Igh an Brockley Ill iss auw the Edgware
        Raoad
    Where mao'or-whys crank up araound the Wa'ford Bahpass
        Laoad.
    Bu' South ter Marbuw Arch an on an daown to ni'ive
        Brixton

Where me ole groowp'll tike mey back to rap ou' the aole
    friction.
Thems tricksters auw an slick sick pricks Ah'll ge' ou' to
    Nahgeeriah
Where top ter taoe is all corrup an everywahn's inferiah.
Mybe Ah'll ey whass this? Trip aover legs from doorwhy,
Collapse aover a man oo sits an looks ou' in a sorewhy

Sorry. Ellaow.

Grey beard black-rimmed glasses grey hair like a mop. Long legs sticking out of grey blanket. Buttoned up old black coat the other end of the
blanket.

Well, now you're down stay and sit with me. Or are you in a hurry? Are
you hurt?

Nao. Jes surprahsed. Wasn lookin.

High on Ecstasy?

Cauwse no'. Rappin ter meself. Yer beggin?

No. Just resting. Waiting for the night to fall.

Iss fall'n.

Not really, not to sleep yet, just winter dark and iodine lights. I found
this nice doorway and want to keep it.

Waon the lah's an traffic keeyp yer awike?

Used to it. Traffic dies out and I can wrap this scarf round the eyes.
Real problem is to find a carton. What are you called?

Blike.

That's a poet.

Ah am a paowet.

Is it a surname?

Naow, iss me nime. An' you?

Ulysses.

Wha' kinduv

Greek hero. And famous novel. Call me Uly, Where d'you live Blake?

In care. Yoowth plice in Kiwb'n.

No parents?

Brixton. Thy spli' ap, me dad wenter prison. Ah was tiken awhy. Years an years agao.

How old are you then?

Fou'eeyn. Near fifteeyn.

Don't you go to school?

Well, yeah, bu' no' todie.

And can you work there, I mean, homework?

Nao. Daon' lahk aomework. Bu' there's the telley. Ere, whah' yer in the streey'? Ah meeyn yer

You mean I talk educated, don't you? But you know, Blake, the way we talk is only the dialect we were born and brought up in, and it stamps us forever, and dates us after a while, in fact, all old people complain they can't understand the young, that's because language changes so fast. And your way of talking's rapidly ousting the old way, even at the top. Even on the sacrosanct BBC you hear announcers saying 'on the beey beey ceey' in pure Estuary, as it's called now. People like me are the ones with the quaint dialect now, just as proper English is the quaint dialect compared to American. But we manage to decode each other, don't we? I mean, when you said Blike I immediately understood Blake and when I say Blake you hear Blike.

Yer shooar tauwk a lo'. Sao, whah yer in the streey'

Yes sorry, professional deformation. I got derailed on a pet topic instead of answering your question. Unlike you, you answer clear and quick. But you know, it's not because one talks educated; that one doesn't end up in the street.

Yer mayn ejikiytion's naow yeuwse?

No, I don't mean that, education's more use than no education. But some education turns out to be useless in the modern world. And when they can't use you, well, there you are, useless. And it's not just accents, but ideologies that change. Did you ever read Scott? You know, Ivanhoe and Rob Roy, you surely saw the films. Splendid stories, but Scott wrote down how people talked, in a Scottish now changed, and what they talked about, long religious sermons by Covenanters and so on, unreadable today because those wars are dead. Like the gobbledegook of modern ideologies, incomprehensible even thirty years later. Where are your people from, Blake?

Nahgeriah.

He comes alive suddenly.

I know Nigeria well, I spent many years there, and in Togo, and Ghana, and Cameroun. I love Africa. I was a teacher. First I worked on cooperation programmes, then for the various African governments. But I tried to keep away from their chaotic administrations and work alone when I could. Yes, I love Africa, and Africans.

He talks he talks, he talks like a book, them questions was just to get the ole self on. Ey, dyer knaows abou' ar origins?

Whose origins?

Well, ipes an gorillas an tha'. Ah meeyn thy says on telley the first man ris up on is ahnd legs in Africa.

I see.

He does too, same as Sam. Same piercing look, behind the thick glasses reflecting the dull afternoon growing pink from the early orange lights. Looks old, at least fifty, lor.

That's only where they found the earliest skeletons, Blake. But I guess you're right, mankind began in Africa. You should be very proud.

Yer kiddin.

Are you good at school?

Aow come off of i', thy all aasks tha'.

I meant, do you like it?

Middlin.

You know, you were asking about mankind, and how it made the jump to brain development and articulated speech,

Was Ah?

Indirectly yes. Well, you know, there's been very little biological change since then, but a huge accumulation of knowledge, I mean cultural, technological change, from the first stone used to smash a nut, on to the sharpening of silexes, the wooden plough, and so on. I believe every child in the world is born with equal chances, but doesn't get them. I don't mean just schooling and all that, but constant stimulus from day one, through eye-contact and play-sharing with parents who should know by instinct what kind of attention to give, not just silly babytalk but real words and sentences, and smiles and encouragement to agitate all the limbs until they find which one is needed for which action, activating all those dendrites that grow with each activity. And most kids don't get that, so that only some dendrites grow, you know, like those lit up signs with half the letters missing. A lost inheritance. Parents are split, absent, quarrelling, drunk, distressed, struggling with poverty and the rest. So there's synaptic sclerosis. Tell me, do African mothers still strap their babies on their back while they work?

Dunnao.

I believe that's a guaranteed way to fabricate under-development. Oh there's oodles of physical contact, yes, and that makes for the sane physical well-being and warmth the Africans are famous for, but gorillas get that. And what are the eyes looking at? A piece of kente cloth on the mother's back. What are the limbs doing? Where's the curiosity, the stimulus of the brain, of the concomitant limb-movements, the exchange, the gurgling conversation? In Europe we took a long time too, and some regions still swaddle their babies into immobility, but we were eventually given that primary stimulus, if not from parents then from nannies, and later discipline, producing the West's canny, inhumane intelligence, but we lack your clever ways of surviving in jungles and deserts, above all your warmth and ease. In a few hours you can assemble hundreds for a celebration, well, perhaps not from a rival village, but far and wide locally. And I attended Christian masses where the whole congregation would sway and lilt in rhythm, almost dancing, to their dialect versions of the Kyrie or even the Sanctus, so different from the gloomy dead services here. And look at the streets here. Children used to play in them, people used to trade, as they still do in African villages and Lagos ghettoes, women pounding yam, making and frying yams, washing clothes, selling peppers and kerosene and cigarettes and water. Shouting, hating, loving each other but at least not indifferent. The car killed all that.

Daon be daft. Africans are auw massacrin eaych ather.

True. It's only a theory. An idea I mean. But the world forgot the idea in ideology and kept only the id. Or only the I.

Ah daon' ge' yer.

Yes I do stray a bit, that's what wandering the streets does to you, to me I mean. But wouldn't that answer your question?

Wha' question?

The one you asked, Blake. There was a huge rift in Africa, and to the East of it, it was all savanna and early men needed extra protection and so developed quicker and learnt to make fire. That's called the East Side Story. But bones were found in Mali, that's thousands of miles West, so the scientists are still quarrelling about it, I mean the East Side Story. Anyway those early men slowly spread North, and East, all over the world, into Asia, and Indonesia, and right up towards Korea, and further North to the Bering Straits and over to America, and of course into Europe. Over millions of years of course, I can't remember the time-scale, but they slowly changed their physical appearance during all that time, adapting to new circumstances, to different climates, getting paler, changing their eyes, their mouths, their size. But Africa is believed to be the cradle of mankind.

Blahmey.

I can't stop him.

And then there's the problem of modern education. It's going to the dogs anyway, everywhere, what with new teaching theories that change every twenty years or so, each time sacrificing a generation. But Africa al-ways posed a specific problem, as did other parts of those far-flung em-pires. The French imposed their system, you know, our ancestors the Gauls, stupid don't you think, though of course some argue that it's very generous to share your ancestors. And the British just ran mission schools, well, they did their best, according to the beliefs of the day, but of course, as in everything, their best was never good enough, they believed in their way, but then things change, you see

long speech on

        education   yeah

         the human genome project

    wha'ever tha' is I

                   culture not nature

   but the new gurus of ethnic diversity

     shi'

                all highly suspicious and

> falling back on nature and pseudoscience
>
> towards a new racism
>
> bugger all he's a fucking Goth guru himself
>
> well good, a babyboom hipster
>
> well Ah muss bey

Yer clever. . . Sao, whah the streey' mister?

You're right, Blake, I'm still not answering you. But it's a long story. And boring.

Or mybe toow many others was even cleverer?

Maybe. Maybe I prefer it.

Whass i' lahk? Aow dyer eey'?

There are food centres, hostels and things.

Freey?

Mostly. But I'm on assistance. Called Benefits, as if we made vast profits.

Aow 'bou' sex? Mybe yer daon neeyd if? Caowl wah' an auw ey?

Well no, not cold white fish. Yes. That is a problem for many of us. But not for me, Blake. I'm over seventy.

Weuw fuckauw.

And just surviving tends to drive it away. Mostly. Especially in rain or frost.

He seems to switch off like, go into a daze. Drooly Yooly. Eyes look dark behind the glasses, like the hair and beard used to be black, but I can't see in this greypink light. The traffic trundles by, like farting hippos, the smells sick-sweet at this street level, Dung Sour Pee like that Chinaman, the legs and feet clump and clicket past, eyes miles up and unregarding. The doorway's not deep, that explains the legs sticking out, but quite wide, enough to sleep sideways, offices maybe, but nobody comes in or out ey, waon thy be cammin ou' of them offices soown? He starts.

What offices?

Ere where we're sittin.

He peers at a wrist-watch in the bloodlight. Yes, you're right. Better move off a bit. But I want to keep an eye on the spot.

There's a coffee aover the raoad ow bou' i'?

Coffee would kill the night's sleep, but tea would be nice. Let me invite you.

No' on yer lahf, Ah fell on yer dinn Ah? Ah mikes a bi' o' cash yesterdie on an odd job. Ere's a brike, cross quick.

What sort of a job?

Never yoow mahnd. Yer neeyd a bi' o' scrambled eggs aforethe nah'.

Oh they wouldn't serve that it's a pizza place.

Thy'll serve somethink, no' jes teey. Ere we are. Tible in the winder toow, yer can watch. Bu' wha'll yer doow if the doorwhy's liken? Can' rice back ou' canyer?

Good point, Blake. But if the office workers come out they'll prevent that won't they, same as with us? Anyway, there are plenty of doorways in London, even if that's a nice wide one, though no good if it rains again. You're a nice boy Blake.

No' reely. Go' tahed ap wiv a gang reycennly, small tahm jobs an all, an pushin crack.

That'll shock him off. It does, there's a pause. Fact is I roused the school-teacher again.

You speak in the past. Did you leave them?

In a wie. Yeah. Todie lahk.

Fuck it I gave him a handle instead. Here it comes.

You're too bright to touch crack, Blake.

Yeah. Toow teeys pleeyse and somat to eey'.

Pizzas aonly anchaowvy an olives, cheeyse an tomah'er, shrimps an

Cheese and tomato. Two. Okay Blake? Forgive me if I seem to scold but crack means other drugs, then down and down, and you deserve better than that.

Aow Ah knaow. Pushin ain' tikin. N"er worry erm, Yoowly, Ahm all rah'. Me brine's brill active, no' on the rah' thinks mybe bu' all there.

He seems to feel the irritation in my voice, looks troubled, is silent, but shit he was at it again, just because he's older and white, fuck him he's the one in the street. All that guff about decoding accents but he still meant he knows which is the right one and how clever he was to decode mine an how we go on making our own underdev after the white departure but he's the inferior one just at the moment isn't he? No roof to sleep under while I oh balls he's a miz and I'm turning nasty but he does kinda

There yer gao, toow teeys toow cheeyse an tomah' er.

Plates clatter down, bill for him as white dad type, I snatch it, the feel-good factor. The pizza's tough.

Lahk car'board ey? Fuck i' yer could bah twenty of theeyse an sleeyp reel good on em.

Might be a bit messy. Well, we'll just chew hard.

Sorry mi'e.

Don't apologise, I'm so hungry I could eat leather, it's a pleasure.

You're a nahce man toow erm, Yoowly.

Chew. What next? Is he going to moralise again?

What do you want to be later Blake?

Here he goes, work hard an finish school fat lot it helped him what to say?

A star. A rap star. Aow no' the orrocore gangsta-rap or the 'op boo'leg-gin' bu' me aown. Useter belong ter grouwp, back in Brixton when Ah was a kid. Bu' tha' was aiges agao. Ah gone on to meself bu' Ah can' fahnd any-one in care, thys auw damclacks.

Did you try?

Yeah. No' intrested, Ah can doow the rappin bu' yer needs a band, a bi' o grunge ter back the tahmin lahk.

The rhythm.

Chewed.

Yeah.

Chewed.

I could do that for you.

Yoow?

Chewed.

We could go round the pubs as a two-man group, called Black and White Whisky, no, that's old hat, Black and White TV, what d'you say? Do me a bit of rap.

No' with this cardboard in me maouth. An yoow, can youw doow me a bi' of battry? An ow dyer fahnd the drams?

Yes. Pity. It was a nice idea.

Chew. Tea gulps to send it down. He looks sad. Silence as we both chew.

A couple sits down at the next table, blondish woman mature and an older man, dark, talks Italian at the waitress who's flummoxed. Pasta the woman says loudly we're always eating pasta. Weuw yer didn neeyd ter mike fraozen canelloni for lunch did yer? A nahce bi' of scalopina frinstance. As if I could find the time Leao. Or the money. He smiles and strokes her hand marital row averted. She's staring back at me I look away but catch a surprising smile so it wasn't a racist stare so I look again to smile back. Yooly intercepts and joins in.

The pizza's like cardboard you know.

Aow we doow knaow. But it's the nearest and my husband's Italian so we walked daown, didn't we Leonardao?

Yeah. No' lahk I'aly, where pîzzas meuw in yer maouth.

So you're Italian then?

Me father was. Pee Aow Dabbleyoow. Then married an English girl an se"wed ere.

I'm Ulysses. Pleeysed ter meey' yoow. This is Stella.

And this is a young acquaintance Blake.

Included back in at last, I nod, I was beginning to feel out of it. Must get out of it out of what where am I going what am I doing here? Drums! He must be barmy.

Well, erm, Yoowly, Ah mussbe gaoin. Nahce meey'in yer, daon' yer mowve Ah'll gaow an pie the biuw.

Oh. All right Blake. Good luck. And thanks.

An' for the istry lesson. Cheers.

There's another one lost I must be repulsive. Oodles of people coming out of that doorway now, soon I can go back.

Waon't you join us and eeyt another pizza?

She snaps but smiles, odd mixture.

No thanks, one's enough.

More teey then? Come on, come on aover.

All right, it's very kind of you. I'm watching that office doorway opposite till it's free of office workers.

Doorway? Freey, why?

To sleep in.

Good, that shocked her, wide-eyed distress or is it sudden repugnance and regret?

Yes, I'm in the street.

Another one!

What do you mean? We're thousands. Millions. Billions if you include the world.

I work at the Jobcentre in the West End.

Oh that one. Yes.

Never seeyn you there. Saw a funny little man yesterday. Scrawney. Among hundreds of others of course, but I remember him. Well-spaoken like you, been on the streeyts for seven years he said. But he never told what he was doing before, until yesterday, that's why I remember him. A manager, think of that.

Shey ge's upse' bah er work.

The husband chews away, disgust undisguised around his mouth and eyes.

Can we, can we help you, in any way?

Tears sparkle her eyes.

No, thank you. You're very kind, but I manage you know. Please don't worry.

The doorway's been quiet now for some minutes. Time to go. Can't stand self-indulgent sympathy slurping over me. Thanks for the friendliness, that alone was welcome. Good evening.

Goodbye, Mister er

Well it's a small world isn't it, despite the craowds. Look at him Leonardao, he's crossed the road and, damn the bus, yes, settling in that doorway. It's going to be a long night for him it's barely seven. Why daon't I ever see him at the Centre? Must be registered raound here. Seems like he likes it that way. Like the other, what was he called, Quentin Stockwell, that's it, seeyms they get attached to the streeyt and daon't want to reintegrate. I wonder what he did before. They never tell, those that were a bit further up, maybe they're that much more ashamed, the higher they are the laower they fall that's what I say, must be very hard and they can't blame a bad start like the others, they were given every chance and somehow couldn't seeyze it and keeyp it.

Aow shu' up Stella we're eey'in' ou'.

And then it happens, the very next day, a manager's job in a small electronics firm comes up on the computer. Oh, probably means nothing,
already filled in advance, put in just for the offerstats but there you are,
Mr Quentin Stockwell is beyond reach. Unless he comes in again today.
Unlikely. It'll get put up on the walls automatically by the girl at the main
computer so I can't hoard it. Maybe there'll be no candidates qualified for
it until he does come in. Silly me, of course there will, if not here then in
all the other centres. Next please.

But miracles do occur. Around eleven. Intensity of thought transfer-
ence perhaps. Out of eye-corner a glimpse, pink and green anorak. Glance
over the shuffling pale black man at the counter and the queue behind
him and yes, the black backwards cap and wide black elastic over the
gingery brown hair. Our eyes meet. My eyebrows go up and my head gives
a slight nod in some probably untransmissable message but he joins my
queue. Interminable. By twelve he's there, and I tell him, barely suppress-
ing my excitement. But it's not communicated. He seems tired, uninterested.

I told you. I couldn't do it any more.

But then there's an electronic-sized gleam in those eyes, as if I were
clicking on a file-icon and opening new windows, possibilities, persua-
sions, hopes. He agrees to try, to go for an interview at least. I ring up. But
dressed like this? Icon pink and green. Iconoclastic click, it's all right, say
you walked across the Heath it's in Putney. But take off that cap. Mouse
on Finder, what shall I tell them about the last seven years? Mouse on
Search. The truth. Oh not the streets, Cancel, but Unemployment, odd
jobs, temps and so on. He clicks Help. They'll want reeycent references.
Mouse on Format. Temps rarely give refs. Mouse on Style. And, yes, your
charm. Mouse on Save. Etc.

Well whatever next?

Who could expect?

Nice woman that, seemed personally concerned like

a mum

Or blow the fortnight's Benefits from this morning on a

black jacket?

Over the black jeans should look okay.

appointment's two o'clock.

no time for lunch even.

And what if there's a whole queue of candidates

and still no job is it worth it?

Oh hell don't go.

One forty-five in Putney, lunchless in pink and green anorak.

Fifteen minutes to find the place.

Why old Croaky? Why not ?

In a chemical suspension of particles

being and not being

wanting and not wanting.

Jesus where are the old ref and diplo?

Yes, here they are.

Bit dog-eared, trotting alongside all this time in hifi

trailing old self only half-desired.

It's a computer-firm after all, not general electronics as said. Cuter Computers, what a name. Straight into an office cluttered with large desks themselves littered with diskettes around screens, some on the edge about to fall into empty cartons all around on the floor. At each desk a screen-faced microserf downloading in screen-trance or carpal tunnel syndrome and behind them a wall of piled up cardboard boxes. Yes? I was given an appointment with a Mr. Day. Two o'clock. Ah yes go through that door please. Into a narrow corridor with four people waiting by a door.

Craoakey!

It's Elsie. Coffee-faced and cute as a computer in her black rabbity fur. Third in line. We talk across the fourth, an elderly man who glares till she swaps places with him and he's pacified. Fancey meey'ing yoow and so on.

Aow there's no' much aope bu' yer never knaow, thaough Ah'd ai'e ter ge' i' if you daon', Craoakey, Ah meayn yer wai'ed sao much longer.

Well, me too, I almaost didn't come you knaow, after seven years one gets used

Shsh daon' sie tha' ere, Ah sie, wha' a mess, thy sure neeyd a manager daon' thy. Wha' tahm were yer taold ter come?

Two o'clock.

Sime ere, muss bey a block appoin'men' lahk a' the doctor's.

A fortyish woman comes out and the first in line goes in. Haow's Tek?

Aow Ah soown give ap on im ee's an ambulant alphabe' of los' cauwses.

That's good. But we're all ambulant.

Sao Ah ambuwed a bi' wiv im yesterdie, bu' no' seeyn since, an yoow?

Nao.

Don't ask her where she slept and she won't ask me. We all know any-way one doorway's much like another and the hostels all seem to be for young home-leavers. The interviews are fairly quick, and the middle-aged man who's just gone in won't stand a chance.

You'll be next Elsie, hey, a word of advice, keeyp tha' caoat on.

Whay?

I meeyn that teeyshirt, underneayth, not too cleeyn.

Aow. Cheers Craoakey. An yoow, tike tha' cap orf.

Sure. Here you are. Good luck, and no hard feeylings ey?

She goes in. Takes a longish time. It's true she was a computer-operat-or, but no managerial skills presumably. Still, it's the young women who get all the jobs these days, anything from editors or engineers to business consultants, soon there'll be nothing left for us. Boys work less well at school and rapidly become negative lost young men. Read that in the pa-per. Two others, both young, boys really, line up behind me. One with red hair and glasses. Shit I feel like skidaddling. She comes out, all smiles. Not bad she whispers, good luck.

It's a woman at the desk in the tiny office, why didn't they correct me? Late twenties, elegant and bland in computer grey. Sit down, Mr er Stock-well. I see you're thirty-eight. Said with the ambiguous poise of the young to the crumbling. Studying the diploma and reference. Turns to a ma-chine and Xeroxes them as she chats pseudo-amiably. That's a long time ago isn't it? Did you lose that job? Ah, it went bankrupt. And you've been on Temps and Benefits ever since? Hmm. Well, you do seem to show more managerial experience than some of the others, but none in computers, where things move fast. Tell me, what are your impressions of this firm?

Well. Go on, be bold, win or lose. Mind the accent.

Go on, be bold, I don't mind.

It's very small, isn't it? And looks a bit chaotic out there.

How right. Smoothly. We're doing very well though, and are about to move into larger premises. That's why we're looking for a new manager.

New? Isn't she the manager? Or is she the owner, the boss, who's sacked her manager?

Managing is more important than understanding what you manage, would you say?

Well,

It's the salesmen and technicians who know the wares, hard and soft, but you would be prepared to learn a little about those wares, wouldn't you?

Whereas Elsie knew about hard and software more or less and would learn a little about managing, surely they can find someone with both, easily?

I did use a computer in the job. And of course I'd be prepared to

Of course. But take a look at this.

She hands me a pamphlet on the infohighway binge. Windows 99. Large black letters.

WE ARE EMPOWERED
TO BEGIN THE WORLD
OVER AGAIN

Like God to Noah after the Flood.

Tell me a bit about how you'd change things, from what you saw.

Well. If you'll excuse me, I was shocked to see so many diskettes scattered on desks, I mean supposing a customer brought in a portable and his set of system diskettes, and one of them fell out in one of those cartons, or just got mixed up with others, and the customer was blamed for losing it, and made to order a new set?

A hypothetical case. But worth entertaining. Of course in our new premises there'd be more room and less, chaos as you put it. But that's a criticism. How would you put it right?

I'd insist on fixed trays on every desk.

Any other criticism?

Not on the face of it. Oh yes. if you'll excuse me again, since you ask. The offer said manager for an electronics firm. That's what I was. I know computers are electronics, but if it said computers it would sort out the candidates and save you

Don't talk yourself out of an opportunity before you're offered it, that's not good managing, I told you. Managerial skills are more important than the wares. Did you know anything technical about . . . electronic gates?

Well, yes. At least I learnt.

So there you are. What else?

Well ma'am, Ms Day, when I was in work I began to notice, besides it was hammered into us at business school, that the grander burotic firms become, the more inefficient they can be on little things, personal touches that don't get tucked away in databanks.

Such as ?

Well, for instance . . . Mouse desperate on Search. That funny article in the paper . . . A customer's just bought a computer, installed on say the 15th, gets an invoice impossibly dated the 10th, posted on 20th, payable without fault on let. The accompanying letter, when there is one, offers a maintenance contract, details enclosed, but they're not enclosed. The guarantee asks for the distributor's number but it's nowhere stamped on any of the manuals, nor is it on the letter. The conditions of sale start by saying READ THIS BEFORE UNPACKING but the document is packed, and printed so small even good eyes can't read it, on purpose no doubt. The user's manual is crammed with every instruction except the one you need. Er, well, that kind of thing. I'm not saying this firm's like that, but it's more and more frequent. With all products.

I see. Is that anorak what you normally wear?

No. I took a long walk on the Heath.

Why? Do you live around here?

No, I came by tube, and needed exercise. Nice sunny day for once.

Ow-kay. Erm. How odd, there's no address on the e-mail.

E-mail, he-male, she-male.

Can you give it me?

14 Andover Way, Kentish Town.

Post code?

I'm afraid I keep forgetting it.

Hmm. Never mind, that's where we'll be moving to or thereabouts, I'll put in the first three digits of ours. Phone? Fine. We'll let you know.

And out. No handshake just a nod.

Misery. Ring Hilary at once, or go there, a shock a reproaches the lot.

Elsie's gone, didn't wait to compare notes the bitch.

Back to the Tube change at Westminster, cup of tea and a

bite first

lunchless pangs

Brilliant remembering that funny article

memory's not so bad then.

It said Plato foresaw it all

the invention of writing would make man lose

his memory

putting things outside his head onto stone parchment or

whatever

though he wrote it

or we wouldn't know would we

and printing made it all worse

now computers are finishing the process.

Only hints of course, in the interview.

Jesus maybe she read it too.

And next? well now

    to face Hilary

        After seven years.

   Click Help.

        But Help's never any help

just produces a text of generalities.

          And she'd Save it all with an interminable

          print-out vomited from her mouth is it

          worth it?

      Damn Elsie, wonder what they asked her. But she's

    addressless too.

C'n Ah come in?

Euwsey! O'cauwse, lahk sam teey?

They're around the table in the window, saw me coming, Xavier, Adelina, Diogo and Vasco. Lucky I didn't come earlier they might be in bed before the kids came home, happened once before.

Ah'm no' stylin daon' worry, Ah jes neeyd ter aask yer somethink.

Si' daown Euwsey, yer looks dead bea'.

Weuw, jes a mini' thanks, Ah'm no' feylin toow good.

Ere tha'll pu' yer rah'.

Cheers. Sorry, Xavier, saonly jes a mini'. Lin. Ah wen for an intervioow fer a job. An thy arsked for an address, ter le' mey knaow lahk. An Ah give youwrs, an yer phaone Ah aope yer doan' mahnd iss aonly the wahnce.

Silence. Xavier glares. Kids glance their wide black eyes from one to the other. Lin's distressed.

Bu' wha' can wey sie luv? An aow'll we ge' aold of yer?

Jes sie Ah'm ou' and yer'll gimme the messige, Ah'll cam in the mornink, iss jes for a feuw dies an jes fer a feuw mini's lahk. Or give yer a lesson.

Nāo!

Xavier, yer never ere in the morninks. An is jes the wahn-orf, an i'll be aover in a few dies.

Nāo! You não come. Nunca mais.

Okye Xavier. Cheers for your co-op.

Lin see me to the door and in the area murmurs Teuwbe Stition, eleven, till end of weyk.

Queeynswie?

Yea. Bye.

Sari hug.

Fresh air

brings back fast receding consciousness a bit

Up the steps into the street

pain tearing inside like a swollen rat gnawing

six rats gnawing

quick, doorway

not this one the next

hell six more steps

train through brain bare sunbeach glittering sea walk in alone

deeper and deeper cooler and colder.

Slowly the porch again

then

the inevitable nausea no.

Breathe in, deep, slow

and again.

Every month it's like this.

Took aspirins with the tea surrep but can't be working yet

Breathe.

Oh no, it's coming up.

Tea first aspirin and all.

And the cheese sandwich.

        Everything since the breakfast sausages

retched out until there's nothing left

   and the tract grips and writhes.

Finish. Handkerchief. Relief.

Though the lower pain's still there, the rats,

what caused the upper wrenches.

        Head full of ice not brain. Cold sweat.

Head down on knees.

  Acid smell of sick makes me retch again.

       Can't stay here.

Wait just a moment and crawl down the steps before

anyone comes out or up oh lor

  clickety steps someone's coming

down quick and away

     at least to another door.

    Motorbike sound, no, moped, like a low lone-mower.

That don't matter. Stopped.

   Oh for a beaker full of the warm South warm bed hot

   water bottle on tum.

The chemist.

    That white clay stuff they give, And a chair. . .

Can't make it.

Must.

Slowly, hand on railings, cotton wool legs. Head like icebox.

     Men in the street don't suffer this at least.

Doctor used to say, when there was one, it'd all

disappear with kids as if all girls before kids fainted and

vomited every month look at chorus girls.

Guess they exercise more

but you'd think with all the walking.

Was that the back of Yuppy's sheepskin across the road?

No, it's walking away, round the corner.

Here we are. A crowd. A body with no legs and two clay feet and head an empty globe's a cockeyed construction, zing, silently thundering train through brain again breathe in train glides into station lady in pink emerges and waves to crowd little girl gives her flowers and curtsies man in golden chains bows. Faces like planets above. White overalled woman leans over. Voice from outer galaxy zooms in Stand back will you please. There now, feeling better? Jennifer help me raise her. We're going to sit you on that chair so that you can put your head down. There. What? Oh I see. Put your head down now. Terror, another retch but no, nothing left to vomit thank God as if he cared. I'll get you something hold her head down Jennifer. Yes madam I'll be with you in a moment Ann come to the counter will you. There you are, drink this. The white clayish liquid. You'll feel better in a moment.

I do. But ashamed. Must buy something. Last few pounds on painkillers and sannies no tampax for me I bleed too bleeding much. Into the plastic bag. Yeah Ah'm all rah' thanks ever so kahnd and out on shaky legs towards the Park and a bench but the sunny afternoon's long over the pink streetlights are on. Western sky deadly white but the dying light down here's pregnant with growing dark.

If only, oh for that job.

A little flat somewhere, a room a kitchenette a bath a loo

of one's own.

That's all a girl needs. Isn't it?

Maybe call at Tyburn and beg for a bed?

Why not their number instead of Lin's? It vanished anyway.

But couldn't expect the portress nun to take messages for someone not there.

And guests pay for rooms.

Oh they'd be charitable but no.

Other way.

Cross over to park.

Feeling better. Lor there he is sitting on the bench.

In that red balaclava.

Has he been there ever since?

No, not same bench, that was miles up, near Marble Arch.

Can't face that damn alphabet A for Apartheid, I for Indian Reservations an all

but he's staring the ground out ruminating the ills of the world walk away and find another bench.

There isn't one.

Walk on. No, don't pass out, roll head round for circulation there's one over there, can't.

Go on.

Roll head. J for Jihad K for Khmer Rouge no doubt.

Hey, aitch for withering?

Here it is. Oof! Head down?

No it'll bring attention.

Roll on.

It's dark now, he won't see me.

Funny how the posh accent wouldn't come

at the chemist, too ill.

But it did in Putney that was great.

She was nice. Seemed impressed.

Gave out hope.

But that probably don't mean a thing. Wonder how Croaky did.

Turn cap round and ring. Pause.
Who is it?
Hilary, it's mey, Quentin.
Quentin! . . . Go away . . . I don't want to see you.
Pleeyse Hilary, it's urgent. Just wanna tell you one thing.
One thing! After seven years!
Pleeyse.
The door opens a fraction. That Quattrocento face, with its huge eye-lids and pale blond lashes and invisible eyebrows chiselled and silver in the dim streetlight but the whole silhouette dark against the golden hall. Slightly more cushioned now, fantom grey eyes glaring.
What do you want?
Kids at haome?
You can't see them.
I only asked. It's you I want to seey.
What's happened to your voice?
Smaoke too much. Pleeyse, let me come in. I'll explain.
I don't want to know. You can't disappear without a word for seven years then just turn up. Not one word.
I knaow. You see the firm went bust.
I know that. So why couldn't you tell me, like a man? Where were you all this time?
In the streeyt.
In the — ? Don't lie to me again.
It's true, Hilary, I tried at first to set up again, without telling you, then I felt sao ashamed. And I was sleeyping out all this time. On meeysly Bene-fits. Eeyting in centres an all.
And, and, you never got a job? I thought —

Nao, Hilary, I didn't. Nor Another Woman. But this afternoon I did get an interview, for manager, in Putney, but they're moving raound here, aonly they neeyded an address and phaone. I avoided that till now, so as not to bother you, but this time I

You should get that croak seen to. All right. Come in. They're upstairs doing their homework. I don't want them to see you it's too late for that, we'll go into the kitchen but

Nao, I'll stay out here, they might come daown. I said all I wanted to say except this. The firm might ring or write, during the next few days, a weeyk, two at most, here's the name, and all I wanted was to warn you, and to come once a day. Or even just ring, to find out if there's a message or a letter.

Pause. Long look, grey in the dusk and low street lighting.

Okay then, but better ring me at the office. Round noon.

You got a job then? That's nice.

I'll write the number down. Not the name or address, I don't want you calling there.

Thanks Hilary. Real big of you. And if I get the job, maybe we

No. But I wish you luck. Goodbye.

Forgive, Hilary, forgive, it's good for the psyche.

The door hesitates in its closing movement but closes.

Trudge through the minuscule front-garden to the minuscule gate.

Cold sweat, prickly.

That wasn't too bad.

No scene to speak of.

But steely.

Guess women left alone get steely if only to cope

then get blamed for steeliness.

But no, no feelings.

What are feelings anyway they drown under words.

Or get twisted and transformed, and vanish.

Yes, they vanish. Gone. None left. Drizzle back. Business

done, think no more about it.

HEY, WHAT THE

    Tall dark figure bald, face blotched like a thermal image

        punch between eyes

                going out

        punch on mouth

Out.

        Head throbs. Greyish glow.

           Dribble from mouth

  Drizzle on face.

      Pavement wet under hands

What hap — No! A mugging!

          In the darkness between the bluewhite

streetlamps.

    Sit up.

      Street fluctuates.

Head down, brow on wet flagstones. Cool.

              Cold on chest

  Still dribbling.

      Hand to mouth.

                 Black.

Jesus it's blood not saliva. Jaw hurts too. Teeth? Tongue round.

Taste of blood. One a bit loose.

    Why's the anorak zipped open?

            Christ!

    Hand inside.

        Wallet gone.

With two weeks Benefits.

And the dog-eared dip and refs.

Stay down. Think.

Blood drips black on dark grey flagstones.

Brain lunges.

Quiet now.

Handkerchief, mop, hold.

What next?

Back to Hilary?

No.

Night Centre in Caledonian Road.

A bed

A shower.

How far is it?

Crawl to low garden wall and gate.

Here.

Hand on wall.

Gently does it.

Oh-kay.

As ladyboss slowly said.

Hey! She xeroxed those papers!

Legs shaky.

Hollow in tum. Hungry

Nausea. No. It'll pass.

But if no job no papers back

And if job it won't be

necessary

Or else, yes, always

                            necessary

Steady there

      gingerly to end of street

                into Camden Road

                      There'll be traffic and people maybe

But won't beg

                  aggressive begging they call it now

                    There's Camden Road ahead in orange

Cross it and take Murray Street into Agar Grove and on to York

Way then cut across to Caledonian, shit, it's all little streets and

a maze. What's that?

   No!

      Yes!

         No!

           Yes!

                The wallet!

Is it? Yes.

      Thrown down, too shabby to sell.

            Empty of money

but papers left

         Those dog-eared faithfuls.

Tuck it all in out of the wet. All? Not all.

             Here's Camden Road;

   rain falling fast now

         in golden shower

like Zeus and whatshername

Or the Coronation of the Virgin room 7

What's money anyway

Cross over

Murray Street that's it.

Shortish.

Aow!

Sit down. No.

So, two weeks without a cent.

Oh, small change in trouser pocket

Sweet Jesus! Ten, twelve, sixteen, seventeen pound
bits and odd! But that won't go far.

Far. How far is it? There's Agar Grove. Turn left.

Just remembered. Across York Way into Brewery Road
leads straight into Caledonian.

Not a soul in sight. Just as well, must look drunk.

No. Feel better now.

But it'll be a long way up Caledonian.

Idiot! Camden Road meets Caledonian further up. Doing two
sides of a triangle

trying to

cut across.

Too late.

Don't meet for ages anyway so much the same
and this is quieter

Hilary real tough

Course she couldn't invite, but still

a little friendliness, gentleness

as if that was still around

Oh for that job.

Here's Brewery.

So dark. Lights too far apart.

Black warehouses and, well, a brewery.

Nearly there,

well no, quite a way to walk still.

Pentonville Prison in silver and blue

in the golden distance, might be in the Uffizi

nice to be in an office again

Wonder where they're moving to.

Fra Angelico, that was it

with the potato heads looking up at the basket

shot up on golden beams like shuttlelight satellite

but more gold beams above.

Fat lot of use

Oh Hilary,

She's giving 'em dinner now or washing up while they watch

the telly

Or maybe they help her they're not kids any more

They won't grow up delinquent not with her

Or maybe it was Neil who came out and did it!

After she told'em.

Impossible

The man was tall.

But then how tall is he now? Shut up.

Brain jellied.

Feet gravelling

Gravel one end

and jelly the other

Walked across the Heath indeed!

She suggested it though, that woman at the Centre

Came in handy

Young and strong any job shit.

Feel like sixty-five

Orange lighting

all drizzled through like dust in sunbeams

Caledonian Road

Turn left

The sodium light smells, iodine on grazed knees no,

a dead smell, like a graveyard,

street filthy with litter

polystyrene packages and other trash.

London's not what it was

not here anyway

no nightlife

only in the West End

and suburban pubs and discos

all closed in.

Here there's only muggers.

Another five hundred yards or so or metres whatever

Why Quentin?

Why not Quentin?

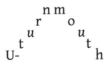

Postoffice bags of humanity in doorways.

Man passes them looking away.

And another.

And a couple hurrying.

Here it is. Ring.

Long wait.

Shouting and yelling inside and thumping

Yes?
Please, would there be a bed?
Peering.
Aow, iss yoow? Quentin inni?
Yes. Hellao er
Martin. But this plice is for yangsters naow.
Pleeyse Martin. I was mugged. Punched on the head. And robbed of Be-
nefits, drawn today. Can't face a doorway.
Tell that to the
Pleeyse, Martin, pleeyse believe meey. I don't feeyl well.
Pause. More peering, though I must be lit from the inside light behind
him.
Yer bleeydin . . . Rah' then, cam in, there's a few beds left.
Thanks Martin. What's all the raow?
Jes the usual. Yang thags.
Thugs!
I stop dead in a freeze-frame. What if
Yer frah'ened? C'mon.

Yes. Sorry. I'm shaken up.

Cam along. Muss sie Ah regre' the aole dies when adauwts cam ere. Thy coul' be drank or arf dead, bu' there was stiuw a bi' of deycency left in em. Thass auw gorn naow. Ere, Ah'll give yer this separa' cubicuw. Wanner eey'?

Yes.

Rest ere an wash a bi', shaowers an byes'ns daown ter the left, remembah? Bu' yer'll be ficin em in the canteeyn. Unless thy 'r auw watchin telley bah naow.

Thanks Martin, I'm real grateful.

Knaow the wie? Iges since yer kime.

Yes. Preferred doorways in the end. It was so, military, here.

Tha' was Zeb. Ee's gorn, Ah took aover. Bu' ee did keeyp em quiert, be"er than Ah can Ahm soft. Tike i' eeysy lad. Ere's a meeyl ticke', and wan fer b & b. Muss gao naow, seeyer.

Seeyer. Thanks Martin.

Zeb for Zebedee. Yea. Real Nazi-type. Liked to show who was boss round here. But then, Martin used to be one of us. Christ what a racket. Can't face it. Must eat. Maybe a shower then they'll be gone from the canteen. No, they'll stop serving just wash face. Nine already. Street so much freer why be down to this? Hate people. Oh for that job God please, Can't take any more. Wouldn't hate people then. Promise. Tears! Hey, pull the old guts together no use giving in, or praying to non-existence.

The canteen's empty.

Hi. There's only steheuw left.

A bald young man. Like the mugger. Can't be.

Fine. Where is everyone?

Watchin telley, iss the aonly thing'll keeypem quier', when the fiwrn cam on.

Thugdrug I suppose?

Ahspaose.

What was all that raow before? Fighting?

Dunnao. Thy was plyin guitars an rock, saounded lahk an auw nah' rive cep the meuwsic wasn technao. Then somethink appened. Eey' i' ap pleeyse Ah wanna cleeyn an claose daown an gao an watch.

Aow!

Whass the ma''er?

Sorry. I must eayt slowly. Lip's swaollen.

Someone bashyer?

Yes. Look, this'll take ages, why daon't you gao and watch, I'll wash up the plate and stuff. Promise.

Weuw . . . Rah' yer are. Bu' Ah muss bring the blahnd daown. Yer can ge' in thraouw tha' door seey? Ah'll leeyve i' anlocked an cam in an seey te i' li'er. Bu' leeyve i' claosed wiuw'yer.

Ey, can you put some of this back I can't eeyt it all it'll take me all night. Or is there a bin back there?

Yeah. But mussn wiste i'. No' ungry then?

Yes, but even more tired. Want to shaower while they're in there and bed.

Okie mi'e. Ere yer gao. An cheers.

Peace. Pain. Silence. Munch. Meat tough. Just eat the potatoes. At least it's hot. There. Last bit. The little door. The bin. The sink. Shootings from the tellyroom.

Too tired to shower. Sink into bed.

Suddenly it's all banging and yelling again. Telly over? Lor it's seven! Longest night for years. Quick, shower while they're still in the canteen.

But the canteen's crowded, caterwauling, cacophonous. Can't face it. Must, no money. Q for T.

And sausages, better stock up, Stockwell very funny. Fried eggs too, the lot. And nobody looks at me I'm an oldie. That corner over there. But a threesome makes straight for the same table. They'll either abuse or ignore please God let them ig

Yeah, thass im. Says one of them, mildly familiar.

They sit around me with a clatter.

Didn' Ah seey yer in Pu'ney?

Did you?

Yeah, in the queuew fer tha' job. Yer shooar took a long tahm.

Food is still difficult. The youth looks about fifteen, they come younger and younger, even among potential managers. Redhead, that's how I somehow snapped him into the old databank. In a dark green polo under a black leatherlook jacket. There's a girl in black leather pants and zip-jacket open on a red sweater and another boy, or man, slightly older in a once elegant loose ocre outfit, or is it sepia, siena who cares, now very shabby, at least twenty but I can't tell ages any more.

Yer look lahk yer bin in a figh'.

Got mugged. Last night.

Aow, thass tough. Feeylin all rah'?

Yep.

They tuck into the yuck food.

Nime's Rickey with a mouthful of sausage. An this is Olley ao sorry where are me manners this is Pavlaova. Weuw Paula reelly bu' used ter bey a dancer.

She laserbeams above her teacup and adds ballet dancer.

Her dark hair drawn back tight into a sort of invisible bun. How come then?

I wasn't re-engineered like those two. She talks posh. Is she slumming, on an urban plunge as they say now?

Sao?

Partner dropped me. Back broken. Too long off to start again. Learnt nothing else you see except useless steps and positions and music. Tried to go in for teaching it but too many retired or failed ballerinas around. But plenty of suppleness for walking the streets.

Olly ogles her goofily and eats. Dark and distinguished despite the scratched ocre outfit. Looks like a grated carrot. If the floppy brown hair were green he'd be a carrot, just pulled out of the earth. Come to think of it he was there too. Seems inarticulate like so many of the young. Maybe she came as well, later. With that poise she'd win. Anyone can be a man-ager.

You didn' give us a nime, did yer? says the redhead.

Sorry. Quentin.

Ooh la. Pavlova says coolly. With a name like that you're sure to get it.

Yeah, an yer stiyed ever sao long. Wha did thy arsk yer?

At last the excruciating eating is done. But even sipping tea hurts.

Oh, the usual. As if I went for interviews every day. You know, how would I change things and all.

Did she naow?

Rival eyes pierce me. I take out a cigarette.

No smoking in here, sorry. Says Pavlova, firmly but courteously. But you can go into the tellyroom.

Godsent excuse.

Well thanks I will, can't shake the habit.

Expensive one.

So they don't? I thought all young people did, or drugs.

We'll join you there later.

Is that a threat? She waves, Olly nods politely.

Well, that'll be nice. See you then.

Go straight out, into the street. Shit, so tired still and looks like the weather's turned cold. It's bloody cold even in the tellyroom. Telly on. Still breakfast news, perishable info, someone interviewed against what excites sound engineers, loud traffic, walking on gravel, making words inaudible then sudden flash of the Prime Minister on his opponents: You're talking about perceptions, I'm dealing with reality. Arsehole. And now a news girl frumpy in crimplene pink suit that crinkles round the armpits and across the sleeves and chest, staring at the camera, can't they get girls smart in every sense they're paid enough aren't they why put them in suits anyway they look like air hostesses each one a different colour and pastel shows the creases more, instead of silk shirts or soft chunkies that fold where they're meant to?

> Polish workers used to cross into the Soviet Union to earn better pay. Today it's the Ukrainians who cross illegally into Poland for the same reason. A government spokesman picture heavy accent Yes we know of zem but zey help our economy. If it grroos a serrious tret we take action.

In other words use em while you can then expel them when they become a problem.

> A young woman of African or West Indian origin was found strangled in Kensington Gardens yesterday evening around six colour picture of a startled pretty girl black curls police suspect rape — It's Elsie.

Next, the Business Summary. But first we'll take a break.

Stay with us.

Out. Buy paper. It'll cost a precious pound but

Icy wind, whipping, lashing.

Where's the newsagent? Down there looks like.

Front page but tucked to the side. Gory details, maybe a prostitute soaked sanitary towel sidetracked and blood everywhere oh shit leave all that to the videonasties it's Elsie all right passing witness says saw a man sitting on a bench not far black leather jacket on blue jeans red woolly hat. Tube to Edgware Road change at Kings Cross and Baker Street maybe Tek'll still be at the other Centre. Smell of electricity and unwashed cattle-crowds along corridors. Guitars, trumpet, violin, voices singing, clashing groups of different music echoing through the glazed tunnels. Another pound fifty gone. Thundering like arteries under London's skin. Why bother? Train packed can't even read the paper. Feel sick. Out. More cattle-crowds along glazed but stinking corridors. Eight thirty. But he likes to linger over a cup of tea and a smoke.

He does.

Hi Croaky. Hey, why no breakfast? God what's happened to you? Got bashed?

Seeyn this?

He looks under the pointing finger. Chokes on a cigarette.

Reeyd it.

He reads.

I sit, pushing the others down the bench. A bench, somebody said, one-feels good on a bench, the invention of the chair was the beginning of selfishness, each for himself. Was it you on that bench?

Yes. But early. Fivish. Dusk falling. I saw her. She saw me, then turned away and went to sit on another bench further on . . . Croaky! You don't think

Gaowon.

This jacket's brown not black.

Very dark brown, and in that light

Oh God. She was rolling her head, erm, in a strange way as if to say she didn't er, care to talk to me. I stared at the ground, pretending not to see her. Wondering if I should, well, join her. But I didn't . . . You don't believe me!

Gaowon.

Croaky, I swear to you I didn't. She vanished, yes erm, wrapped in darkness and I went off up the er Bayswater Road to find, I mean towards Marble Arch and bussed up the Edgware to a berth.

And nao witnesses I suppaose. Then walk away from here, Tek, or take a bus and a truck aout of London, North, or Eayst, West but not Saouth. Change thaose jeeyns back to the braown corduroys and get rid of that red balaclava.

Come with me Croaky, I'm all shaken up.

Nao. I'm shaken up too. I was mugged last night, lost all newly drawn Benefits, slept at Caledonian Road. Neeyd to be alaone. Here's the paper for company.

Pleyse Mister pleece-man.

Yes 'm? Yer should call me constable dear.

People push and jog around the kiosk in the Queensway Tube Station.

Ah've jes bouw' this piper. Ah can' reyd.

An yer expect may to reyd the piper for yer?

Bu' Ah knaows this girl. Shey's me friend.

Yer do do yer? Sao?

Pleeyse, tell mey wha' i' sez.

He glances at the headline, and down.

Yer knaow er ey?

Wha' das i' sie? Whass shey dan?

Shey ain' dan nothink, shey's bin dan in.

Dan in?

Murdered. Strangled. Riped.

Nao!

Man seeyn sittin on a bench no' far orf as darkness feuw. Probbly a prostitu'e.

Nao!

Nao wha'?

She ain' a pros — prostituta.

Weuw yer'd be"er gao ter the police stiytion an tell em.

The pleece stiytion? Is i' far? Ah go"er ge' back aome to ge'

No' far. Up the Byswa'er Raoad ter Nottinkiuw, turn rah, then fowrk immej ut left, yer knaow wha' a fowrk is? He gestures with his left hand. Ten mini's wauwk.

Bu'. Ah muss ge' back aome.

Look lidy, if yer knoaw tha' woman lahk yer sigh, thy'll wanner knaow Waon' thy?

Yes. Thanks mister.

I'll never remember all that I'll ask again at Notting Hill. Tears down my face. I'm cold in my thin blue coat. It's Xavier's fault she stayed round here, in the park. And they rang this morning about the job! They wanted to give it her! And see her again! If only. It's a long way.

The man at the desk is barely interested.

Rough sleeper probably. So you say you knaow her?

The piper sigh shey was a, a prostituta.

You daon't wanter belieyve all you reeyd in the pipers. But rough sleeypin daon't rule it out do it? Well, give me your nime an address, and phaone if you can, we'll contact you if wey neeyd more information. Friend you say? What kind of friend?

Wey me' cleynin a' Tahburn Couven'.

Tyburn ey? We'll make inquiries. Thank you dear. Sign ere will you.

Ah can'. Shey was teeychin mey to reeyd an wrah

Was she naow? Did you pie er?

Nao. Ah feeyder samtahms.

I seey. Well, put a cross. Can you find your way aome?

Yes. Shey me nime an phaone fer a job shey wen' for an thy rings this mornink an warmed to give i' er.

What sort of job?

Dunnao. Thy sez manager job.

He fills it in.

Did thy give yer their nime? Or phaone number?

Well? Did thy?

Nao.

Surely thy gaive you a message for er, asking er to ring back?

Yeah. Bu' Ah lost i', or euwse iss a' aome.

Well, you must fahnd it and give it to us, they'd give us more details.

Wha', will thy . . . ? Where, is shey? Can Ah seey er?

Not naow. We'll let you knaow about arringements.

It's all over in a moment. Oh Elsie.

Why did I hold back that office number ?

Love's born of poverty Father Reilly said and

sleeps in the street.

Why her?

Pleeyse, where's the Tuwbe Stiytion?

They tell me. Kindly. Tears streaming. You all right dear?

Nod vigourous and away.

Born of poverty and something else.

Occasiao. No, Opportunidade.

But why?

Here's the Station. Now I know where I am. Get bus in

Bayswater Road.

Where to? Tyburn. Yes. They'll help me.

The park shimmers in shy sun after the rain. No, can't look.

Why couldn't I — But impossible in one room and beds.

Rosario's empty.

Oh Rosie be careful.

Come back.

Here's the stop.

It's turned cold, feel frozen in my skimpy blue coat.

Tall brown house among brick and white ones.

Big brown porch. Told me she

slept there sometimes.

Why didn't she . . .?

Door to outer lobby open now but closed at night.

Ring bell.

Long long wait. Portress-nun always miles away.

Ah, she's coming.

The little window opens, frames the nun's face framed in white and black.

Adelina! You're crying. What's the matter dear? Come in.

Side-door clicks. The hall smells of polish, is bare except for the phone corner behind glass and white wood, with a chair, nowhere else to sit, by the tall glazed window, nuns musn't see out.

Sister, iss Euwsey.

Who is Elsie dear? Compose yourself.

Useter cleyn ere wi' mey. Lass year. Then yer couldn'

Oh, yes. What about Elsie then?

Shey's bin murdered. In park. Shey was me friend.

Come into one of the parlours dear, and sit down. I'll make you some tea.

Nao, nao tey thanks. Ah jes wanter ask yer

It won't take a minute and it'll perk you up. Go along to the middle par-lour and at least sit down, you're distressed.

Past the long guest-kitchen down the corridor, deep into the building, to the middle parlour, the one with the two rickety armchairs.

And out it all comes, all jumbled with Xavier, the paper, the police, the lessons, the job, the request refused, the Tube arrangement, the message never delivered. Thy gives er the job, Sister, everythink was goin ter bey auw rah'.

My child, you mustn't blame yourself. You must pray for strength.

Sister, shey's all alaone naobody ter look after er naow. Can yer doow er a Mass in the Chapel lahk? If thy gimme the . . . body? Lor an wey can' afford a coffin.

My sweet Adelina, it's not up to you to pay for the coffin. But we only do Requiem Masses here when a sister dies you know.

Aow.

There's a church you go to isn't there?

Yeah bu'

You must go and see your priest, dear, Father Reilly isn't it? But I'll speak to Mother General about money for the funeral if he can't provide. Come back tomorrow. But go and see him first.

Auw rah' Sister, Ah'll trah. If yer sie sao.

I do dear. Tell me her full name, so that we can put it down in our prayers for the passed-on.

Bus back. And to the church. Closed. No idea where the priest lives. Can't read the notice on door. I'll come to Mass tomorrow and see him after.

What do they do with unattached bodies? Who pays? Meu Deus! Never rung that office they should know she ain't available. Didn't want police to tell em. Why did I say about the job? Can't at home Xavier'll be there so he'll know I took the message. Phone at Station. Here's the number I took it down, but couldn't write the name, Mrs Day I think. Doesn't work. Try next one.

Ellao? Can Ah speyk to Mrs Die?

Your name, please?

Oliveira, bu' shey won' knaow me nime.

Well, I can't —

Shey left a message wiv mey this mornink, for a friend, wha' was given a job wivyer.

I see, you're the cleaning lady are you? Just a moment.

A very long moment, more cash quick, no, yes, who is it?

Yer spaoke to mey this mornink bou' a job for —

Yes?

Weuw shey's dead.

Dead?

Sudden lahk. During nah'.

Oh. I'm sorry. How — click, gurgle.

Oh well, she don't care I've done me duty lucky I thought of not saying murdered or they might link it up. I'm barmy, as if it could count against her now. Oh well at least the job can go to someone else. Well it would anyway if she didn't ring. My brain's a regular curry. But the police wanted to know more about not being a, a prostituta. Now I bury her right, somehow. I'll go and see the police again. Think I can remember the way. Sandals hurt.

Well, you've brought that number lidy?

Nao. Ah meeyn yes, ere. Bu'Ah wanna see er. Ah wanna pie for the funeral.

She's not here madam, she's at the morgue.

The — ? Where's tha'?

Look lidy, ere's the nime of the undertiker oo looks after theeyse things. Gao and seey him and talk it aover with im.

Can't read the address, I'll take a taxi.

Past and Xavier's in one of his furias, shouts at me Portuguese. No lunch, and don't say you've been shopping you're empty-handed where were you whatever next what a family an all the rest. I put the paper in front of him. He can't read either so I tell him. Consternation for a minute then more furia. I don't even listen. All the month's money's gone now and I can't tell him. Then the kids come in, then Joaquim. Two days ago he came back with his motor painted black, wouldn't say why, was it an omen? Or advance mourning? To the kitchen while the row goes on. Joaquim follows, holding the paper.

So yer read i'?

Yeah. Sorry bou' tha' mum.

Shey was me friend, wha'ever yer sie, Joaquim.

Ah sez nothink mum, jes sorry.

In a low voice: Listen Joaquim, shey's alaone an nobody to bury er. Sao Ah gaoes ter the funeral man and pays fer a coffin, the cheeypest, bu' Tahburn sez thy 'd elp mybe an tomorrer Ah'll seey Huey Father Reilly fer a Mass.

Thass bigguv yer. Sao?

Ah spends all the month's money Joaquim and Ah can' tell IM. Yer daon', yer wouldn'

Yer muss bey jaokin.

Bu' yer mikes money Joaquim, Ah daon knaow aow an Ah daon ask.

Syour problem mum, yer gaoes all genrous lahk fer nao reeyson an expec mey to elp.

Shsh. Daon' shaou'.

Well tell mey, whah should Ah ?

Jes to elp yer mum.

Some mum. Spens all er money on a bladdey coffin, yer knaows Ah couldn' stand er!

But he stays there awkward like. A monster image floats above the onions.

Joaquim! Yer didn' —

Didn'

Kiuw er?

Wha', mey? Mum! Yer mussby barmey. Ah wasn' eyven ere yesserdie when shey come.

Aow dyer knaow shey come then?

Dad taol' mey.

Ah seeys yer maoped tahed ter the rilins ap there, bu' yer no' come daown. Jes after shey gom.

Yer allucinitin. On drugs eh? Some mum, lahk Ah sie. Gao fuck yerself.

And out.

Into the room? Or out altogether? But it's night already! I peep. I shout.

Joaquim, yer no' ter gao ou' in the nah', iss dyengerous! Xavier cauw im back! Whah can' ee stye an eey' wiv us an watch the telley? O Santo Deus!

Too late. Xavier shrugs. Back to the kitchen to cry into the simmering curry.

Dear God, whatever next!

How's Derica's doing on her slippery soap? For instance

Derica can't understand why Gina accepted a job as

Claire's assistant

Is there a Claire? Never mind.

But the intriguing Gina is determined to succeed where

others failed

She alone will subdue the millionairess.

So Claire is a millionairess.

We create mental money.

But what about Rex and Doug and Rick and Cindy et al?
On the Metropolitan Line full of metrognomes. Well no, not
many at this hour.

Shooting past Kilburn without stopping,
And others.

Reflection in black window pouched and pained.
History's too palimpsestuous. Willesden Green.

Dollis Hill, can't even read them.
So, in for a thorough repsychling. A floppy disc-rumination.
But discrimination's good for PGP on brain's internet,

despite Virtual Communities.
Ah, Preston Road.

Nine more stations to Watford then hitch
North to wherever

Didn't watch this morning. You needn't watch, Tek, she said
Hence the shock when he brought in that tabloid.

To Birmingham or Leicester accordingly or even Leeds.
Damn, the ins not to mention the outs of London
doorways were just becoming nicely familiar.

The street. Who would think? Over-generalisation they said.
Refusal to face
the nitty-gritty of one decade. Then the offshoots
of academe

journalism, publishing et al, just as bad.
Did you hack the wrong boss or back the wrong horse?
What a world. A Welteranschauung. Play respects to it in
playback or back pay.

How's that for a mise-en-trope?

This ride cost over four pounds.

And it's turning cold, must buy a wool cap, different colour.

Histoires de cul, tail tales. Stop it.

And those lies to Croaky, making up an identity as crapped

out war-hero.

As if this century's obsessive search for identity wasn't just

a sick humanoid joke

Everybody egoshiating over and over.

What to do? Oh Elsie. Her damn cheerfulness. A for orses,

and now Z for effect.

Couldn't help her with aitch though, or jay. Chafe or

strain? No, not good. J for jitterbug she said. Jig, java. Jihad.

Juntas. K for konga is that a dance? Karaoke? Kigali. Katyn. We

didn't find an I. L for lambada. Lambeth Walk. Walk walk walk

we do nothing but walk.

Like Richard Feverel. Or Jeanie Deans. Or Nicholas

Nickleby. He walked from Yorkshire was it, then almost

to Southampton.

I for Israel, born in the parturition of the Red

Sea no not that. Go away.

Fornicator 3 ad through the window where are we?

North Harrow. Just two jeaned legs hip to thigh with a bulge.

Nobody apologises, not for My Lai or Nagasaki or

Nankin or Treblinka.

Uganda Vietnam Verdun, hell who cares, X for

Xenophobia.

Only Willy Brandt knelt.

And didn't need to.

Houses stuck side to side like Siamese twins for ever. The Underground should remain underground. Everyone cosy at home. Hind fences high enough to avoid eye-contact as they say from kitchen to kitchen, those in front lower for neighbourly pretence.

But now it's all vertical. Tower blocks. Inner cities outside.

And further out there'll be the fearful rich in their

new compounds

behind high walls with barbed wire and electronic

gates and code numbers and private vigilantes. Don't

park on driveway or is it don't drive on parkway.

State of the Nation. A state-of-the-art nation. But the artists

gave up. End of Nation State.

We were two billion on earth when dad was young, and

we're six billion now. In one lifetime. But they say the

growth is steadying now.

If he's still alive.

Ow canyer walk sao long when yer sao aold?

Well you know, Blake, people walked much more when I was young. And even more before that. Jeanie Dean now, in one of Scott's novels I was telling you about, she walked all the way from Edinburgh to London, to see the king and save her sister. In fact she saw the queen. And Nicholas Nickleby walked from London almost to Southampton. Met a theatre troop before he got there though and joined them.

Oo's eey?

And as for Africa, well everyone walked. Even in the hot sun. Till the buses came. And then everyone crowded in overnumerous, hanging dangerously out like a swarm of bees on a crocodile. Unless they bought second-hand cars, cluttering the traffic. In Lagos you can hardly move.

Ah knaow, Yoowley, sauw i' on telley. Ah daon' give a shi'.

A shit is just what you are giving, Blake, simply by saying it.

Silence. I've gone too far again.

Where are you off to, Blake?

Jainin me mi'es. On a buiwdin-sah' orf Kiuwbn Igh, afore i' ge's cauwed Shoouw Ap Ill.

Not for a shoot up I hope?

Nao.

But he doesn't laugh, or even smile in the iodine light. Must quench those brief attacks of authority.

A building site. You mean you work at night?

Nao. Iss abandoned. Uge plice. Way meey' there reglar. Ere i' is, beyahnd tha' door in the fence. S'long Yoowley, nahce bampin inter yer.

Hold on, Blake. Can one sleep there?

Weuw,

You don't want me to join you. I understand.

Thy's all yang, Yoowley, yer'd be

But I'd go straight to another part, you say it's huge. A future commercial complex I take it?

There's nao roowf anywhere Yoowley, jes wauws, biesements bu' aopen skah. Nao good ter yer if i' rines.

I see. But it's not raining now. It's turned cold and windy, and walls would at least

Saokay fer us, wey jes tauwk an plan, an gao orf.

Plan what, Blake?

Aow ere's Joakey, hi Joakey!

A slim figure rides to the door in a black helmet on a black Vespa thing. He raises his plastic vizor. Very young, seems, Indian as far as I can tell in this orange light. All very young. More and more young people, more and more old, only the middle ones left to pay for them.

Tara, Yoowley, seeyer mybey, aope yer fahnds a plice.

They vanish behind the fence.

The Welfare dream dying in the street.

Where next?

What's the time? Nearly eight. Ravenous.

There's a drab block of flats across the road, big doorway.

Shops all along, blinds down or metal gratings.

Must eat something or I won't sleep. Only two
pound and odd left.

Four decades ago a pound could pay a week's rent in a shabby
rent-controlled.

Now it barely buys a newspaper.

There's a poky restaurant a bit further down
in the block of flats.

Too posh.

Well, not really, only posh for me.

But there's nothing else.

Why isn't there a and chip shop they'd give me
a cornet free. It's Indian or something. No, Bangladeshi. Could
try and beg.

White car parked outside, the only one, gleaming pink in
the sodium.

Who knows.

Green walls with red moons haphazard, round red neon circle above,
green formica tables and circular red plastic mats.

Not many people. Stray couples. Young. No waitress around or would it
be a waiter? But older couple there, in the corner, they might be kinder.
Sipping tea in glasses and nibbling poppadam and pickles. I'll join them,
may I?

I put down the big plastic bag with the blanket against the chair.
They're deep in conversation and look up, annoyed, then pointedly at
other tables, still empty. But I sit. Professor-type, I know it; wife too prob-

ably, both well fed and groomed. Kind, usually, full of liberal ideology. That other couple last night, offered me another pizza. What are they doing around here?

They continue their conversation, a bit too purposefully, something about quantum physics, to cut out any small talk from me.

A dark waiter appears, in a spotless white pyjama thing, a dhoti, is it, brings them two plates very full of chicken meat in diarrhoea sauce, with rice. And two nans on sideplates. The sauce smells very spicy, tickling the nostrils and almost turning the empty stomach inside out. The waiter looks at me with polite scorn and moves away as if I weren't there.

Gingerly I stretch hands, take the professor's plate, may I?

He grabs it, looking up at me amazed, no not even, indignant, furious. Tug of war. His tea-glass topples. The plate clatters to the floor, breaks, and the chicken korla or whatever it is and rice flattens out like a cow-turd. And hot tea all over the table, and on his trousers and on, aïe, thighs burn.

What the hell do you think you're doing?

Too abashed to say simply I'm hungry.

The waiter arrives with a pail and shovel and mop. He seems to think the man dropped it. I will brring you one otherr sir, you are not to worrry accidents will happen will they.

The man glares at me, patting his trousers with his red paper napkin.

The food's gone, I must go too. But I stretch out for her nan. She grabs it fast and furious. Not even that. I get up, and in the bending movement upwards swipe his roundly bitten-in nan and stride outside into the Bengal night.

Well! Whatever next!

Why did we stray into this area Vivian, I told you we weren't far from home.

I know, George, but I was so hungry, and didn't feel like cooking. It was such a long drive.

Herre is your korrla, good sir. And another glass of tea yes? And nan. Did the other gentleman leave?

Gentleman! He was no

Shshsh darling, no fuss.

Yes sir. I saw it all sir. A verry shameful conduct is it.

Yes, you could put it that way. But er, never mind. Thank you so much.

You are verry welcome sir.

Silence as he looks at us. Then goes.

George.

Yes darling?

I feel ashamed.

Ashamed? What ever about?

Well, I don't know really. I can't quite put my finger on it. I mean, I'm thinking. I mean, there we are, working hard in our sphere, researching for humanity, and, well, somehow, I mean, we do get a bit, cut off, from other spheres, don't you think? Shouldn't we, well, to tell you the truth, George, I'm appalled by the fact that, without this er incident, I would never even notice such a person.

Notice? How is noticing relevant? He thrust himself on us, we couldn't help noticing him. There were plenty of empty tables. I never saw such behaviour.

Yes George, you're right. Eat up now or it'll get cold.

Silence as we eat. I expressed myself unclearly. Of course noticing is irrelevant. So why am I upset? I can hardly swallow. Excuse me a moment. I get up, rush to the door, open it, look up and down the street. Then back to the table.

There's no-one there.

Well of course there's no-one there. What's the matter with you Vivian? Why was he in here anyway, he shouldn't be, even this shabby place.

The waiter brings hot cloths in thin plastic envelopes. They look like white coconut nans.

I knew that we — oh dear, what a lousy end to a pleasant conference. Not that Carlisle gave us anything but rain of course. Still, it was a success, wasn't it? Your paper

Watching the restaurant in the darkness opposite,

well, a little way off, back near the wooden door,

to see if the car is theirs when they come out. Why?

It's turning cold. Bitter cold.

Just to see.

Munching the nan. Couldn't happen in Africa.

That was quick, there she is in the light of the door.

Pop inside behind the fence, leave the door open a chink.

But she's alone.

Stares up and down the street.

Waits.

Goes in again.

Good grief, what does she want?

Or suddenly ashamed at their bourgeois reaction,

coming out full of true caritas to offer me a meal?

Try again?

No, not worth the risk.

But can't cross the road to that doorway

now, they might come out.

Yes. Here they are, coming out. Didn't linger over a

desert anyway.

They get into the pinky white car, laughing excitedly. They

drive off.

Good, can cross now.

Ere, whass this aole wreck doowin ere? Ge' off aour backs.

The gang surrounds me in the lurid light. I can see Blake's Urhobo face gleaming orange and his white eyeballs pink then he looks away. Are they going to beat me up? Hands up helplessly, the plastic bag with the blanket in the left, I stare at the gang leader then at Blake, but he's still turned aside. Please, I just thought I might sleep here.

Aow, a raff sleeyper.

This ain' a sheuwter yer damclack. Gao on, ou' yer gelo, we're on a job.

They jolt me onto the street, I stumble, fall, pick myself up and cringe along the wooden fence, too frightened to cross the road to that doorway.

Ey tha' car, Sam, is gorn.

Cauwse i' is Ken yer cre'in, nao yuwse ter us in tha' cayf lah'in'. Ere iss freeyzin caouw, c'mon.

Their voices drift off. The chill drizzle or rainless damp of the last few days suddenly dropped at least twenty degrees. Raise the scarf over ears and mouth. It's like wading through an iceberg. Hope it doesn't snow. Except the paramedics come out in cars to pick us up when it's real cold.

On and on, treading Shoot Up Hill towards Cricklewood Broadway. Something'll turn up.

The neon or spot-lit shops behind their metal fishnets make bright white shores for the greypink sodium sea, well, river really, with us bathyscaphing smoothly along the bottom. Two static goldfish ahead, two round white creatures like owl-eyes approaching on the right, passing, and again, the deepsea world illuminated by Cousteau's invisible flaremen and amber, red, or green animals watching for us along the left in a diminishing line. And now, the two white sharks like sentryfish standing erect and waiting.

In the garishly lit phonebooth the fat grey and green bundle looks like a baby whale, but huddled on the floor, knees up with a pink woolly head bowed down upon them.

There shey is Charlie. In the sime boowth.

But she waon't come you say?

Nao, she's nuts. Thass why I — ere wey gao.

Pity to wake her Frank.

Aow shey likes to seey mey. An she muss eey' a' leeyss.

Shu' the door you chump, phaone's vandalised.

Shouted muffled into her knees.

Iss Frank, Ivey.

My words make a puff of mist like a small gunshot caught in the white light of the booth and disintegrating in the stink coming out of the door. She raises her face, blotched and infragreen in the light and framed in the dirty pink wool with grey wisps sticking out like fins.

Aow, Frank. Iss yoow.

Cam with us Ivey, pleeyse. Another gunshot of mist. Yoow'll die freeyzin', eeyven in there.

Ah will if yoow daon shu' the fackin door.

Wey can tike yoow to an ostel Ivey.

Ah ite ostels, yoow knaow tha'. Shu' the door.

Now it's her words that steam as the cold seeps in.

Jes during the caol' spell.

Caold? Iss never caold till Christmas. No' till Januwary.

But it is, Ivey, temp belaow zerao. Come along.

Our mini gunshots barely meet before disintegrating. The smell attenuates the cold.

All them bunks in big roowms, and yang oowligans flinging their jeers and sneers araound.

Bu' a' leeyst i'uw be Warm, and there'll bey foowd.

Nao. Er . . . Did you bring anything, Frank?

I did. I knaow yoow by naow Ivey, you're cussed independen.

Thass nahce.

She fumbles in an old black leather shopping bag and brings out two zinky dishes and a plastic spoon.

Tike theeyse then Frank, they're from the laass caold spell in Octaober. All washed ap. In the public toile', bu' the wa'er's cleeyn. Bin trilin em all throuw the mahld weeyks.

You're amizing Ivey, cheers.

I shut the door.

Back to the van and the hot container. Another hollow metal dish, covered with a second, and a plastic spoon.

There yer gao luv. Nahce stcheuw. Tha'uw warm yoow ap.

Thanks ever sao Frank. Nao whiskey Ah spaose? She cackles.

Nao, but my friend ere's a nurse, he can give yoow a medicai'ed pickup.

Premeditai'ed murder more lahk. New pal, ey? Whass his nime?

Charlie.

Charlie is yer darlin yer darlin yer darlin.

Who gives her the pickup in a tumbler of thick glass the size of an eye-wash.

Shu' the door naow, lahk the good boys yoow are.

The door must close before she'll eat anything. The door closes.

Do they knaow you do this Frank?

Aonly the chef, sao-called, but iss eeysy. I bough' the ho' continer me-self and the me'al dishes and he give mey the foowd. I doow i' every nah' soown as the caold cam on.

I start up the bathyscaph and move away. And what happens when you're off?

She arf starves I spaose. I alwise warn er.

Rum lady. Why doesn't she want to come?

Well, yoow eard. The ostels are maostley fer the yang oo leeyve aome an cant fahnd work an waon gao back. Iss taff on the aolder ones naow, thy feeyl anwahnted, thy faold in on theirselves.

Why's she in the streeyt?

I never ask. Sime as everyone else I spaose, nao job, nao money for the rent, an all the rest. There's anather bandle. The nigh's jes star'in . . .

The bundle in the doorway's a long one, a gangly boy in a dirty sheep-skin jacket and black shiny shellsuit trousers. He cringes a greypink face.

Ah ain dan nathink, leeyve mey beey.

Daon bey afride sanny, we're the paramedics, prahvi' lahk. Wey pick ap the aomeless when iss caold.

Aow. Sao whah can' yer doow tha' every nah'?

Rules is rules, c'mon ap, wey'll tike yoow to a meeyl an a bed.

He hesitates. Gets up slowly, long legs taking a whole twenty seconds to unfold. He stamps on them a bit, then follows us to the van. First catch.

Yer aour first catch.

Lahk a fish yer meeyn?

I meeyn yoow' si' pietiently in the van while wey pick up athers, ere's one.

An old man. Like a floor mop under a large floorcloth, grey hair stick-ing out of a thin grey blanket, with black-framed glasses unremoved for sleep. Half dead in a doorway.

Hey's dead!

Nao he isn't. Very weeyk pulse. I'll give him an injection.

The man lies motionless as Charlie slowly frets up the sleeves, the plastic one and the woolly one. He jolts at the needle prick, the eyes open and blink behind the thick glasses.

You'll feel better in a maoment. We're taking you to a warm bed and food.

What? Where. Ow!

Can you get up? Weuw help you.

Hands under the arms and up he goes but yells and half crumples in our arms.

Legs are gone. Was I run over?

We put him down again gently.

Hypothermia. Get the stretcher Frank, weuw must take him to the hospital.

The gangly boy offers to help as I detach the stretcher and unfold the sideseat into a bunk. He follows me.

Thanks son, help Frank with the shoulders, I'll take the legs, they'll hurt. Fragile, This Side Up. Gently naow, one, two three lift. He yells again but he's on the stretcher.

There. Pick up the laower end wiuw you boy, while Frank gets the thermos aout.

And in. Thermos. Spout-mug. There naow, sip this quietly. Haold it in your hands, it'uw warm them.

But the hands are dead and can't take the spoutmug Charlie holds out. Righ' san, haold it for him will you.

Can yer gimme wahn toow?

Later. You hold the mug for him.

He sits on the opposite bench and bends over. Charlie gets out to join me in front. I talk over my shoulder.

Whass the nime, boy?

Never yoow mahnd.

Simmer daown, jes miking conversaition while ee drinks.

Thy cauw mey Yuppey.

Aokey Yuppy. Mine's Frank.

Ah knaow.

And this is Charlie. Ee's a nurse.

Stop nattering Frank, put the heayting up, move off and daon't stop again, whoever we seey. They'll wait.

Righ' doc.

He talks up three hospitals, third okay. At Emergencies he gets out and walks in. At last two cloaked nurses come out with a long trolley and help him with the transfer, causing more yells. He follows them in, I tell the boy to fold the bench back. I give him the hot broth, he deserves it.

Cor iss 'o'.

It's menter bey. Sao thy call yer Yuppy.

Yeah.

Still daon wanter give the reel nime?

Ah daon care ter. No' oblahged am Ah?

Nao, pleeyse yerself Yuppy. I'm sorry abou' this delie.

Weuw, iss nahce an warm in ere.

As long as I keeyp the engine ranning. Wha'

An daon aask mey nao questions lahk whah Ahm in the streey'.

I wasn gaoing ter. I was abaouter sie whass keeyping Charlie? Admin crap I spaose. Bu' why didn yer gao strigh' to an ostel? Thy welcome yang peoyple like yoow.

Dunnao.

Yoow daon like them ahther? Lo's of peoyple daon. Thy prefer the streey', and the solituwde.

Srah'.

Yer no' oblahged ter cam yer knaow. Bu' I advise yoow toow, iss turned reel caold.

Yeah.

Ere's Charlie. Wey'll doow a bi' more unting Yuppy and then tike yoow all to the Emergency Centre. Finished the drink? Daon wanter spill i' all aover tha' nice sheepskin doow wey?

Yeah. Cheers.

Called Ulysses Something. Off we gao. Ulysses. The weary traveller. Wife waited years and years, plagued by pretenders while he slept with island nymphs. There's another one.

A lumbering jogger in a dark tracksuit, middle-aged, springing up and down gingerly on one spot in a doorway and gushingly grateful. A young woman curled up in a brown blanket, her teeth chattering instead of her voice. A fattish man, fortyish, on a carton with no protection but fat and a skimpy black coat. An old couple huddled together under one khaki blanket. That's enough for the moment, more urgent to drive out quickly to the Scrubs Lane Emergency Centre. But the silver and gold oceanic night will be a long one.

Five o'clock. And screaming aches all over as usual.

Should be used to sleeping hunched up but no.

Same every morning.

And the phonebox full of carbon die oxen, warmed it up, yes,

but another couple of hours and off, dead.

Still, always wake in time. But it does make for dizziness.

It probably stinks like exhaust-fumes to anyone

coming from the fresh air.

If it is fresh.

Twenty billion tons of carbon gases a year they said on TV.

Come on, up. Turn over on knees. Ouch. Grab the door-handle

and press the glass wall.

That's one big snag here, arms half dead and no

strength in them anyway.

And agony ants in the knees. There.

Lean against the glass and open the door a bit.

Damn, forgot the bag. Leave it down there for now, blood

back first.

Wow it's freezing. Come on, plunge into the

greypink sea.

It's a sea all right, can't never see the stars through that lot.

Nobody around. Hands against the glass wall during knee-

bending, ouch,

three inches only and up,

and again, like a sewing-machine but slower,

down, up,

down, up,

and again. Knees full of gallstones.

Go on, they'll disintegrate with the laserlike blood.

Coming to life. Down a bit further now, six inches

and up, down, up, regular fucker, how long now,

minutes like half-hours, must do at least thirty.

Yoow auw rah' luv?
A gingerbread man in police uniform.
Aow, yes thank yoow officer. Just doowing mahraobics.
Did yoow sleeyp in there?
Yeah. No' a crahm isi'?
Nao bu'
Dahying ter peey officer, sorry, can' stop fer a cha'.
Yer've left a bag on the flooar.
Aow yes.
He picks it up, not so much out of galantry but to examine its innards, dirty zinc dishes spare undies and all.

Thanks officer. Ah daon carrey bombs. Off nao fer a brisk walk, tara.

Bugger him, that delay's going to cost a dribbling, can't

hold it too long, how far is it?

Has he gone? Yes. Do it in the gutter.

Fuck it, a car. Go on. Feet not yet come to life they feel like

burning ice.

Too late, it's trickling down between the legs, it'll

show on the grey trousers.

Lucky it's still dark in this orangey shadow.

Hot breath hot pee, regular auto-heater.

But it freezes fast.

It's stopped. It'll start up again soon. It comes fast and often these days, and only for a piddle then minutes after it decides to come again like a coy ruddy virgin.

It'll be the hostel one of these nights.

That'll surprise Frank. He's a lovely man he is. There are the toilets ahead.

But no, never.

Just a few bad moments. Nothing to the Bill days thank God he died even if he did leave an unholy mess. Wash the pants down there and dry them at the Drop-Out. Here it comes again

proper flood now just as the steps go

down. And the warning

twinge in the bowels, quick.

Oof! Just in time. Regular as clockwork. Course it's that stew.

Dear old Frank.

Must wash at the basins and hope nobody comes down. Or do a wash with the flush water? That's right, get the worst off by hand.

Where's that towel? Ugh, it's filthy.

Tapwater freezing. Now the pants. Fact is, better change everything, the grey trousers for the green ones and the windcheater, using the machines at the Drop-Out.

Now for the plates.

The gravy's gone dry, where's the nailbrush? Rub a dub dub three men in a tub.

And in, can't dry them on that towel.

Long walk for breakfast. But feeling better. Nothing like exercise and a clean-out.

And it's going to be a nice dry day after all that rain.

The white dawn's rinsing all the bloody sodium to pale gold, like sun.

Three cheers for freedom, whatever the price.

Here it is. A queue. Well it's worth it.

Nice people mostly, not like them ruffians in the hostels.

Only the older ones come here, the real rough sleepers, and they don't cling or try to gang up, just a friendly chat and away.

Who's the little man in front ? Seen him before. In a pink and green plastic and funny cap.

The front rim behind as if beckoning.

Bangers pleeyse, an a bi' of bicon.

Take the bread, as if sausages weren't all bread, tea at the end.

He's gone ahead. It's early, most tables are empty so I can't sit beside him. Can't I? I will.

Ellao there. Cnah si' withyer? Ah've seyn yer ere before.

That's not a reeyson.

Oaw well sorrey.

Nao, excuse me, pleeyse sit daown. I'm feeling terrible.

Oo dazn?

I daon't usually. But I'm upset.

Ah can seey tha'. Samwahn magyer?

Yeah. Two nights agao, but it's gone daown a bit. Benefits staolen, just drawn.

Aow yoow pore think. Ey, wey match! Yoow in that pink an greyn jacke' an mey in a dark greeyn traouser suit an pink hat.

Seey this tabloid? Back page. That girl, dead. Murdered in the park two nights agao. They're still trying to find aout who she was. She was sitting there, on Mondey, just where you're sitting. Her name was Elsie.

Aow dear. Ah'm sorrey. Bu' if yoow kneuw er, wha daon

I didn't knaow her. Just her first name. She sat there and talked, just like you're doing, and I daon knaow yoow doow I?

I'm Ivey.

I'm Quentin. But the few peoyple I knaow theeyse days call me Craoaky. Cos I smaoke too much, daon say it.

Ah wasn gaoin toow, aow shud Ah knaow you're still eeyting.

The place is filling up. People always sit, on an end chair, then at the top of the bench.

Haow d'you manage, er, Ivy, I meeyn

Yer meeyn Ah'm a bi' aold fer auw this?

Well

Yer neeydn be galant, Craoakey, Ah'm wie paas tha'. Sixtyfahve laas birthdie. Aonly son killed in Belfast iyteeyn years agao, fahv years widaowed with much relieyf but nao provision. Aonly the meeysley aold-ige pension. Aow Ah did work for a bi', servin at Tom the graocer's, an then cleeynin jobs on the QT bu' then i' cudn last, an the pension waon pie the rent will i', le' alaone the lah' an 'eayt an the foowd. Streey's rent-freey an lah'-freey, there's aonley the caold's a problem at nah', specialley in winter. Aow abaou' youw?

Aow, toow complicated. But I went for a job, an intervieuw I meeyn, couple of days agao, seeymed to gao well, but

Aow doow thy le' yoow knaow then?

I gave the wife's address.

Aow, sao

Beeyn in the streeyt seven years. Left without a word when the firm went bust. So I was obliged to gao and warn her.

Thass ard.

It was. Well, not as bad as I expected. But she wouldn't let me in cos of the kids. Well, not kids any more. Gave me a number at her office to ring and find aout. I didn't yesterday cos of, well, this murder, anyway it was too soon, but I'll try today. I'm not eyven sure I want it.

Cauwse yer wanni' yang man.

You daon knaow wha' seven years in the streeyt can do to the brain, and management skills, and memory.

Aow yes Ah doow. Well, no' seven. An no' — Sao yer was a manager?

Small-time yes. But this murder's upset me.

Was shey, a girl-friend?

Nao, nothing like that. Not in this kind of life. I hardly knew her I taold you. But she was bright, and cheerful, and funny. Then I met her again in the queue for tha' job. Maybe she eeyven landed it, she was competent enough. And that very night — aow I can't bear to think of it. I can't eeyven bear to get it naow you seey.

Yang man, er, Craokey dear, daon gao ter pieyces. Srah', smaoke an reeylax. Ah'll tike wahn of me aown withyer. Bu' yer muss promise mey ter ring. Ah meeyn, yer mah' no' bey chaosen, bu' yer mah' bey, an yer'd hite yerself for ever no' knaowing wunn' yer?

I dunnao. After all, they daon't necessarily inform the unchaosen, sao eeyven if I ring and there's nothing I wouldn't knaow.

Aow yes thy doow, if yoow was intervieuwed lahk. Common courtesey.

Whatever's that?

Yeah you're rah', daon meey' much of i' theeyse dies. Ah muss gao an wash some claothes . . .

Sao must I. I forgot. I usually do it first, sao that it dries while I eeyt.

Aol' tahm-an-maotion abits ey? Thass good, yer kep something. Ah loss all tha' faas, whass the yuwse of siving tahm when there's all die? C'mon.

Go' a phaone ere mister?

Two booths down the corridor.

Cheers.

They're not booths they're wall-phones with mica helmet things. Is it too early? Nine.

Loitered at the telly till offices open.

Better wait a bit longer that Mrs Day won't be in at nine and not too much cash left. Back to the idiot-box. Seen all the business news fat lot of use. Footsie slightly nervous today.

Smart girl in red pantsuit against mountains. However
big the screen is she says it can't do justice to the
scenery, you must be here to appreciate it. Goodbye till
next week. Screw you.
I'm more and more out of things. Never felt it in the City,
too fucking busy and crapped out
after a day buying and selling too quick
almost to think.
Don't even know the faces on the screen or covers any more,
even on the titzines. Used to know'm all, through that cult film
fad, fucking awful, kind of MontyPy parodies.
Ten years ago there were maverick films about Mean
Street and that, used to watch them as videonasties,
never thinking that one day
And the new singers, handing out sick words on
outstretched arms
under laserbeams who are they? And the hit-tunes?
Boring and repeatful when one of them come on, compared
to eighties and even seventies when a kid.
Though never heard many at work, never went to discos,
But at home in that hitec pad, and dancing
to them with Debbie. Ah Debbie.
She decamped when the dream bounced. So did everyone else.
Fuck it this is boring, politics again.
Used to be hip with them on the markets but now they
can polycrap themselves. Oh no, it's a filmstar, or pop, an
exclusive interview that's good he slipped up there didn't he.

Never heard of her. What's she saying? She doesn't want to be just a sex symbol, bullshit, she probably made her rep on it, with those tits bulging out of her tight daycol. So what does she want? Missed it.

Nine-thirty. Beetle along.

Ellao? Cnah speyk to Mrs Die pleyse?

Your name please?

Jimes.

Surname?

Tha' is the surnime. First nime Jesse.

Hold the line please.

Tinny music, something classical, hope not too long.

Yes Mr James, good morning. I'm glad you called. You've been short-listed with two others. But we'd like to see you again, do you mind?

Doow Ah mahnd, Yer mussbey jaokin. When?

Eleven suit you?

Rah'. Ah'll bey there.

We'll see you then, goodbye.

Who's this royal we, she means I don't she?

Ey Mister, where are wey? Ah was brou' bah van.

You're in Scrubs Line.

Tuwbe Stiytion near?

Well, no' exactly near. Willesden Junction's nearest as the craow flies but you're no' a craow are yer. Seey ere, there's railway lines in between us and i', long way raound up ter Harraow Raod and left, an left agine after the bridge. Where dyer want ter gao?

Pu'ney.

Aow well, better turn rah a' Harraow Raod to Kensal Greeyn, iss on the Bikerloo lahn, chinge at Paddingon. Cauwse yer could wauwk daown ter Shepherds Bush, whah wauwk North when yer gaoin Saouth, bu' yerd chinge twahce, Nottingill an Earls Cour'.

Cnah wauwk auw the wie?

If yer go' threey aours. Is i' Saouth or North of the 'Eayth?

Saouth Ah think.

Ah can xerox this bi' of map for yer. Scomplikai'ed.

Cheers mi'e.

These cruciating hesitations. Not like the Stock Exchange.

Grey area this. Wormwood Scrubs on the right, prison

isn't it, or was.

Warehouses and scrapyards.

Over a railway bridge. Long walk in the freezing sunshine

saounds good, arriving topform. Would save on the fare.

Could ask for an advance if the job — No,

wrong impression.

As it was couldn give her an address. Seemed

understanding though, proper commiz and told me to ring.

Still, there are two others.

Red brick houses with pointed roofs. BBC TV on the right.

Better go by tube and walk all the way back.

If the sunshine holds.

Or I'll get out at Putney and walk the last bit.

That's it. Good choice. Half past ten. Tube mostly empty

bar three giggling girls then fucking phased out and station

stops produced a few more lulus and bimbos.

How's it possible to stop thinking all that time? It's that kitkat.

Can't remember a single thought, that's no use for

manager.

But why do they want a city man anyway? For

quick use of computers?

Maybe pity? City pity bitty witty.

Titty. Ditty. Pritty.

Twenty-nine years old and this. And still look a mere boy. That man in the van, kept saying boy and Sonny. Sunny. Ey, snap out of it. How can it be sunny and so cold? Never saw the sun on the markets. Not many people on the Heath yet.

A wrapped up black girl with a pram, passes smiling at what's in it.

Motional rump even under her coat.

Man in a pink and green jacket ahead, marching fast like a soldier or a tail-chaser.

Why can't all London be like this, green grass for ever and few yobs? Streets full of beggars. The old just sitting hopefully the young more aggressive and insulting, can't accept what's happening to them after all the promises and the cheerup stats saying the economy's recovering fast and all.

Ey clamp output or there'll be a blank at the buying moment. Relax, breathe etcetera. Breathe in the green breathe out the dream. Explore explose exploit.

Electrodal election selection. Revalorisation of manual labour they was saying fifteen years ago well that's all gone now manual labour's just a manip.

That little Malaysian boy on telly, Indian or whatever, asked what he hoped to be and answering a millionaire, so as to help the poor. As is they ever did.

Here's the place, Cuter Computers.

Well, millionaire yes, practically, and I didn't help the

poor, so

The narrow corridor. The man in the pink and green jacket.

Hellao Yuppy.

Iss, iss,

Craoakey yes. Remember me? Breakfast at the Drop-Out, Monday wasn't it, with Tek and, Elsie.

He's staring at me like a madman.

Weuw Ah never. Yoow infer this toow?

He nods. Lip's swollen. Eyes still piercing me, can't hide alarm surprise fury thinks how come, me, a mere boy is that it? Well I'll show him. I'm as much a beautiful girl in black leather from top to toe prances out stream-ing a silly smile they sure shortlisted a variety of human wrecks. You next Quentin, she says, good luck.

Quentin! What a name. He seems to know all those shortlisted, well, the two of us. She barely glances at me as she strides past up the narrow cor-ridor like a princess. He's taking a long time. Don't know about the bird who just left but at least two of us are drop-outs. That means the pay's too low to tempt other managers, forget what it was, funny that, losing touch when anything'll do. So they're trying for someone cut-rate are they? Well it'd be a springboard anyway.

Maybe the choice is just personal? Or social? Whoever needs it most. Priority to the middle-aged cos there's no hope left for them? Or to the young cos there is? No, it's always business first. The most competent, ef-ficient, labour-saving time-saving space-organising speed-generating, productivity-producing product, well that's okay, or the most custom-er-satisfying, self-confident, authority-inspiring that's not okay. But it'd come with the job wouldn't it, she'll see that. If she ain't iffy.

He comes out. Signals me in with a sideways jerk of the head, eyes switching at once elsewhere.

There are three people behind the desk now, Mrs Day in blue today, and two young men, a bit of a crush.

The questions are much the same as before, about working in the City and handling computers and Internet, how long and all that crap. Seems the young men are technicians only there to see if they can bear to be managed by me. Seems they probably can't. Minge okay seems to like me and that's the main thing. I don't go inartic like so often in fact I amaze myself by the ease I feel, the way the right words come flowing like a printout, but not one of them you can't stop or that clamps the output sudden despite desperate unclamp instructs thank you very much Mr James, well, we'll talk it over and let you know.

Erm. Cnah wite aou'sahd then?

No, we'll be submitting our conclusions at a meeting tomorrow.

Bu' weuw, c'n yoow teuw mey

Tell you what Mr James? You didn't tell us much did you? Oh you talked all right but did you hear yourself? You gabbled away without ever finishing a sentence before leaping into the next. You'd made such a good impression the first time, what happened?

Bu'. Aow. Nerves Ah spect.

I understand. You do want the job very much, don't you? Oh, you're the one without an address or phone. Yes well, ring me tomorrow at three. Goodbye.

Bugger all. Worse'n the Last Judgment.

Bet they already made up their tiny minds.

Three o'clock!

Gives em time to contact the fucking winner ey.

Head empty again. Leaden feet and leaden heart

to carry all the way back across the Heath

and all the way into London. Too cold to sleep on

the Heath.

But where and what to eat on two quid? Screw it all.

Oh Debbie. Oh Nikkei, Dow, Dax,

Hang Seng where are you?

Dow down, Hang up, Nikkei nicked, Dac back in,

Dax Hoonded, Footsie Whoopsie.

Aow did i' gao Pavlaova?

Well, very well, Ricky. I may even get it. But there are two others in now. That man we met at breakfast yesterday went in after me.

Wha' man? Less wauwk back Ah'm fraozen.

You know, the little man who was mugged.

Aow weuw, ee waon mike much of an impression, with tha' swaollen lip, looked lahk a streey' urchin after a fah'.

And the other, well, he didn't look like anything.

Didn thy mahnd, Ah meyn

The total lack of experience? Well, they knew that the first time didn't they? It's the looks that count Ricky, the poise, the confidence, and the long habit of a very tough discipline. Oh isn't it a beautiful day.

An yoor a beauw'ifuw person Pauwla. Ah spaose yoow forge' auw abaou' mey then? And Olley.

Oh, Olly. He's inarticulate. Oily Olly. Just adores me and never says anything. He'll never get anywhere.

An mey?

Now Ricky stop that. I can't stand possessive people.

Mey, possessive?

It was sweet of you to accompany me Ricky, I appreciate it, especially as you tried too and weren't short-listed. But

Bu' wha',

Well, you do cling so.

She stops in her tracks. I stop too. As if quarrelling entailed standing positions. Position Number One.

Ah seey. Yer daon eyven knaow if yoow' bey given i' an yoow awreadey be'ive lahk

Like what? A prima ballerina?

Lahk an employed person. Oo coudn care less abou'

Oh, go fuck with a gatepost.

She whisks round on her black leather legs and walks off, with her prancing gait, as if about to occupy centre-stage in Position Number Three or whatever, back towards that office. To take the Tube probably.

But no, no following her. If that's the way she's going to be.

Others can drop her like her partner did and she

sure paid for that.

Go North young man. Across the Heath.

In fact she's doing the dropping. Looks like.

Hope they don't take her. That'll teach her. The dying swan.

Besides there'll be jobs soon. What with Christmas coming up.

They'll need extra salesmen and tourist guides, so there.

A bit of a bite somewhere then walk to the Jobcentre in Kensington.

Iceblue sky and icewhite sun, glorious. Women. Just minge.

Two fuzz are striding fast across the grass must be after someone.

Jesus it's me.

We'd lahk you to accampaney as to the poleeyce stiytion lad.

Wha'? Wha'for?

The other one's staring at the red woolly hat then looking down at his little book.

Jes to elp us with aour inquiries.

Ey wha' is this? Ah'm jes wauwkin across the Eayth on a caol' sanny die.

Cam along sanny, there's a car in the raoad, waon tike long.

Nao, Ah waon, unless yoow expline.

Jes lookin fer samwahn, in red wool 'at, black leather jacke' an bleuw jeeyns.

I stare downwards in astonished acknowledgement of the description.

Iss leatherlook, no' leather.

Weuw, wi'nesses wouldn knaow the difference.

Wi'nesses! An wha' am Ah spaosed to bey guiw'ey of, in theeyse ever so common claows.

Better cam along yang man, we're aonly doowing aour deuwty, if it's a mistike yoow can expline a' the stityion.

Deuw'y deuw'y. Of cauwse iss a mistike.

Then i'uw bey cleared ap waon i'?

Aow auw rah. Ah aope iss on me wie, Ah was gaoing North towards Shepherds Bush.

Wey'uw drahve yoow ap there afterwards if yoow were inconveeynienced for nathink.

Weuw, thass somethink a' leeys. Ah was gaoing to the Jobcentre in Kensington.

Thass ou' of aour area. Kensington ey?

The other jots it down in his book.

Ge' in.

The other gets in at the back with me, as if I was going to leap out. The car takes off.

Were yoow gaoing to wauwk?

Yeah. Ah lahk wauwking.

And did yoow wauwk auw the wie ter Pu'ney?

Nao, Ah kime bah tuwbe. Wha' is this?

He writes in his little book.

Yoow soown fahnd aou'.

Bu' yoow mah teuw mey.

Bey quier', we're nearly there.

No' in this traffic we're no'.

The driver switches on his swirl light and siren and speeds through. I feel very grand.

Ere we gao.

And out. Oh they're polite enough with their just a check-up an all. There's works just outside the station with pneumatic drills. They're always digging up roads everywhere.

And then it all starts. In a little room, the drill punctuating us at a muffled distance like a dragon rumbling in a cave. With a dark-faced dark-haired dark moustached Inspector. What do I do, oh, why then, where did I go to school, dragon, where do I live, oh, so where did I sleep, where do I eat, dragon, where was I and all the rest.

Pleeyse can' yer teuw mey wha' iss auw abou'?

Dragon.

Right, lad. A girl got murdered two nights ago in Kensington Gardens.

Wha'! Murder! Naow look

Simmer daown young man, just tell us where you spent the night, not last night but the night before, Tuesday. Can you remember at leayst?

Oof! Dragon. Thank God!

Of course I can remember. A' the Nah' ostew in Caledaonian Raoad. Auw evenink an auw nah' an breakfus. Wey was plyin 'ard rock in the tell-ey-roowm tiuw the cam on, Corrup Cops i' was.

Who's weey?

Dragon.

Aow a lo' of as, capuw of friends of mahn an a lo' of athers Ah didn kna-ow.

Right, we'll check up. He lowers a small lever and talks into a machine. Get the Caledonian Raoad Hostel on the line Hughie. Thanks. Oh and bring a cup of teey for the lad.

An a biscui'?

And a biscuit Hughie. Thanks.

Weuw cheers, nan toow soown. Ah'm arf starved after tha' wauwk. Iss Mar'in Gardner. The man in charge there.

He notes it.

Aow bu' ee mah no' be there in the dietahm. Cheers. Ah dunnao.

Keeyp quiert young man I'm on the phaone.

Dragon. I didn't notice the phone ring. I sip the tea, hand trembling, and I spill some on the floor. I put the cup down on his desk and search for fags. He offers me one and it trembles too as he even lights it for me, talking down the phone all the while. So somebody's there. Okay thanks very much, sorry to trouble you.

Well you were registered there at seven. And you're right about the noisy craowd. And you did sleeyp there.

Sao tha' le's mey ou'?

The dragon's gone ominously silent.

Not quite. The girl was murdered araound six, after dark already, park empty, and a man in the same clothes as you're wearing was seeyn sitting on a bench nearby.

Aow'd ey bey seeyn if i' was dark?

Would you like my job, smartey? She was in the dark, further on, but he was visible from the Bayswater Road and the buses.

Look, andreds of peoypuw wear jeeyns an black jacke's.

And a woolly red hat?

If i' was red, in the streey' lah'. Ah spaose thy sauw the red air toow, an the glasses an freckuws. Isn i' saodium lah'in there?

You're not conducting this enquiry young man. Pity thaough, you're brighter than some. But okay I believe you, and it is rather a long way to walk to Caledaonian in one hour, thaough not if you didn't walk, eeyven in the rush hour. But as you can't give me a fixed address we must keeyp you here overnight.

Wha'!

While we check.

Listen, Ah was with theeyse twoow friends auw afternoown. I' was rinin, wey wentervideao arkide an then ter the ostel, tergether.

Names?

I give them.

But' they're aomeless toow. Thy'll be there agine ternah'. Ah kime ter Pu'ney with Pav — Paula, oo was gaoin fer an intervieeuw.

Where?

Plice cauwed Cuw'er Cumpew'ers, the ather sahd of the Eayth.

Did she get the job?

Shey didn' knaow. Shor'listed with toow athers.

Right, we'll check. But we must keeyp you here I'm afraid.

Fuck auw.

It's almost as comfortable as the hostel and you'll get fed. Nao rock music thaough.

The custody cell is a narrow cage behind a barred gate with a high barred window and just a low bunk to sit and ruminate on the sinuous ways of chance in poverty and exclusion. Jesus it's only one-thirty! Hope they bring me food. They do. On a knee-tray, no table. A cheese sandwich, more tea and an apple. And an Evening Standard to read. They point to the backpage. The girl's been identified, by the nuns at Tyburn Convent where she did some cleaning last year and by a friend. Never eard of er. Nao well tha' daon proowve nathink does it? Aow gaow awie Ah meyn cheers. Tyburn. That's where they hanged people.

Still hungry when they come to take the tray away. Read the paper from cover to cover, chain-smoking. That fucking drill starts up again. Would be nice to be a journalist. But school never taught me nothing. Nothing like the fruit-machines, the discos, the videonasties, the cyber-shops. Pavlova wafts in with arms gracefully akimbo then up over her head like petals and fluttering down on him like a bird. She lifts him with amazing strength to the ceiling where he floats turndown on her finger-tips while she pirouettes slowly round on points, downing one foot at every turn to make the twirl so that he's bouncing on an airy trampoline, higher and higher till suddenly there's nobody under him and he's float-ing unsupported and finds that he can fly. It's marvellous. Natural. He's Superman. Out of the window and over skyscrapers and scaffoldings, swooping down over Jap policemen in khaki helmets running around looking up at him and shouting. Then up again. A cloud passes and he's lost in it, he is the cloud and the street canyons below go dark. A tall scaf-folding clanks down. A light is switched on.

Well yoow slept a long tahm. Rah throow all tha' drilling toow. It's stopped naow, for the nah'. That's bad, yoow waon' sleeyp ternah'. Ey, yoow smaoke toow much. Ere' s a bi' of supper. Nahce meey' pah.

Aow yuck. Ah meeyn cheers.

More tea. Another apple. Two doctors away.

Out of cigarettes.

Wide awake.

What the fuck to do?

The tray is cleared. The clearer's a different man, not so chatty. They're dealing with a murderer, a rapist. Somewhere to stay the night anyway. But if they find Pav and Olly it'll be all right, they'll confirm everything. But will they be there? We didn't always go to Caledonian. And Pavlova — no she wouldn't do that. She can't. A quarrel's a quarrel but

Seven o'clock dear.

Oh. Hello nurse. I dozed off again. The night-nurse woke me at five just to ask me how I felt.

Tahm to check aout Mr Grant. We're all rah naow aren't we?

I suppose we are. It was nice here.

But we neeyd the bed. This is a hospital you knaow, not a hostel.

Same root though.

What was that? Come along, up we get. We washed aourselves didn't we and ate breakfast?

Did we?

We did. And naow we must shike aourselves up and tike up our bed and walk mustn't wey?

Whose bed?

Aoh cam on Mr Grant, Ah was aonly speayking literally. Ah'll draw your curtains. Your claothes and blanket are in your plastic bag in the bedside tible.

You sure they're not your clothes?

O' course they're not, what are youw on abaout? In ten minutes you must be at the checkaout desk. Leayve the hospital shift on the bed.

Ten minutes. Four to dress, six to get lost finding the desk. Then out in the cold again. To walk walk walk to eat to sleep to dream. Thank you for all your kindness goodbye.

At the check-out desk there's a tall man in front of me in a brown leather jacket, well, leatherette, a yellow knitted hat, brown corduroys and uncombed pale caramel hair. Some trouble with the name. So there'll be with Ulysses. He turns to look at me and smiles apologetically. Thirty-fivish. Grey eyes. I'm not in a hurry I say besides I'm called Ulysses, they're sure to muddle that too.

I'm Tek, short for Wojtek, itself short for Wojciech. Grandpa Polish. I've always shortened it even further.

He hangs around waiting for me.

Like a coffee somewhere?

Sure Tek, that'll be nice. If you can spare the time.

Oh time, all the time in the world I'm a drop-out.

Why, so am I.

What, at — ? Must be tough.

And out along a glass corridor into a strange street that climbs left and slopes right. Tall narrow redbrick houses with white windows, antique shops and such, empty of coffee places. He turns left and we climb. It hurts those stiffened legs.

Oh we'll find something.

Yes, that's what I said two nights ago when the cold fell. They found me in hypothermia.

They found me last night, under the motorway. I came down from Manchester.

Manchester? Say where are we? Looks mighty smart here.

Pond Street.

Bond Street? No, how come?

Pond. There are ponds on the Heath. That was the Hampstead Royal Free Hospital.

Hampstead! We could walk on the Heath then?

If you like. There are some coffee-shops up in the Village. Oh, stupid of me. The Heath's much nearer if we go down Pond Street to Lower Hampstead and the coffee'll be half the price. They're very erm, boutiquish up in the Village.

We turn and walk down. That's a relief. And it is very near. More tall red brick houses and lively shops facing a sort of avenue of trees. With more red houses high behind.

Is that the Heath? Looks very small.

No, no, that's just the beginning, it widens out over there. Here's a coffee-shop.

Still empty at this early hour, except for two old men playing chess.

What were you doing in Manchester?

Oh, I hitched up there on the spur of the moment, thinking it . . . But I couldn't draw Benefits up there, seems it's all localised. No freedom of movement for vagrants isn't it odd. Like immigrants. In the global economy money is free to move but not people. Unless you're rich of course. Or a New Age traveller, but they're in luxury compared to us, old cars and vans and caravans. Sort of back to the land, but they seem to create havoc in the fields. Er, they're Opt-Outs not Drop-Outs. No Opt-Out Centres, see. So I came back, yesterday.

He's gazing at a paper left on the next table.

Mind if I take a peep?

No, go ahead. Lost interest myself.

He looks at the front page, then the back page, then fast through it, nervously shutting and opening it like an accordion.

Looking for something particular?

No, just glancing at the world.

That's all it deserves.

He puts the paper back.

Cigarette?

No thanks.

He takes out a small tin box. There's only one there.

So, how are things with you -lisses?

I grin at the old joke.

Sorry. People are always greeting me with Hi Tek, so . . . But you worry me. How old are you?

Seventy-two. The chronologically advantaged, they call us now.

He guffaws dryly. Never heard that one.

You wouldn't need to.

And how

Oh, years of teaching work in Africa, but for both French and British and then independent governments, total admin mess, they never saw to a pension somehow. French admin language is unusually opaque, you know, not a single word self-evident but a code-word for the ordinary citizen to learn. And when it's not opaque it's aggressive. Where we say 'liable' or 'not liable' to tax, they say 'frappé', which means hit, and 'échappe', which means escapes. That expresses the long historical relation between people and prince. Oh I know admin language is the same everywhere, but here at least there's a Gobbledegook Prize, so they make an effort to avoid it. There the gobbledegook mania goes all the way down to reading-manuals for tiny tots. Either old with archaic turns of phrase, or new with footnotes at difficult words. When they can barely decipher.

I meant how do you manage, not to exchange causes.

Yes, sorry. Anyway, I came back too old to work.

I mustn't bore him with the past as I did with that black boy.

No, please, if you want to. I meant I wasn't prying.

I understand.

There's the silence that usually follows that phrase. He volunteers to fill it, though in a monotonous, uninterested tone.

All institutions develop their own jargon against the public they're sup-posed to serve, look at doctors and their illegible prescriptions and the way they still need to dazzle their patients with jargon, no change since Molière. And lawyers. And insurance. And er, it gets . . . look at architec-ture, the inner void of Lloyds in the City, with all its complex utilities on the outside. Same with the Pompidou building, but there the void's for culture.

I wouldn't know.

He sure leaps about, from the ridiculous to the sublime and back.

That's in Paris. I spent a few years in Paris way back, doing research.

Research?

Yes, well, I started out as a historian. But it didn't come to anything.

So that's why we clicked! It's so hard never to meet anyone educated any more. Sometimes I lecture to myself, on Africa, on education in the Third World, on Under-development and all the rest, but of course it in-terests no one.

I know. Old ignorant discredited opinions thrust out at you as if new, round and round, like damn prayer-wheels.

Silence again. He's not forthcoming about why history came no noth-ing. Give him time. Time is history.

Shall we go?

In a minute. Nice and warm here, why hurry.

But the voice is still one-toned, obsessive, unappreciative of the warmth, or me, or anything. He drones on.

You know, I learnt to walk in Paris. Less huge of course, you really feel you're moving from one quartier to another. Well, here too but it takes so much longer. And meeting the Seine at the end of so many streets. Lon-don can seem quite riverless when you're stuck North or South, odd when you . . . And there's a boulevard I lived on, oh not the elegant ones, this one was drab and dreary, it goes from the République to the Bastille, and it's where all the manifestations take place, I mean, demos, protest marches. The bit of it I lived on was called Boulevard des Filles du Cal-vaire, but the Parisians always twisted it round to le Calvaire des Filles du Boulevard. Friends also called me Disco, you know, for discothèque.

I giggle nervously. The voice doesn't alter for the jokes. Rum customer. And there was I explaining French words to him. But I want to stay with him. How can I interest him I've become an old bore. I lived so long ago.

Why are you called Ulysses? Are you American?

No. But the family name's Grant, and old dad mad about the American Civil War. Parents do saddle their children.

Anti-slavery anyway. Any connection with those African interests?

No. Careful now . . . Just chance.

He picks up the check and counts out some money. Oh Christ, not enough.

That's okay, let me. Damn, same here.

Okay we'll go dutch.

Was he just cadging a coffee then? Both generosities crushed but he doesn't look crushed. And away.

The Heath's not far. Just like open country, should cheer you up after the drab London streets.

I thought you liked drab boulevards.

That's different.

We cross the street into the avenue of tall trees, and walk along it with the shops to the left. Baggy ladies in and out of them. Much busier compared to Kilburn. I try and talk.

When I was a boy the streets were alive with people shouting their wares. They lived and loved and hated publicly. And street-criers. The knife-grinder, the ragman, the ice-merchant. The last relic of that was the invisible-mender visible in a window, but even that vanished. Now it's each for himself, hurrying by.

I'm not sure that's not an improvement. If you go further back there were the leech-sellers, the child-hirers, the meat-hirers, yes, butchers hired a piece of good meat to put in the window, selling bad meat inside.

Good heavens.

Now advertising does that. But we learnt to decode. Children still work, however, though illegally.

The brief avenue opens out into a huge space. The shops on the left move back as tall white Regency houses with black doors and balconies and long front gardens. There are ponds to the right in the distance but he lets them be and walks straight on. Not like a Common at all, a real piece of unspoilt wilderness, well, ordered and landscaped, with hills and dales, and skilful clumps of trees. We cross another avenue of them. It's still very cold though the sunshine is slowly waking. Breaths precede us like ensigns. The houses to the left are now far and uphill and become Victorian, less grand, not exactly opulent like the white ones but comfortable, and obviously costly now with such a view. Are we comfortable dear? No we are not. We are walking on a crisp cold day with no notion of where we shall sleep next. Uphill tugs the soleus in the right calf, not to mention the tendo calcaneus lower down in the ankle, and as for the left there's a leg-splitting ache behind the knee, whatever that muscle's called. Regular spindle-shanks I am. I pause and turn as if to admire the view behind us.

What's that monstrous white rectangle behind the trees?

That's the Hampstead Royal Free, where we were. Looks like a giant electric grid.

And up we go again. Up we get now and take up our bed and walk. Never been here before. Always kept West somehow, Gladstone Park, Clitter House Rec, Hendon Park, even West Hendon Rec by the Reservoirs. Hampstead frightened me, like Mayfair, Westminster, Chelsea, Kensington, Knightsbridge. The rich don't give.

I find myself telling him of that adventure in the Bangladeshi restaurant. He laughs. Intellectuals you say? Yes, they would. Take out the t and change double l to double f and you get ineffectuals. Well-meaning liberals I expect. But then, Liberalism always lacked a political . . . And now Liberal Economy means Market Economy, at least in French, in other words, turbo-charged capitalism, Free Trade with a vengeance. But intellectuals always were muddled and ill-mannered, treating the world as their oyster.

We're not like that.

Maybe not. But then we ceased to be intellectuals.

One can't cease! The brain doesn't stop.

Oh yes it does. It gets inescapably de-structured. And out of touch. But I meant, professionals. An intellectual is someone who thinks continually, and communicates his thoughts to others in reasonably intelligible . . . er, intelligible at least to other intellectuals. Oh, or another definition, someone who can contribute, or thinks he can, to changing things.

Yes, I see. Yes, you're right.

A wave of deep depression moves into the heart area, or is it the brain, from some invisible chattering girl at an unseen weather map.

But we're striding heartily like two gentlemen on a country walk. Except that each of us is carrying a bulging plastic bag. One contains the folded blanket and a toilet case, the other is closed at the top. But people pass us as if that's what we were, gentlemen. A young couple intertwined. A woman with a pram. A muppet-sized muppet-faced lady with a long line for a mouth. He seems to feel no real need to talk. He stops to look at a grey squirrel in its accelerated nibbling followed by an accelerated scuttling away up a tree. The Vale of Health, he announces after a while, pointing to a pond with tall Regency houses on the other side. In fact most unhealthy, he goes on, too near the water.

You seem at home here, Tek?

Oh yes. Brought up in Hampstead. The Royal Free was quite small then, well, comparatively.

I see. Family lives here then?

No.

He's silent. Then, as if to answer that envious wonder, he adds: Dad ran a delicatessen. We lived in Gardnor Road, a very unposh street at the bottom of Flask Walk, further back, we passed that bit, in fact. Hampstead's full of unposh streets you know, where tradesmen lived. But they only rented. It all became too expensive, and even drab little houses sold for fifty times their value in the sixties and on.

But he doesn't say where the parents went, or whether they're still alive. He's both open and shut, natural and wedged in. A real intellectual I suppose.

Let's go to Kenwood.

Is that far?

A bit, and uphill. I'm sorry, are you feeling tired? There's a lovely country house there, a sort of museum, and they serve coffee.

Well

He laughs.

No cash, true. And you'd like to sit down a bit. Of course.

Look, there's a bench. And we can talk. Easier sitting down.

But when we reach the bench he plonks down like a sack of potatoes and drifts into a reverie. Or depression, seems. I hate benches, he says suddenly.

Oh. Well

No, no, I'm sorry, you must rest. Wasn't thinking.

Thinking's just what he is doing. I thought he said we'd talk. Brain's a blank, I don't know what to say. I could be the father but feel like a son.

Shall I tell you why?

If you like.

Oof! He's opening out. But staring at the ground.

Earlier this week, I forget when, one evening, late, the darkness was falling

It's coming out staccato.

No, I'd better start earlier. Do you know the Drop-Out Centre in Maida Vale?

Yes of course. Day only.

Well, I was breakfasting there with a friend, Croaky. Monday I think. And a stunning West Indian girl joined us. In a black rabbit fur all be-draggled with rain. Called Elsie.

Yes?

Oh. Yes well. Croaky went off. And she and I walked to Hyde Park. I was very depressed. She tried to cheer me bless her but I couldn't somehow float out of it. On the way to the Park she told me I was an Endist.

What's that?

You know, all those people who speak at Speaker's Corner or write books about the End of the World, of Civilization, of Capitalism after Communism etcetera etcetera, and there's no end to such gloomy prophets, especially now, round the millennium, nor do they even refer to each other but shout alone in the wilderness. It didn't get any better when we reached Marble Arch and sat on a bench near Speaker's Corner, which was empty of speakers. And er, finally she walked off, rather fed up with me.

He's silent again. Is this a dropout love-story, a street soap. Suddenly he diverges, as if on the same wave-length.

You know how soap dialogue never lasts more than one minute? Like MTV rapid editing. Super-articulate, then quickcut to another scene, also super-articulate. Span of attention and all that. Not like life at all, where people can't talk and yet go on and on, never getting anywhere.

Take the time you need, Tek.

And he does. A monotoned and muddled story, in long sentences full of subordinate clauses and hums and ers and sudden breaks in mid-sentence, with manic alphabets which he seems to treat like the butterfly wings of the chaos theory, capable of moving mountains on the far side of the world with a mere flutter. And another long digression on modern history as ideologised fiction, yet over-documented, too cluttered for clear interpretation, gorging its archives and its aerial encyclopaedias, for that's what Internet is, Diderot's dream but with snippety entries on everything, plus Chardin's noon-sphere, do I know the noosphere? I do. A planetary envelope of thought, he nevertheless explains, a bit like Hegel's World Mind but less ponderous, more of an international mièvrerie on the one hand, a software simpering and sighing, and on the other a criminal network, for porn and ordering hard drugs with a mere bankcard number. Whereas the further back you go the less there is, so that historians can talk about say popular feeling during this or that half-century or even decade from one chance indication, without a clue as to how ordinary people actually experienced things. Of course the Annals School and the New Historicism tried to remedy that by clogging things up again, scanning parish registers and trade invoices and leapfrogging disciplines. And further back still, mere fragments of the Presocratics, and in prehistory, well; only archeology and geology speak. And geophysics, paleontology, paleontochemistry and biology, climatologists, astronomy and the rest, never used in modern history. But today there's not a starlet or pop singer or petty criminal or minor minister who isn't recorded somewhere speaking or wailing into a mike or shaking hands or entered into Internet with one famous remark if any. All of which he suddenly scatters again with our sophisticated political incapacity to catch primitive war criminals, blockage at all levels, compared to the defeat of Germany when we captured not only the men but all the documents, the Germans being so methodical. And on to the death of memory crushed by the perpetually new, the death of history for other reasons I stop following. People pass us as if we were two forgotten memories sitting there. I'm getting frozen again. I'd almost like another stiff climb.

So what happened?

Oh. Yes. I went back to the Park the next day, oh, not in the morning, not hoping to see her, I don't know why really, just to think. It was getting dark. I was sitting on a bench. Not the same bench, it was further up, in Kensington Gardens. I could see Ambassadors Row and Kensington Palace looming out of the deep twilight.

And then?

I daren't interrupt him to say I'm cold, so I try egging him on instead.

I saw her emerging from the Bayswater Road, into the corner of an eye.

He glances awry at me out of the right eye.

I think she saw me too, I'm not sure. At any rate she walked off towards the palace, and was absorbed in darkness

And then?

I can't understand what he's on about. Then he takes out a crumpled tabloid from the inner pocket of the brown bomber jacket, all folded, and unfolds it.

Croaky brought this in to the Drop-Out the next morning.

I look. A blurred colour picture of a pretty girl with dark curls. Strangled. Raped. Well the other way round. I can hardly read the text under the headline.

It happens every day, he says, but not to someone you just met. Look down here.

He points. Glasses steamed up and I take them off to finger-wipe them. Impatiently he snatches the paper and reads out: A witness saw a man sitting on a bench nearby, in a black leather jacket, blue jeans and a red woolly hat. That was me.

You changed clothes then?

It wasn't a woolly hat it was a balaclava. How they could tell it was red in that sodium lighting I . . . or the jeans blue, after all they saw this jacket as black. Anyway Croaky told me to get rid of the balaclava and go North at once, and er I changed the day-jeans to these brown corduroys which I wear at night. Erm, I swore to him it wasn't me, that I left the bench and walked back to Marble Arch and bussed up the Edgware Road to . . . Well it's much quieter up there compared to the tart areas. I'm not sure he believed me. Er, I'm not sure I even believe myself.

How d'you mean? Is that why you were hunting through the paper?

Observant of you. Yes. To see if they caught anyone. Then er, I'd feel free. But in fact would I? It's hard to . . . well, you know, I said earlier that we lose brains in this game. Memories too. We walk and walk, take in this and that, and I suppose think. But I can never remember what I was thinking. I can never reconstruct it.

You mean you went blank, and did it perhaps?

I don't know. How can I if it was a blank? She certainly irritated me the day before, with her damned optimism. But not, surely, er, to that extent. All I know is that I saw her walk away and I moved off in the other direction. And went into shock when Croaky showed me this paper the next day.

And that's why you went to Manchester?

Yes. I bought this yellow hat there, and er, a packeted plastic raincoat to sleep on, saves finding a carton. I burnt the red balaclava with a lighter in a scrapyard. And I hitched back, and slept under the motorway. And er, was picked up. Broke. And broken.

Yet you offered to buy me a coffee.

And couldn't pay for it! Oh I'll get Benefits today. Well, this afternoon.

And you suggested walking with me instead? Even to that smart house far away, for another coffee. But I believe you Tek. You wouldn't be telling me if you weren't innocent. You're a nice man.

A muddled one, say. But you're right, it's too far. And completely out of the way.

What way?

I mean, no buses up there I think, posh car-borne area and miles off the usual haunts, near doss-houses and such. But you must be frozen, erm, Ulysses, I am. So sorry. Let's get going, towards the Village, I'll show you where I used to live.

Is there a lot of uphill?

A bit. But it'll warm us up. Hands are twanging. Come on. Up we get.
Up we get and didn't we wash etcetera.

It's only the legs. They hurt more uphill. Like a wedge twingeing behind the knees and down the calves.

We'll walk fast now, downhill first and on the flat to get warm, then up to the Village. And after that it'll be downhill. Thanks for listening Ulysses.

But Ulysses is quiet. Old Ulysses on his travels. Seems afraid of talking about the past. Well, so am I, and I hardly let him after all, almost blocked him off, doing just that. Well, a bit, nothing concrete. Why are we all so anxious for human contact then block it off somehow? Exactly as in society, but you'd think those glitzy habits wouldn't be carried through to the drop-outs and all that supposed solidarity. We were full of ideology that declared personal problems insignificant. And he did the same for other reasons, it wasn't done. He's in pain I think, limping along behind me. I slow down. He nods politely when I show him Gardnor Road, a small cul-de-sac of narrow terraced houses in dark yellow brick that used to be dirty black with steps up to the so-called ground floor. Of course it means nothing to him except perhaps I'm not as overclass as he thought. He's in palpable agony as he struggles up Flask Walk past its poshed up cottages with brightly painted doors, red, yellow, blue. We reach Haverstock Hill. Hampstead Tube Station up on the right, but I daren't say so, though I suddenly want to get rid of him. No cash either of us anyway.

Where are you going?

Nowhere in particular. Pity I can't offer you another coffee and a sit-down, it's well past eleven.

Not round here, it'd cost you three pounds a cup. And anyway you mustn't spend money on me. We're in the same rowboat.

It comes out as robot and he looks puzzled. Why did I confide in him, he's going to cling like a father. A father-confessor, but then he shouldn't know me behind the lattice-work. Pig-selfish of me, I feel better he feels worse, as if he'd taken over the burden. What burden? White man's I suppose.

He stands there indecisive behind the thick glasses and I'm not helping him

---

I must go and collect, I help him.

Where?

Kilburn High.

I'll come with you. That's where I go. Where that restaurant was.

It's a long walk, Ulysses. To Finchley Road and across to Kilburn.

He winces. He understands, but somehow won't let go. As if he felt he deserved company for patiently listening. And he does of course. I give in.

But all downhill. Come on, if you're game. I'll give you lunch when I've drawn.

Oh no, I can draw too.

And off we go down Heath Street, into Church Row and down Frognal Lane. He's very silent, as if intimidated by the clean streets for people who pay high Council Taxes, the rich eighteenth-century houses, the rich nineteenth century houses, the rich twentieth. The filthy rich, always with us. Endless Benefits our Deficits they say. Oh the money exists all right. Et nous, les nantis, les hommes purs, les cent grades. That's how Françoise used to parody the famous Rostand line. Sums up that suncult ballsup she dragged me into. We turn South along the hideous Finchley Road, flat at last, and he seems to perk up.

That's better, he says, nothing like walking to unstiffen. Though that steep downhill was as muscle-tearing as uphill.

At Swiss Cottage we can't cross, and go down into an underpass, then up again. I hold him by the arm patiently.

Just one more road, Belsize Road and we're in Kilburn High. You seem to know the way like a tourist guide.

Oh, tourists don't come round here. It's still downhill but gentle.

But the Dole's just closing for lunch, isn't that just dandy? Oh please! It's only ten to one. We're broke!

He seems hysterical.

There's a Drop-Out just down the road. Says the official woman, officially. We must eat too you know.

So on to the familiar Maida Vale Centre and a queue. Sausages and mash, bread, tea. It's crowded. Nowhere to sit. Oh there. Can you push down a bit and make room for two? Nao chum, if there's roowm for toow ere there's roowm for toow laower inni? Thanks. There is, only just. He squeezes in, I squeeze in opposite. It's impossible to talk in the cockfight clamour. Just as well. But it's good to sit down, even for me.

Back to Benefits. At least we're among the first and it's fairly quickly over. Then the postoffice to cash the old giros.

Now let me buy you a coffee, Ulysses. Or a drink. Ay, there's the pub. But he misses the feeble joke. First I must get cigarettes and an evening paper.

You are nervous, aren't you?

Well, yes, wouldn't you be?

I sound a bit sharper than I meant. He feels it. He waits patiently while I buy and we go into a scruffy pub. Almost empty by now, yet the floor's strewn with fagends, cashew shells, empty crisp packets. From lunchtime or last night? I suggest a whisky or a gin to perk us up.

But there's nowhere to sit!

He looks desperate.

Yes there is, over there.

On collapsing shabby red upholstery between fake wood panelling and three wobbly tables.

I open the packet of fags and take out the little tin, put three in it and return the packet to the inner pocket. Ration for the day, I explain. I light up. Lovely. He tries to make conversation, to reinvent and prolong, without touching its content, this morning's intimacy. I try, feeling guilty, but heart's not in it. Probably it wasn't then, either.

Cheers. D'you know about the Five Per Cent Nation? You mean, financiers?

That's good! I force-chortle and he smiles feebly. No, the Black Muslims in America, the Nation of Islam. Call themselves that. Or did. At least they feel a nation. But the Unemployed are a Fifteen Per Cent Nation, on average, all over Europe, around Ten Per Cent here but er, Twenty in Spain and Italy. Twelve in Germany officially but double that since reunification. And worldwide the average must be at least thirty since some badly developing countries are saddled with eighty percent unemployment. And so on, And near Twenty all round for the young, though in Poland Eighty Per Cent of them don't find jobs after getting their diplomas and er I think Seventy Per Cent of those under thirty-five are unemployed and drift into crime. We put the clock back a hundred years. And Street-sleep-ers, say around Five all round, but we don't feel a Nation do we? Thank goodness. Er, virtual communities without even Internet to communicate by.

But Ulysses seems too downloaded even to take that last bit as an apo-logy.

We're the pollution, they're the polluters. But personally I like being cut off. Oh I know I get depressed but I'm glad to be out of touch. Can you understand that?

No. I don't like being cut off. Even the young don't. But at over seventy the social exclusion gets mixed up with the feeling that so many exciting and highly complicated changes are on the way for the twenty-first cen-tury and I won't live to experience the results. The young will.

So what? Excluded from what? The ex East Germans rushed through the wall-breach to the forbidden pleasures of the West, and are no happi-er. Do you really want to see every city a slum and skyscraper megapolis like Mexico or Cairo or Rio or er, Calcutta, with the poor at . . . Or every village in the world, if any are left, drinking coke and videoviolence and dancing to the same music, dreaming prefabricated disneyland fantasies and speaking tele-hostish in whatever their language, their own legends forgotten? Or floods everywhere due to glo . . . oh and bad barrages fois-ted by the IMF? Let the young cope with the errors of their elders.

Well of course I didn't mean

I know. Sorry. But we all miss things, Ulysses. Voltaire and Rousseau both died the same year, missing the French Revolution they indirectly started, and er, the Terror.

Oh I know, but I meant

Technological change? That moves faster and faster of course. But you know, it takes two or three hundred years, three or four average lifetimes, for one rationally decent notion to spread from a small minority to the whole of society.

Such as?

Well, that consensus can be merely the sense of the con-men, that the State, or for that matter the status quo, isn't ipso facto right, or that na-tional identity is a cultural construct, er, like identity you know . . . that there is no national essentialism, and no national exception, in other words, Ulysses, men can't invade other people's land, economy or culture with their shaky notions of right, even to the point of genocide. Or that all people other than the white male, or any male, are not for that sole reason lesser human beings to be outflanked or ignored or interrupted or otherwise manoeuvred out of basic human rights. And as to that, there's a growing infertility of male sperm in all species, due to the chemicals man has invented, and eighty-six percent of Russian children are being born sick. So life, let alone male supremacy, may die its natural death. And er, well, some of these notions, though at last recognised in official discourse, must still be fought for, they're not automatically accepted at all levels of society, or in all societies.

Well,

But even future technology is unpredictable. Take Mary Shelley for instance.

He's off again.

She placed her novel The Last Man in 2073 but couldn't imagine men moving on anything but horses or, for special urgency, in a balloon. Or fighting with anything but cannons and muskets, with the war still between Greece and Turkey. Or the end of man as due to anything but the Plague. And er, or the role of government as anything but putting up new buildings. Not to mention her notion of women as merely passive and compassionate. Strange for the daughter of Mary Wollestonecraft and the wife of . . . well, the novel is about the failure of art, so I suppose it's all right for the artist to fail. But then, er, imagination's out of fashion, both with the Fundamentalist Right and the Literalist Left, with both it's subversive. And of course politicians are by definition unable to imagine beyond the next election. Hobbes said a sovereign power protects people against each other. But who protects them against the prince? And today, who decides? Intensive farming, intensive fishing to the depletion of stocks with quotas always fixed too high for political . . . and er, globalisation, numeric systems, you name it, things fall upon us without any decision being visibly made, in fact governments don't understand the systems they're trying to control, they merely administer the consequences. Elsie said, that morning, that if politicians take a generation to digest the changes they've caused, then there'll always be long and painful trans-itions for everyone else. That was the price of progress, and she seemed prepared . . . But there I go again. In fact, when I said I liked being cut off, I meant, well, I can be serene about failure. I used to think I . . . but I get too tired to communicate. Except as tedious ranting. Very unpopular.

Ulysses looks crushed at this verbose transformation of that timid per-sonal fear. But it also gave him time to recover. And even attack.

You seem to relish that. But hand-wringing and generalised lamenta-tion is a conservative, nostalgic attitude. Besides, you're communicating now, and you did all right on the Heath. Even if I couldn't always follow.

Touché, by Ulysses the wily one.

He's silent. I pick up the paper. Mind if I glance through?

Nothing on the front page. I open it quickly, through to the pack page. Heart stops. A young man is helping the police with their inquiries. Few details. Red woolly hat etcetera.

They've found him. Look.

He takes the paper and reads where I point.

Well Tek, that must be a relief.

It is. Though it may not be the right man of course. Anyone dressed like that would change, I did.

Still, you should stop worrying. Hey, d'you know Kensal Green?

Somewhere South of here I think, on the Harrow Road, why? It says the girl's funeral's taking place there, at three today. At the Kensal Green Crematorium.

Does it now?

Will you go?

No.

You should, Tek. She may be, well, all alone, with no mourners.

And be recognized again? You must be joking.

No, Tek, you won't be, not now. I'll come with you, it's only down the road.

Hell, he won't let go. Another split second and I was using that as an ex-cuse to get rid of him but like a fool

Well, I'll go for you. And say a prayer. It'll be something to do. And I'll sleep at the Scrubs Lane Emergency Centre. I hate those hostels, they're so rowdy, but in this cold.

Okay Ulysses. Thanks. You represent me. They won't arrest you at any rate, you don't correspond. Erm, I'll meet you at that Centre then tonight, and you can tell me all about it. Thanks for everything. And out.

And into the small chapel, crossing myself. Santo Deus,

there's no one else.

Won't be able to watch what other people do. I'll

stay at the back.

Xavier went into one of his furias. But I stood firm for once and

just came.

Not like a church at all. More like a meeting place.

Oh I know I said she warnt religious like but still, what

with Tyburn paying

and Father Reilly a bit too

you'd think they'd ask for a Mass and a proper funeral. In

the earth.

But the taker under was hard. Unknowns get cremated he said.

Well they didn't always did they.

The cheapest coffin, very plain. And no flowers except my

scraggly bunch.

The priest in black and white comes in and looks

around at the empty seats. Well, not a priest I suppose.

Must be economical.

He starts intoning some kind of prayer.

Ah, there's some people. I wonder who they are.

A little man in a pink and green plastic jacket.

Hardly right for a funeral.

Not that my skimpy blue coat would be any better but the police gave her clothes to Tyburn and Sister insisted I take the black fur coat and I feel terrible in it. Said I wasn't to but I do.

He's with a fat woman in green trousers and green jacket who can hardly walk.

He helps her into a front seat on the left.

Is it her parents? No, he's much younger, with dark red hair, hers is grey, sticking out of a pink woolly hat.

And here's a dark man in a white mac, he slips into my back row on the other side.

The priest's gabbling now.

Oh Elsie! You looked so cold and away in that metal drawer.

And I'll never learn to read now.

Here's another one. Didn't know she knew so many people.

Tall and thin, with a grey beard and glasses, must be her father, he'll join them.

But no, he goes and sits in front on the right.

It's all so empty, so sad. No statues or pictures or votoes or anything. And no proper altar behind the priest, just a kind of low cupboard.

I cross myself all the time to make up for it, and kneel.

Avé Maria cheia de graça. O Senhor é convosco . . .

But what's the use of that if I can't pray? Santa Maria Mãe de Deus rogai por nos, pecadores agora e na hora da nossa morte Amen.

But she won't stay with me.

The cupboard opens.

The coffin suddenly slides into it for it's like

that scanner thing that frightened me so much.

And it's gone. And unlike the scanner it won't come out.

And it's all over. The priest hurries out. Why pay for a coffin if

it's to be burnt at once? At least in earth it keeps a while.

I stand up again, O Deus, tears streaming down. The man in

the mac is gone. The fat woman is hobbling up the aisle and

nods to me as if I belonged.

The little man holding her arm. Then the old man.

They go out. I can't stay and pray. I follow them out.

Outside in the kind of cloister garden they come up to me. The fat woman asks me, You were relited dear? I shake my head.

Then they ask each other. Nobody was related. Just a friend you knaow,
says the little man in pink and green. She was nice, he says.

But the other two say no, they didn't know her at all.

How is it possible to be so alone in the world? And to leave it so solitar-
ia?

The fat lady nudges the young man.

Come on Craoakey, we'd better gao.

Oh, so you're Croaky!

It's the old man, seems relieved.

Yes, who are you?

Ulysses Grant.

Aow come off i'.

No, it's true. I was picked up in hypothermia two nights ago and taken
to a Hampstead hospital. And checking out this morning I met Tek.

Tek? What's he doing in London?

Oh, I know, he went up to Manchester but couldn't draw Benefits there
so he came back last night and was also brought to the hospital.

Triple idiot.

No. He told me all about it. We walked on the Heath. Someone's been arrested.

The fat woman looks impatient.

Look, daon less stand ere an freeyze, less gao fer a cuppateey samwhere. Lahk ter join us, Mrs er

Oliveira. Nao thanks ever sao. Ah'm upse' lahk. An Ah muss bey ge"in aome. Bahbah.

I wonder who she is. Elsie's aonly true friend I guess.

Aow cam on Craokey, yoow were a friend toow, after awl yoow kime.

Yes. And Tek didn't.

He was afraid.

You meeyn he thought the police might be here?

I don't know. No, he jettisoned the red hat and bought a yellow one and the jacket's brown and he wore the brown corduroys. I offered to come with him. But he seemed set against it. So I said I'd represent him and came alone.

And you didn't eyven knaow the girl, except as part of that story?

Well, nor did Ah, Craoakey. Ah can unnerstand tha'. Cam on, Ah'm fraozen.

I give in. We walk out of the gruesome grounds, St Mary's Catholic Cemetery on the left and Kensal Green Cemetery on the right, towards the exit with its black brick lodge like a miniature castle. The gate gives out onto a half-circular lay-by in the Harrow Road, with a few cars parked. There's a clump of trees opposite and skewed black rowhouses to the left, one taller than the others above a cluttered shop full of extinct lamps. Beyond that it's just low yellow brick houses with wide white stucco pelmets above the windows all the way along like interrupted lines on a motorway. Not a teashop in sight. But a Mason's Arms pub to the right further up the Harrow Road near the main entrance of the cemetery and apparently there for gloom appropriate.

I'm shrouded in shock, dejection and loneliness. To fall back on Ivy whatever next? The baggage we pick up. I can't even talk. But the old man does that for us, holding the floor about Africa and whatnot. Ivy listens well, as she listened to me earlier when I told her I didn't land that job. Crushed to pieces. So who did? Can't be that Yuppy narva, so it must be the girl, Pavlova, a fallen ballerina. What's the world coming to? Putting poise youth and charm above experience. And Hilary fake sympathetic on the phone as she gave me the message. Jubilant probably.

How to get rid of this lot? Ivy clings like ivy. Goes on about preferring her phonebox independence to hostels but that seems to be nights only. And this nerd lecturing. The whole in surrealist crosstalk like the Pinter plays of old. When we went to the theatre. If Tek was here we could just walk off as we used to. Not that he deserves it he made me walk off that morning to go with, with, Elsie. She's the only sane person I ever met on the streets these seven years. Was.

Well — stroke of genius — I must call on the wife.

Bu' yer said

There's some business to discuss.

Ah seey.

They say I see together. Clearly she doesn't want to be left with that old gook. But one must be cruel, she'll be all right.

Nice talking to you Ivy. See you at the Drop-Out maybey.

She struggles up.

Ahmuss gao toow. Bu' in anather dahrection she adds hastily to reassure me. Goobah Mister er

Grant. Goodbye.

An thanks, good lack.

Oh wickedness. We leave him to pay for the bitters. He's

plunged in muted anguish but not for that, he doesn't even

notice. Still, can't entertain anybody till next Benefits day.

And Ivy must be stuck in older dispensa-

tions of women not paying.

But she's understood too.

Outside she just raises a woolly grey hand,

nods her pink woolly head

and shambles towards Kensal Green Station.

So, away towards nowhere, well East until both are

shaken off as he'll soon come out of that dismal pub
and I can't go towards Scrubs Lane as he said he'd be going
there tonight Oh God

how far is the Caledonian Road from here ten miles?

Valuable footage of footwork screened through the head.
Ulysses Something. Quentin, Ulysses. U always after Q. IQ for
you. No. Messenger mows past on a moped in a long low fart.
Mopederast. End of tether. End of life.

Sleep out round here and freeze to death. Slowly.

Nice death they say.

Just fall asleep.

How to find old Quentin again?

How to reenter that vanishing species that works

and earns and therefore lives?

Croaky's quite other, not just other than the others but
other than Quentin.

Here's a crossroad. Hate crossroads, always a decision to make,
freedom but cancelled at once.

Left towards Kilburn? No, straight on along this
endless winding Harrow Road,

cross over the Marylebone and on to Euston Road
and towards Caledonian. It'll take two hours.

A boy passes in theta-state under walkman.
Beatific. But not like that Virgin at heavenly message. Walkman,
that's what Croaky is, not even walkietalkie.

Don't want to talk to anyone ever any more.
Jehovah's Witness thrusts a pamphlet. Throw it away.

Streetlights switch on, drenching the clear
twilight in a sea of pale pink blood. Cold
cold people swimming frantically
in the nebulous shimmer
like microbes under a microscope watched by
unemployment statisticians, the doctors of society.
But it's not night yet, it's the bloody rush hour.
Teeming humanity among queueing spewing machines.
They say old diseases are reappearing in now
welfareless Russia, TB, cholera.
So many walks on so many nights, cut off from the stars by this
anaemic bloodred glow. Just as we can't see to the next day,
ever, never beyond the dosshouse for the night.
Or die.
But Croaky knows Quentin, Quentin'll be back at
that Jobcentre with the motherly blonde
if at first, try try etcetera.
Hilary's a real bitch.
Not one word of hope, not a hint
of maybe sheltering me protem. Steely.
Here's Marylebone Road.
And at the door that night, not even a fiver or a tenner
to help, oh but that was before the mugging, how could
she know, doing fine said Quentin stupidly proud.
Still, steely.
Why couldn't she understand and
forgive? Or at least forget?

Man with toothache, hand up against left jaw.

No, mobile phone. Everyone in frenzied communication.

Euston and King's Cross. Taxis and travellers and

trudgers and tarts. Into Caledonian.

Hope Martin'll go on overlooking the

age-limit. In this cold.

He did so far. Till you get Benefits again he

said, but not after. This cold won't last, it's

always mild and rainy till after Christmas.

On and on. Past Pentonville Prison on the right,

in blue and white, Brewery Road on the left

in gold.

Maybe prison would be nice. Looked after.

Arrived at last. Good sort, Martin. But then he used to

be one of us.

No private cubicle though, sick man in it.

So dorm it is. With double bunks. It's okay. Thanks Martin. I'm fagged out.

Lip's b"er anywise.

Yeah, but everything else is worse. I didn't land tha' job.

What job?

Oh, didn't I tell you? I forget who I talk to theeyse days and what I say. Anyway it was zero, from the zerocrats. Quiet tonight.

For the maomen'. Ere 's the ticke's. Perk up Quentin.

What for?

Okiey Quen, yoow se"uw in. Nao smaokin in ere remembah, aonly in telley roowm. Ahmuss gao. Bah fer naow.

Settle in. Not in but on. The bed's hard but pavement's worse. It'll do till supper. Nikes off, ballbearing feet up. Used to believe the world was on the whole just. Now it's all climax porn from the comfort of deep extropian armchairs. All depends where you are. From here it's thugs and junkies and ball-shrinking glares and acid allnight raves and the woeful dolers as inflatable screams with dysmorphed feet.

Most of the bunks are already occupied by other fagged out faggots. Need a fag. Tellyroom. Go in socks. They're all watching Eastenders, those lucky ones with home tizzies.

Quentin! How are you?

It's Pavlova.

Shshsh.

She sideshoves her elegant head to indicate out.

Nao, I wanna smaoke.

Later then, at supper.

Shshsh.

She's with that inarticulate stick, Wally or Olly, the grated carrot. He's holding her hand but she now disengages it gently. Her profile is pure Gisèle. Or computerfirm manager. Cuter Computers.

Seven at last, she leaps up. Time to eat.

I follow them out. Still in socks. With holes in. Who cares?

Congratulations she says in the queue.

For what?

For getting that job. I suppose you don't start till Monday.

But I didn' get it. I thought you did.

What! You mean they gave it to that nerd?

Yuppy.

That's right. Yuppy. The golden boy. We know him, don't we Olly?

Ow. Do we?

Well, not so that he'd know us. I ignored him at that place. But we know all about him. Here's a table, come on Olly.

She surfs towards it, holding her tray like a sail. We sit down more clumsily with ours, of stew and bread and tea. Place filling up fast.

What about him then?

He's on drugs.

That's nao great shakes. But he can't be. Seeymed quite normal to me. If a bit off.

That's just it. He's not yet demolished. Just a sniff or a kitkat here and there or an e-pill or whatever, to get by, but he won't last.

Well, even respectable peoyple do that. Nao jabs you meeyn.

Must do, now and then. I've seen him here right out, in that separate cubicle. Martin looks after him then, tells him he can't take in fargone addies so watch it kind of thing, trying to talk him into sense. And he does keep off mostly, Martin says, it's just for special occasions I guess, like interviews. Not quite hooked yet but it can't last. They'll soon find out at Cuter Computers, not so cute either. You knew him didn't you Olly?

Ow. Erm . . . ye-ye-yes. Ectually.

Astonishingly, now that he talks at last, it's in an Etonian drawl. Or Harrow, Rugby whatever.

And what's the diagnosis?

The erm. Ow. Well, i-i-i-i-it's er difficult. To say. On cer-cer-certain days. You see. He-he-he can't. Utter a word.

Apart from the agonised stammer on small syllables, he speaks like a spokesman, hesitating for the most cautious expression to land on the most expected. Whereas she punctures him much faster, the whole body uttering at him, as if twirling on the bum.

Like you, Olly. And other times he'd talk nine to the dozen as if he were buying stocks and shares. Or ruling an empire, which he did in a way. So you told me.

Eb, solyutely. I-I-I-I do er agree.

But haow extraordinary. Nao managerial experience at all.

The conversation is being smothered by the increasing clamour and clatter of the canteen and we're suddenly shouting into it.

Nor me, Quentin. Just years of the hardest discipline in the world. Yet they called me back. I thought — well never mind. And you?

And me what?

Any managerial experience?

Well yes as a matter of fact. And I thought I made a good impression.

So did I. Experience for you, poise for me, and they go and choose a lulu like that. They lose, don't you think Quentin? Good heavens, who's that?

Martin comes into the canteen with a dark moustached man in an incongruously immaculate cream-white raincoat. Must be lined too, in this weather. He walks straight towards us. Those two young people he says. Inspector Hollis. Wants to see you.

Hey, what did we do? Come and sit down, Inspector.

Well, it's hardly the place. There wouldn't be a quiet room somewhere? He turns to Martin, who says Nao, jes the office, an Ah

Well, why not?

He sits down, removing his mac, in a dull grey suit. I shove down, gratefully unwanted.

I'm just checking up on an incident, and want to ask you a few questions.

But this gets lost in the ambient noise. She only catches the last words and almost yells.

Speak up Inspector. Questions did you say? Like what? He speaks up, like a ticked off schoolboy.

I sent a constable last night, but you didn't sleeyp here did you?

Did we Olly? Another bum-pirouette.

Er, n-n-n-no. We erm.

Never mind. That's just to explain why we couldn't find you earlier. Can you cast your minds back as far as Tuewsday?

Tuesday! Jesus, what are we today?

Friday.

She turns again but slowly, imaginary arms arched over him, in fact raising an elegant wrist to cup her chin and gaze at him.

You know, Inspector, one night's much like another, it's hard to remember. Tuesday's prehistory.

It was, I'm taold, a very raowdy night here.

Oh, that! The cupping hand now flutters away. Yes well, we organised a bit of rock. And there were a few knockers around. Not illegal is it?

I was merely attempting to assist you in laocalising the night. Aout of prehistory. What time did you come in here?

How do I know? Do you remember Olly?

No. I-i-i-indeed. Not erm. Clearly.

You were registered at seven.

Good. So why do you ask? What is all this?

He seems fascinated by her dancing hands, but then drops his eyes to his notebook like a crestfallen prince. His manner is quiet but the noise makes him shout inappropriately, just as his creamy coat, now on the back of the chair, clashes with all the shabby trash around, so that his lips don't seem to correspond, a sort of bad bit of dubbing.

I'm interested in the time between six and seven.

Oh, we were in a pinball arcade somewhere around.

Just you two?

No, says Olly. E-e-e-ebsolyutely, not. It was, erm, a vi-vi-video, arcade. And there was. There was, erm, Ricky.

Oh, Ricky!

She looks as dismissive as a fairy queen to a departing spirit, or as a Mayfair lady to a serving wench.

And he was with you in the arcade?

Eb, solyutely . . . He was. Erm yes. We w-w-w-ere er together. All three of us. All a-a-a-a-afternoon.

The inspector cocks an ear to hear this presidency of hesitancy in the hencoop.

Can you vaouch for that Miss?

Look Inspector can you tell us what all this is about?

Can you vaouch for that?

Well. I think so. But where's Ricky?

He booms: I want a yes or nao Miss.

Yes. I-i-i-indeed. W-where?

No idea. I never saw him after that night, Tuesday you said.

The noise goes up and down in football field roars, handball, headball, bumball and the rest, and the conversation keeps shifting from necessary yells to discreet murmurs. This is a sudden still moment into which the Inspector lowpitches a discreet murmur like a verdict.

Yet he accompanied you to Putney yesterday at eleven. You went to be interviewed for a job at, er, Cuter Computers.

She suddenly looks like the ghost of Gisèle. Or crushed in her lie like meat through a mincer. But recovers, sizzling.

My! Big Brother is watching us! We're important at last!

Is that a fact?

That we're important? I doubt it.

Nao use being cheeyky, Miss. I'm asking you to confirm that he accompanied you yesterday.

Well, you seem to know he did.

Yes or nao?

The room is almost empty now, as is her voice.

Yes.

She's losing cool under his inquisition. What's she trying to hide? They say the young aren't bothered by conscience. I wish he'd come to the point. But he's carefully getting the information before saying anything.

I'm sorry, she adds humbly. I forgot. We quarrelled you see and I walked off.

At last he can talk normally, inspectorially.

Right. So that's settled. That's what he told us. And we checked with Cuter Computers that you did go for an interview.

So?

So, you see, he explains patiently, if he told the truth about that, he may well be telling the truth about Tuesday. And that's the time I'm checking on. Between five-thirty and seven.

You said six.

Five-thirty's safer. So he was with you.

Yes i-i-i-indeed, er, ectuelly, he was.

You confirm that Miss?

Ye-es. She speaks slowly, as if the information were being drawn willy-nilly out of her. I can almost see her arms arching down in a swan's dying curve. But I'm wrong. Her voice rises with her resuscitating torso. And now can you explain why this trivial fact is so important?

Yes I will. A woman was raped and strangled in Kensington Gardens on Tuesday evening, in the dark, around six.

The old stomach shrivels. Pavlova's doe-eyes however widen, as if before stage-lights and the dark beyond, taking a bow.

A man was seen, from a bus in Bayswater Road, visible in the street-light, sitting on a bench, wearing a black leather jacket, blue jeans and a red woolly hat.

Why that's

Exactly Miss. Two of our men saw such a man on Putney Heath yesterday morning. Your friend. We took him into custodey. And we're checking aout the statements he made.

I pray quietly that she won't remember I came in here later hat night and met them at breakfast, or they'd start checking on me next.

Another bum-pirouette.

You were here too, weren't you Quentin?

Idiot.

Nao, not at that time. We met at breakfast the next morning. Right here at this table.

Oh, right. Somebody mugged you.

What time did you check in then?

The Inspector turns to me for the first time.

About this time, eight-thirtyish. I got mugged in Kentish Town. Benefits stolen, only just drawn them. The canteen was empty, they were all in the telly-room. I can vouch that all three were here together at breakfast. But that hardly helps you, I add hastily.

No. Sorry about the mugging. You should report to the police when that happens.

I, I just wanted a bed.

As if the police could do anything about a mugging in the dark. I'm dying for a cigarette. The last one, it's hell spacing them out.

I'm dying for a cigarette, if you'll excuse me

Just a minute.

The Inspector puts his hand out as I rise and sits me down again gently.

Weren't you at the funeral this afternoon?

Funeral! Pavlova almost shrieks in the now empty canteen. What funeral?

The girl's. Eyven murder victims get funerals you knaow.

I've been given a few seconds to think. And I speak too loud but clear and true.

Yes Inspector. I knew her slightly. Met her on Monday morning at the Drop-Out in Maida Vale. At breakfast. Nice girl, Elsie she was called. But that's all I knaow of her. Aow, nao, she turned up the next day in the queue for that interview in Putney.

Yes, we knaow. They were going to give her the job in fact.

What! Another almost shriek from Pavlova. So we were just second choices!

It's all past, Pavlaova, what does it matter? I turn to the Inspector. I never saw her again. The next morning, here in fact, I saw her picture in the paper. Nao, first on the television, then I rushed aout to buy a paper.

I seey. Is that all?

Yes. Well — I'm still shouting irrelevantly, then pitch down into the surrounding silence. She was a bright girl. I almaost didn' want the job, not to harm her. Then afterwards I was shor'-listed. But you're not interested in how I felt are you? Didn' get it anyway.

So you must be Mr er Stockwell. He looks down at his notes.

That's me. And I saw this morning that the funeral was today. So I went. And that a man was arrested. Or helping you with your inquiries as they say. But all that's irrelevant isn't it?

Yes. And er, you don't correspond.

I never do, in this streeyt life. Others can spend fortunes on sending in multiple applications but not me. But Inspector, can I ask you a question?

Gao ahead.

If you were there, at the funeral, why didn't you ask us all questions there and then?

Good point. I didn't need to, for the others. I hung around a bit afterwards and heard your conversation, standing nearby, behind a column, and learned that none of you knew her, except you. The Indian lady we knew about, she helped us identify the victim. I thought of questioning you, but as I say, you really don't correspond. Of course if the man on the bench didn't do it, it could be anyone at all, who didn't even knaow her. Still I was late, and didn't want to be found eavesdropping as you left, so I let it go and vanished, leaving you there still talking.

I cringe inwardly. Didn't we go on to talk about Tek and the change of clothes in Manchester? Did he really not stay? But if he did he'd come out. If not, thank God for his impatient inefficiency. Doesn't seem to care one way or the other about a black girl getting raped and murdered. Just routine. Cos if you eavesdrop at all, surely you should wait for the end?

And why does he tell us he did, anyway? But perhaps he's just pretending, laying a trap for me. I change tack swiftly.

Did, did you find out more about her Inspector?

You seem to be interrogating me naow.

Nao, sorry. But it was sao sad, naobody knaowing her. She taold us, I meeyn a few of us there at breakfast, that she was a working mum but her kids were taken into care. Did you trace them?

There are no children, she probably fabulated. Finished?

Yes, excuse me Inspector.

Pavlova's visibly peeked at being out of her star-role for so long.

But Inspector, she's saying smoothly, it can't be Ricky, we just proved it didn't we? You must let him out. Hundreds of people wear leatherlook jackets and jeans and woolly hats.

Yes. It was just that particular combination of colours. But thank you Miss, for being so helpful.

Is he being ironical? She blocked him all the way.

I say, can we come with you and deliver him? And bring him back here. You would drive him back wouldn't you, and there's no hostel in Putney. Is he in Putney?

He is. But I'll just need to make a phone call first.

Before she can speak he takes a mobile phone from his pocket and presses some numbers, then gets up and goes to sit at a far table in the now empty canteen. We wait in silence. After a long while we see him draw in the antenna and walk towards us.

Excuse me. They've just told me the results of the DNA test we did today. It's all right, he's not the raper.

You mean you came here and made all this fuss on an alibi when you could exonerate him more scientifically? Pavlova looks both crushed and indignant, her role suddenly reduced to nothing.

We're obliged to pursue all alleys Miss. Well, come along. I'll need signed statements from you anyway and it'll be easier there. He'll be mighty glad to see you. We wasted last night not finding you so he spent a whaole extra day in custodey, very miserable. The leeyst we can do is to drive him back.

Well I'm damned. I hope there's a flashing blue light and a siren at least.

Streets 'll be empty now, nao neeyd for all that.

How flat and disappointing. Come along Olly. You with us Quentin?

Nao. I'm very tired. If you daon' mind I'll gao for a smaoke and then early bed. Goodnigh' Inspector.

So Tek isn't free of it yet.

Just a maoment Mr Stockwell if you don't mind. I stiffen. I'm afraid I'll neeyd a signed statement and a DNA test from you as well. You'd better come with us.

Aow nao! You were satisfied I'm irrelevant. With no money till next for'night I walked all the way from Kensal Greeyn, you daon knaow what it's like, I'm ill with fatigue. Pleeyse let me sign whatever it is here.

This outburst almost brings tears. He looks at me as a master gazes at a sick dog.

I'm sorry, rules is rules.

So I must fetch the nikes and anorak.

And Xavier's still furioso, railing at me in Portuguese as I prepare the supper.

  If only he could find work he'd become himself again.

  There's no arguing with a man not himself.

Just soup, bread and cheesespread and a boiled egg each.

  In this clumsy kitchen

    with the toilet and washstand next to it, all

    sticking out into the garden.

  Seems all English houses added a bit to make washrooms but

  here the bit was divided.

    And everyone must come through to pee.

      Surrounded by a narrow moat of cement to separate

      us from the garden higher up for the people above

      and they come down iron steps to it. Loco.

Sometimes I feel buried. Oh Elsie. If only

you'd been buried proper.

The door into the front room's half open.

I can see Diogo and Vasco trying to do their homework on the

tressle table.

Joaquim isn't even home yet. O Joaquim. Where

did he go that evening after parking his black motor?

He came in about six. But they've arrested someone

what am I on about?

I wish I could leave the whole lot and just

live alone on my cleaning jobs. No I don't.

Course I don't.

And Rosario, she never visits me now in case her father's here.

Joaquim comes clattering down the steps and bursts in.

Another row. But his Portuguese isn't up to quarrelling with his father
in that mood. Nor's mine really now. But he'd crush me anyway, even if
he spoke English. There's a sudden silence.

Ere's the supper. Eggs in a mini'.

Joaquim is crying. The kids clear their books away.

Down goes the tray with the bread, the cheesespread, the soup-plates,
the cutlery, and I start laying the table. They don't help me, they just wait
to be served in that sudden silence. Things was easier when Rosario was
here. Elsie always said I was one woman against four men. But that's the
way things always was with us.

Ovos quentes! he growls, sempre ovos quentes! E sopa!

And next as I knew he would he throws himself into another railing in
Portuguese against his wife for running to a stupid funeral all afternoon.
Instead of looking after him. And producing worthless kids. He won't
mention Rosario but glares at Joaquim who drops tears into the soup he's
now eating between snuffles. Only these two, he goes on, ruffling Vasco's
black hair next to him who flinches away, and gesticulating towards

Diogo, only these two are good sons, they work hard at their books, they'll go far and they'll get us out of all this poverty. As I thought Joaquim would now that I'm too old, no filial gratitude. But it's years to wait, anos e anos.

Joaquim gulps down the rest of his soup, grabs his piece of bread with the cheesespread on it, leaves his egg and fumbles himself from the table. Ah ite yoow, he shouts at his father in English. Ah ite yoow auw, and slams the door, and out. So now it's one woman against three men. Well, one and two halves. And I love those deeply. For them, I'd bear anything. Anos e anos.

But Joaquim doesn't return. And I don't sleep.

Off to Tyburn after breakfast to clean the parlours, my eyes outside my head, my head outside my body, nerves outside myself. Wrapped in that black rabbit fur that isn't me. She told me she picked it up in the Porto-bello market. So it wasn't her either. But I let it hug me. He's very young to sleep out. Well, no, sixteen.

The phone-call came while I was out. The kids were at school and Xavier can't tell me what it was about. Polizia he said. But he's scared stiff. Then they come themselves. Two of them in a car. Not the one I spoke to. Mrs Oliveira? And all that. They ask me to come with them to the station. No time even to make lunch. Xavier rumbling furious but at least he keeps quiet.

Whah? I ask.

Your son's been arrested.

Wha'? Aow nao! Aow Joaquim! Santo Deus! Whass ee dan?

We daon' knaow ye' lidy, iss a aole gang of em ee says. A black boy, we go' im. Bu' the athers go' awie. Braoke inter a cumpeuw'ah shop. A police-man go' kiuwed.

A whole videonasty bangs through my outside eyes that watch me as I lie on the floor. Voices come out of those eyes on the ceiling. Mike er some tey sir wiuw yer. Silence. Weuw blahmey ee's a ruddey stacheuw. Daon' yer unnerstand English? Jao, gao inter tha' kitchen an dao some-think.

I can't move.

Elp me ge' er inter tha' armchair.

He probably made signs to Xavier. I'm in his armchair he won't like that. My head is pushed down on my knees. On my pink sari, everything's pink. But it isn't. The other policeman brings me a glass of water. Tea coming up. I shake my head, no' wa'er i'uw mike me sick. Okie pu' yer ead daown agine i'uw bring he blad beck. Blood. Murder. Aow? I murmur into my sari then raise my head. Aow did i' appen?

The cup of tea arrives. It rattles in my hand. He holds it for me as I take a sip. Hot. Tike anather lay, youw feeyl be"er in a jiffey.

What's a jiffey? Are they going to drive me in a jiffey?

My head clears. Thy'd neeyd a car officer, aow could ee steeyl cumpeuw'ahs on a scoo'er?

Aow thy daon steeyw the cumpeuw'ahs theeyse dies, aonly the comp-aownens. The mahcrochips an tha'. Very smauw yer knaow. Thy tike em aou' an seuw them ter raogue campaneys. Iss the li'es' crahm wive.

But I feel normal again, strong. Joaquim's not clever enough for that. I get up. Auw okie. Ah'm sorry mister. Pleeyse tike mey toow im.

Yer auw rah' are yer? I nod. Straighten my sari, take Elsie's black fur from the bed, put it on, and he helps me up the steps. Not necessary. I'm strong again. I'm the only strong one in the family.

I'm in the front seat. The car crawls through the narrow streets. But not to that police station. It forks off right, up Pembridge Villas and left and somewhere right again and on and on till we reach a wide road I don't know, thick with traffic and it switches its sickening siren. Very long road. And at last, in a sidestreet, a police station.

And there, horrivel. I can't see Joaquim, he's not here he's in custody they say in some other place. They give me the address on a piece of paper I can't read. I'm sat at a desk and they ask me questions. Endless. What does my husband do? How many children? How old is Joaquim? Which school? Why doesn't he attend this school? So they knew which school. Did he come home last night? Another policeman is typing at a computer. How come he was in possession of a Bowie?

Whass a Baowey?

A Baowie knahf.

A knahf! Yoow meeyn, ee stabbed im?

I can't see it in my mind, such a mixture of the hitech and the primitive.

Nao, in fact aour colleague was sho', an your son wasn' carryin a gun. Nor was the black boy. Bu' wey wanter knaow the nimes of is friends.

Bu' Ah daon knaow is friends officer, ee never teuws, Ah never knaows where ee gaoes.

He'uw be charged with brikin an entrin at the leeys'. Tha' meeyns incarceraition.

Carcere! Prisão! A' is ige?

The equivalen'.

But I don't grasp the word. Some sort of place to make boys quiver? And then perhaps it'd be a good thing, get him out of his father's way, make him see sense. But they go on. He was found with a crackdoser on him A wha? And an aounce of heroin.

Nuns? An eroine? Aow nao, iss a drug!

And a syringe with a dirty needle. How can a needle be dirty, you just put a flame to it, oh but they mean a needle! Santo Deus bu' ee'll ge' ides.

They go blurred through tears.

All rah' Mrs Oliveira, we'll drive you aome soown. Yoow can visi' im this afternoown or termorrer, a' thaose aours. Go' tha' peeyce of piper?

Yeah. Thanks.

Bu' first wiuw yoow pleeyse reeyd an sahn this stitement. I' was tiken daown from yer answers.

The other policeman rips out some sheets from a machine and brings them.

Ah, ah can' reeyd.

Aow. Ah seey. Wha didn' yer sie? Rah, weuw Ah'uw reeyd aou'. Yoow muss listen carefulley befoore yoow sahn i'. Or give us a thumb-print. Aow sao yer waon' be ible to reeyd tha' address wiuw yer? Rah' weuw, yoow' repeay' i' after mey befoore yer leeyve then. Yoow ready? Listen carefulley.

Listen Hilary, pleeyse listen to me.

Silence, she's about to put the phone down but clearly hesitates at the tone-breaks.

Well?

Deep breath intake to gabble before she slams down.

I was mugged just after I left you the other night he took all the Benefits I'd drawn tha' morning just left me with a few paound bits to last a fortnight.

So you want me to tide you over?

Pleeyse Hilary. I can sleeyp an eayt in hostels freey but I neeyd a bare minimum for buses an fags.

You should stop smoking at least.

I knaow I knaow. But buses and tubes anyway. Thaose two intervieuws in Putney cleeyned me aout thaough I walked all the way back . Baoth times. Pleeyse meeyt me, the phaone'll run aou'.

All right Quentin, I'll give you lunch.

There's just time for her to name a pub off Southampton Row.

> Miles and miles to walk once more. Still, the whole
>
> morning's before me.

All the way from Scrubs Lane again where

> the police took us last night
>
> instead of Caledonian.

> Sudden urgency or something.

Got off early this morning to avoid the prima ballerina.

> Southampton Row. No idea whether it's near her
>
> work. Could find out from Directory Inquiries

but not a penny left now. Who cares anyway.

> Don't even know if they give addresses to phonebooths.

After seven years there are so many unknown aspects of

> homelessness still.

> Well, at least there'll be lunch and a nice quiet sitdown.

Doesn't look like a nice quiet sitdown.

Narrow pub in narrow lane.

> Better upstairs perhaps.

Obviously she wasn't going to take this

shabby man to Wheeler's.

It's early. Daren't go in. In case she doesn't show up, can't

afford it. Stay in this doorway and watch it.

Or perhaps she was early too? Help.

No, she wouldn't be, she'd make a point of being late.

But supposing she IS in there?

Then she'd be furious. Even more steely.

Better go in and take an eyeful, just looking for someone.

But then what? Walk out and come in again with her and

they'll know why?

Oh balls and bugger all.

Watch it for another two minutes and then go in.

Thank God or the Annunciation Angel there she is.

In a long bluegreen coat. Tripping gracefully.

Let her go in and up, then follow.

She's deep in a grubby menu.

Hilary.

Oh there you are Quentin. What's happened to — ? Oh, yes, the mugging. Sit down. Not much choice I'm afraid, steak-and-kidney pie or roast lamb with mint sauce.

She still looks ethereally elegant, though tired, in a pale skyblue silk shirt and bluegreen suit under the bluegreen coat now displaying its blue silk lining on the back of the chair. No cloakroom here. She doesn't say why she chose this pub, as close-sitting and crushed and clamourous as the Caledonian canteen. To save time because it's near her work or out of shame for me? Or both. I might follow her afterwards. Raost lamb pleeyse.

Anything to drink? Glass of wine? Or beer?

Er nao, it'll gao straight to those trudging feeyt.

One glass of wine won't, it'll perk you up. Two roast lambs and two glasses of red wine please.

Thanks Hilary.

Her creamy heavy-lidded eyes look down at her folded hands, lashes so pale almost invisible and eyebrows too, blond along the bone arch.

Good, that's done. Now tell me, Quentin. I was so surprised the other night I forgot to ask.

And so panicky in case the kids came daown.

They're not kids anymore, Quentin. Neil is sixteen and Andrew fourteen. You never saw them grow up.

Pleeyse daon't gao on repraoching me Hilary I can't take any more. I'm at the end

Of that famous tether? Right. But I was going to ask, were you being fussy, looking for managers' jobs, or did you try other things, anything?

I did, Hilary, many times. I draove an electric carrier in a factorey, I served in shops at Sales, last summer I was a tourist guide. But they're aonly temps you knaow. And laow paid, not much more than the daole, which I'd lose. And if you refuse a job, nao daole. Well I call it daole but it's Income Support. Daole's aonly twenty-four weeks. Pity cos the daole's according to category, which depends on the years of work, so it was more. There are flats for the impoverished, rent paid by the government, but they go to those in work, or to the young. Sorry, this is boring for you, it's so complicated. Anyway thaose temp jobs enabled me to save tinily cos I went on sleeyping an eayting freey. And helped me avoid the taotal destructuring that years in the street achieyve. That and reayding in public libraries. But jes naow there's nothing in that line.

I see.

She smiles suddenly, that shy quattrocento smile. And lifts her glass. The roast lamb arrives.

We eat. What did that smile mean? A melting? A steely cynicism? I used to read her every mood, but there's a seven year gulf hanging between us now like a meteocloud and won't lift. Very like a weasel. Poor Elsie.

She seems to want to eat before serious talk. As if tanking up for it. She never used to. Quite continental she was, enjoying talk and laughter as seasoning and winesips. It's true the place is hardly like a trattoria or even a bistro. Solid business-men chewing away at leathery lamb and feathery contracts, and the odd lone secretary making do with meat-pie and salad and tea. Hilary finishes. And aligns her knife and fork neatly conjugal across her plate, facing towards me. She sips her wine and watches me as I gulp the last mouthful and place knife and fork to face hers in silent metallic dialogue.

Would you like a dessert? And you?

No. But you'd better stock up.

Well. I'm very short on fruit theeyse days, I'll take a fruit salad.

It'll be canned. I brought you a packet of cigarettes. Here. Is that a peeyce offering?

Oh I'm at peace, Quentin. I'm only sorry that you

Thanks. I smaoked the last one this morning. I was desperate.

You should

I knaow, Hilary, I knaow. But it's a last and aonly pleasure. One's got to die of something.

They're the expensive brand I used to smoke, in a gold ingot. I light up with invasive delight.

Two coffees please, she says as the fruit salad arrives.

Damn, I lit up too soon.

No, enjoy it, the salad won't get cold. But aren't you

In a hurry? No, it's Saturday anyway.

Sao it is. What do you do, Hilary?

We're not here to talk about me, Quentin. I came with a suggestion.

Is she going to . . . ? No, it can't be. I hope she came with money any-way.

We lived a good marriage, until this happened. I can't take you back of course, Neil and Andrew wouldn't understand.

Wouldn't they? Haow can you be sao sure?

So you —? She checks herself. You must leave that to my judgment. But I was going to suggest something analogous.

Analogous? What a strange term.

I'm upset of course, to see you in these straits, whatever the rights and wrongs. It was a shock, as I did distance myself, naturally, it was the only way I could cope. But I'm not totally heartless.

She takes a last sip of wine. What's she on about? She's sure dragging it out in moral righteousness. Though I'll hand it to her she's avoiding direct reproaches, even if it's an effort. I gaze into the salad: peach and pear slices and one slice of kiwi, with a dark, dark green heart. I take a last puff and crush the cigarette.

You remember mummy and daddy I suppose?

I'm so surprised I drop the spoon into the salad and splash the table.

Of course.

I rang them in the country just after you called. And they agreed.

To what?

To lend you their small town flat. For a while at least. Until you get a job. But you must do that. They need it at Easter and they rent it in the summer. They'll forego Christmas, we'll go down there instead.

But, but

But what?

I'm sorry. I'm sao astonished. Aonly I can't afford it.

It's free. They'll pay the electricity and the heating, though you mustn't exaggerate. I'll pay the phonebill, ditto. There's a launderette in the basement. Look Quentin, you'll never find a decent job without an address and a phone number. And here's some money to buy food and tide you over till next giro day.

She passes me a thick envelope.

The throat-lump grows like an accelerated cancer, neck muscles tense to check it but eyes prickle and blink head bent till the almost tears go back in. Of gratitude? Of humiliation?

I daon' knaow what to say.

Just thank you will do nicely. But there are two conditions; One, no drop-out guests.

Okay. And two?

You mustn't try to see me.

I er ... Right.

When you find a job, and as soon as possible another flat, just leave the key with the caretaker, and drop me a line to say so. Finish that salad.

I almost say yes mummy.

The coffee arrives and I give myself the luxury of another cigarette.

I can't belieyve this Hilary.

You mean that I'm not as steely as I seemed the other night?

Steely, she uses the same word.

It wasn't as bad as I expected. I was sao frightened. It was much worse getting mugged and losing all the money. Maouth was sao swaollen I couldn' eeyt.

Would you like to see it?

Seey? The swelling?

No, the flat, silly. You remember it don't you? It's just round the corner, in Queen Square. That's why I chose this pub.

I seey. But daon' you

I told you, that's no problem, though I must get home soon. Come on, finish that coffee and I'll take you there. Could you bring me the bill please?

They bring it to her without hesitating as to who's paying. She pays. She tips. Thank you madam. Thank YOU, it was delicious, goodbye. Oh those days of lordliness.

The short walk to Queen Square. The tall white block. I remember now. She gets the key from the caretaker. My husband, Mr Stockwell, you re-member him don't you? He needs to work in peace from the children for a few months. Yes Mrs Stockwell, you're very welcome Mr Stockwell. My, I'm a man again.

The flat is minute. One double bedroom-cum-sittingroom, small bath-room, tiny kitchenette. Just a pied-à-terre she says, but a luxury terre for a weary foot.

You lie down and rest now Quentin. I can't get provisions for you, no time now, but there are a few shops near Russell Square Station. Don't forget it's Saturday, they won't be open tomorrow round here. I must be off.

Goodbye Hilary, and maney, maney thanks.

I kiss her gently on the cheek. Like an old friend. She doesn't object, smiles, waves and clicks the door shut behind her.

The seventh floor view of Queen Square stares up at me. I watch her emerge below, a foreshortened bluegreen figure, crossing the square to-wards the alley into Southampton Row. I'll find a job now, I swear to her departing self below, I'll go back to that nice lady at the Jobcentre first thing on Monday, with an address and phone, I mustn't, mustn't let her down, mustn't outstay the welcome. The inhabitual wine clouds those fantasies and resolutions for a moment. I want to fall across that bed into an Italian siesta. But must shop first, it'll clear the brain. And then, then, I'll sink into it, dead to the old world.

So you're called Walter?

Weuw, Walley.

Wally. I'm Ulysses. Call me Yooly.

Yoowley, yeah, thass eeysier.

Breakfast conversation's always difficult with us, we sleep badly and not enough, and waking to yet another walking day comes slow. But he's particularly slow. Or maybe doesn't want to. He's big and barrelly. Apart from that woman at the funeral I never saw a fat rough sleeper. Course some people get fat from eating badly. He's stuffing in sausages too fast.

Were you picked up?

Yeah.

I wasn't, I came here before I needed to be. Three nights ago I got hypothermia and they drove me to hospital.

Aow yeah?

Then last night I found myself at Kensal Green. Went to a funeral there. At the Crematorium.

Swill of tea.

So I walked down here, it's round the corner really. They took me in, though I wasn't an emergency.

Yeah.

And someone I met in the morning said he'd meet me here.

But he didn't. Young un?

No. Thirty-five or so. I think he said that to get rid of me.

Praps thy wouldn le'im in.

Perhaps. But I think he did it on purpose. There aren't so many sleeping centres after all and they're miles apart. There's one in Stratford. Or South of the river, Deptford, Streatham. Funny isn't it, London can seem riverless what with the underground and it's all the same the other side.

West's more familiar to me. There's one in Hendon I once went to but I chose this one, because of the cold. It's all right. Don't you think?

Yeah.

Not very sociable are you?

Nao. Is anyone?

He finishes breakfast and gets up. So that's that. But suddenly he looks at me and says lahk a fillup? He's holding one mug and stretches out for the other.

Well thanks. Good idea.

He shuffles off. The place is crowded and I put the plastic bag on the seat. How long will this cold spell last? Why was Tek so mean? Not even coming to the funeral, though we were quite near. And those others. They left me to pay for the drinks without so much as a thankyou. Or perhaps there was, but a take-it-for-granted thanks. I didn't even know them. Perhaps I bored them too. Oh Lomé, Oh Lagos, Oh Accra, Oh Yaoundé. And the villages in the bush. They chatter nine to the dozen there. Everyone's a cousin or nephew or niece or uncle. I took on bad habits. Unenglish, un-european probably. I didn't bore Tek anyway, I listened to him. Perhaps he bored himself and shoved it on to me.

Ere yoow gao.

I take back the bag. He sits down. Plummy face, small piggy eyes, dull straight short hair sticking out in unflattened wisps. He drinks the tea. He smiles, a beaming butcher's smile when about to hack a pig between the legs. What a crude thought.

Ere, thass b"er. Can' tauwk till the second capppoteey.

Oh. I'm sorry then.

But the second cup talk isn't forthcoming. Perhaps he read that crude thought. Then he asks, bin in the streey' long?

A few years. Used to work in Africa.

Wha' conver'ing the niggers?

Stunned, I want to rise and run away.

Simmer daown. Tha' word's back in amang the blacks, thy clime i' naow thy speuw Niggaz with A Z, didn' yer knaow? From neygrao ter calored ter Afrao an naow back ter niggers. Powlitickly correct. The storey of ypocracy.

I see. No, I didn't know. I was teaching out there. How about you?

Ah was a butchah.

Good lord.

Whay good lord? They're neeyded ain'thy? Wha' dyer think yer ay' this mornink?

Yes, yes, of course, I didn't mean

Anywise Ah ain' naow.

So I see.

Wanter knaow whah?

Er yes, of course.

There follows a long rambling yet hesitant story of a rival butcher across the road, whose wife worked in the shop and charmed customers with her woman's wiles whereas he employed, this with a pause and a trenchant look not lost on me, a young boy, first in trining then as par'ner, Dick ee was cauwed, seey wha' Ah meeyn? An ee was black toow. Naow there's oowduws of Aishuns selling an serving foowd, bu' the blacks ain' shopkeeypers samaow, leeys no' ere, an peoypuw didn' lahk no' wiv meay' anywise besands, thy kep spectin mey ter ge' married seey an as-soomed, quah rah' toow, there was somat betweeyn us. An aover the years ee took the castom awie nao no' Dick, the married wahn, bah underc"ing, nao no' the mea' the prahces, in much detail I can't follow, an doow yoow knaow wha' a paoun' of chump chops cost theeyse dies? An leg? An shaoulder? He covers the whole sheep in disorder. Then the pig, every bit of which is edible but fortunately digresses into a totally different story, so incongruous yet so linked to the first that I sit bemused, a doomed listener once again, how one day in a split second while splitting a hanging pig down the middle with an axe, and I shudder at both the image and the weird prescience, he discovered a seer's gift. What he saw in the pig's entrejambe he wouldn't say; but he suddenly knew he was in contact with spirits. He practised at first with Dick, who urged him to set up evening seances, and that was the beginning of the end.

The end? In what way?

He apparently clamps up. But then takes a deep breath and continues, more slowly.

Oaw, Ah star'ed seeyin thinks with castomers. Everey bi' of mea' Ah ca' for them give me a vision of their lahves. Thy didn' lahk i'. Everythink in iss plice, seey, spiri' is spiri' an flesh is flesh. The vodka's good bu' the meay's ro"en, dyer knaow tha' wahn? Thass aow a cumpew'ah transli'ed The spiri' is willing bu' the flesh is weayk inter Rassian. Iss an aole wahn, Ah spec they're cleverer naow. Tride feuw orf. Difficuw enaff anywise, wha' wiv the spandin veg praotess — I see armies of cabbages and cucum-bers marching into a butcher's shop — and vanishing farmers

You mean as a species?

sabsideys. The gavnmen's an assaole.

And he starts remaking the world, politicians naow, they're never on the daole when thy mikes mistikes an are thraown aou' are thy? Or eyven when thy retahr. Thy auw land samethink euwse, on boards of dahrectors an Ah'd lahk ter lie them aou' an axe em. Bu' the beeyf boyco', nao Ah'm auw for i', wasn' the caows were mad but them wha' give em mea'. Them's erbivores yer knaow. Whass more, mea' paowder mide from diseased car-cases, AN didn' warm i' proper, an if the aole world stopp' eay'ing beeyf an poorin pahls of ads inter le"er-boxes thy'd keeyp the rine foress an the plane' in be"er shipe wouldn' thy? An the methane them ruminants eejec, iss almows industrial. Ah'd lahk ter bee a mortuary technician. Yer kna-ow, them wha cuts up dead umans.

He's unquenchable now and I long to leave. And at last after another long detour he lands by chance on the supermarkets, wouldn' work in wahn o thaose if thy paid me.

Well, they would you know.

Daon' knaow where any of i' cams from, an auw fraozen and in plastic.

That sounds like us.

He raises startled small eyebrows.

I mean, rough sleepers.

Aow. Ah seey.

The whole fat body shakes with laughter as if that remark were the last word in witticism. Eats fast, hallucinates faster, thinks slow. I can't bear it any more.

Well it's been really interesting meeting you Wally.

Yer gaoin? Whah? Iss nahce an warm in ere.

It's empty. We can't stay you know, they need to clean up.
There's the telley-roowm. Ah ite wauwkin.
I must, I must go and collect Benefits.
Wha', on a Sa'urdie?
Oh, it's Saturday is it? Yes, well
You're meey'ing tha' friend wha' le' yer daown? Thass more lahk i'. The
wahn wha' didn' turn ap. Ee's wauwkin orf a'ead of yer Yoowly.
A strange fear ices through me. I raise a hand feebly and depart.

Oh God I've done a Tek on him.

Outside the bright cold weather's turned into dull grey

cold, but just as penetrating. The sky's one great mass of heavy

cloud, pregnant with snow.

So it's as alienating to talk of meat as it is to talk of Africa.

Is everyone alienating when they talk of

passion-forming work? Or is it work-forming

passions? Are we now so dead to it all, like plugged off

walkmen, that we don't hear each other any more?

Or even ask egging-on questions?

There was a time when asking people questions about their

interests was fine,

say, the glottal stop in African languages

or mute e in Chaucer. Whatever.

And they'd tell you.

It was, well, not only a nugget of education but

yes, such a flattery they'd hold forth at once

and then think you quite delightful.

It was an art. Opening people up with a golden oyster-knife.

One learnt a lot that way. Especially in Togo.

Where ghosts of unhistory speak in everyone.

Why didn't I stay there? It would be warm

at least, in every sense.

    But then, they're civilized there. Except the regime, and

    Nigeria's worse, and what with the Ogoni business.

    Still,

    Europe's over. Decline and Fall at last. Took its time.

    Posed as master for ages, then source.

      Then destroyed itself in useless massacres.

        As Africa's doing now, before even growing up.

        like those Scottish warlords of yore, few

      of them lairds anyway.

      But it's growing up so fast it'll take over one day.

Europe tried to unite in a desperate last

kick of quivering existence.

    But too late. Too slowly, too inefficiently, too

jingocratically all along the line.

    Yes, Europe spread its intellectual riches and moral

iniquities too wide and

        others took them over.

    The sources are now elsewhere.

So it was paralysed. And died. We're Eurotrash.

Next: Problem Talk-Out, with Bernie Driscoll. But first we'll take a break.

Stay with us.

There's only one other person in the telly room, fat, like me, woman in green with short grey wisps, self-cut too, won't stay down. Grey trousered legs don't reach the floor. She's reading a TVmag, switched off from the ads. Looks a comfy soul, not like that throttled patriarch. She nods at me. Never watch the ads der yoow?

Shake head. Don't want another talk-out let them do it, the blokes on the box.

Didyer ge' picked ap? Ah did. Forced mey ter cam ere, Ah didn wanter.

Sigtune. Thumpthump tinkle. People like potato heads fill the screen on climbing seats one row behind the other. Slim aging heartthrob-type dishing out the problem as camera switches from him to panned potato heads before rushing up an aisle with dick held out to a heavily made up female close-up. What was the problem then? Missed it. Ah think it's a disgrice, a blo' on the fice of Bri'ain, she says. Wey should doow some-think.

Yes, what?

Well, fahnd jobs for the lo' of them.

But if the jobs aren't there?

Inventem.

You mean, the way Hitler did, making armaments? What do you think?

Switch to a lovely pale young man behind her.

Thass a terribuw thing to sie. He says.

A girl next to him, all hair and no face: We mike armaments anywie. We sell them all aover the world, and foster laocal wars.

Well, road-building then?

We built sao many we just creited more traffic jams and more pollution.

But if we don't build roads and cars, that creates more unemployment, doesn't it?

New close-up, old man.

When I was young

New close-up, a battle-axe. Isn't the solution social says the heartthrob, rather than economic?

You meayn more care? For them drop-aouts?

Well, what d'you think?

This is bilge, the fat lady says. Where's the zapper?

Dunnao.

There's Paower Lay an Byeuwtey camin on the next channel aow can wey chinge? About Derica an er trabuws. Nahce to knaow the rich saffer toow, daon yer think? Bu' Ah keeyp missing gri'e chanks of i'. Listen, ere's The Story Sao Far. Doow fahnd the zapper mister.

Ah wanter watch this.

Aow. Bu' Ah was ere first.

There"s nao zapper anywise.

Weuw, the knob then.

We should tackel the prroblem at its rroots. Close-up on a black man, neatly dressed, teacher-type.

And what are its roots? Economic?

They'rre powlitical. Powlitical will is lacking.

Right! So what would you do?

Three young people come in like a windmill, a dark girl in black leather stovepipes and jacket trailing a young redhead and a taller boy in dirty orange, dark and more handsome. They sit further off and overvoice the Talk-Out. The fat woman plunges into The Story So Far. I'd like to axe em, well zap em out.

What a dump! says the girl. But you're evading the point, could you define political will miles from anywhere I mean at the top yes why did they bring us here? But don't you think close-up nice fat boy like me pure laziness that's what well a lot of them just don't want to work you think so how d'you know though there was an emergency thy canceuwed Calledaonian, this from the redhead doow yoow mahnd? from the fat wo-man loudly we're watchin. Oh, that says the girl snootily, the idiot-box turn it off Olly. Olly seems to be the dark handsome one in orange, looks helplessly around as the programme ends with a NEXT, MAKE YOUR MONEY WORK, what money and the idiot-box switches itself off as if by spiritual interference he's got the gift that one and no mistake they heard you, Olly! Though Olly hasn't said a word. Oh well we'd better go for a hearty walk in Kensal Green Cemetery, an unusual haunt isn't it Ricky? And the weather looks grey. Let's go to the Jobcentre there might be Christmas droppings it's Sa'urdie says the redhead oh blast well let's go to the West End if we walk down to Shepherds Bush we can take the Under-ground and she prances out in her stovepipes followed by the two inter-esting but subservient boys.

Wouldn lahk to bey served in a Chrissmus rush bah er would yoow?

Lackily madm yoow an Ah daon gao in for Christmas rashes any moore.

It's damn cold emerging at, er Marble Arch. We're walking through breaths and er, the crowds. Pavlova leads us, actually, towards what is it, Selfridges. As if, as if, we were erm conquering, wild, new, territory.

Come on Olly, don't loiter without intent.

Intent, attempt to get lost, failed. Not wild, territory . . . a human, traffic jam. Try again, later. The heat. The muzak. The er overpowering scent of er, cosmetics.

Ricky.

Yes Olley?

Can you er, di-di-di-distract, you know, her, a-a-attention?

Whah, dyer wanter shoplift? Athers are watching.

I w-w-w-want to, ectually, dis-disappear.

Ah though' yoow adored er.

Y-y-y-es. Yes. Ebsolyutely. B-b-but

Aow Ah knaow, there's a big but. Shi', Olley, wey can' tauwk in this cr-aowd. We'uw loowse each ather anywie. Auw yer neeyd is ter skidadduw.

Stay wi-w-w-w-th me. Ricky.

If Ah can. Bu' look. Pavlaova. Shey dropped us, no' us er.

Oh, d-d-dear.

Ah though' thass wha' yer wanted.

Yes.

Shey was tauwkin ter tha' siles lidey as if shey was gaoin ter bah the maos cossley perfyewm. An naow, vyporahsed. Aow iss a sicknin smeuw, less fahnd men's wear an dreeym a bi'. Or cumpeuw'ahs, wha' dyer think?

Erm. I don't know. M-m-m-men's wear.

I' my bey on the graound floor, wey'd be"er tike the escalai'er, shey'uw never fahnd as in this colosseum.

You m-m-m-mean, emporium.

Wha'? Aow yeah, sam word in oom, yoow knoaw, lahk millenium. Pandimaonium Ah meant.

He studies the list of departments at the foot of the escalator.

Cumpeuw'ahs an Viddyaows, fourth floor, ap wey gao.

But he's already ten feet up as hesitation grips. Always hated that jump on. Though it's worse jumping off, toes may get sucked in. Pushed on. He's waiting at the top. He's so efficient.

Wha' appened teryer?

N-nothing. I was p-p-p-pushed. Er, aside.

Tike eaysy Olley. Whay er yoow sao frahtened of everythink?

I er. I-I-I-I'm not. Frightened.

He helps me onto the next lot. Like a father.

Cam on, threey moore floors. Is i' just a stu"er? In the maouth Ah meeyyn. Or doow yoow think stu"erin? Youw never ge' a job yer knaow tiuw yer ge' rid of i'.

Or, a-a-a-anyway.

Daon bey such a pessimiss mi'e, yer freey naow.

Nice, kind boy. I thought he was a, rival. But he's. Running away with me.

We dream a bit at the computers. One of them I know well. The little green light's on. I touch a knob. Zing! Screen lights up. Welcome. I sit. More screens. Activate the mouse. Windows and request icons. Click. Another window. File. Open. Type.

Bu' yer auw a' aome with i' Olley aow cam? Wey learnt a' schoouw' bu' Ah forgo' i' auw, samaow never tookter i' an never go' ter yewse wahn. Weuw, yer loss ter the world, Ah'll leeyve yer toow i' an tike a viddey a' the viddyaows.

and you're so beautiful

Save As. Pavlova.

you elevate me to the skies, the sun, the moon, the stars oh darling but like a muse you vanish into a noche oscura and I fall crushed to the ground in darkness you bewitch me but freeze me to death when you speak how can you be so cruel when I love you so? The screen is filling fluently without a stutter the lines move down without returns the screen moves up as the soul flows upwards slowly without hesitation don't you see the Inwit inside this machine loves me as you don't seem to and responds to finger touches and liberates me as you could but won't. Its bytes are love bites or the bite of conscience erase, consciousness that's what I always thought Inwit meant, In-Wit, Inner Knowledge, though the official translation is conscience The Ayenbite of Inwit well you wouldn't know it's a mediaeval thing I read in Oxford but I forget it as I forget so much except you or because of you so I am forced to run away or else I'll lose what little Inwit there's left inside the head you suck it dry like a bee to make bitter honey that sometimes seems so sweet

Olly! I knew I'd find you here! What ARE you doing? Where's Ricky?

File. Can't find Erase. Exit. So it'll be saved for someone or other. Not her. Switch off. The Inwit dies with an audible sigh like a man coming and the screen goes black.

In the er, r-r-r-round the, you know, c-c-c-corner.

What corner?

The, ectually, the vi-vi-videos.

Olly, I landed a job! I asked in Cosmetics and they sent me to an office on the top floor. Oh I made an impression I think. Starting on Monday. Just over the Christmas nonsense but still, it's a foot in the door isn't it? I hope it doesn't do me out of the hostels though, can't afford a flat yet can I? Come along, I must tell Ricky.

But Ricky's vanished. Skidaddled. As he, called it. He's so clever. Perhaps he saw her coming. During those. Rising words.

Oh well, he'll turn up. Olly I feel terrific. A small revenge on that wimp Yuppy. Oh I do hope it lasts. Then slowly I can move up the ladder again, run a counter, then floor manager. Come on Olly I'll buy you a coffee, there's a lounge on the fifth floor.

Maybe she'll. Vanish too. When she's. Fixed up here. Find another. Hostel. The Scrubs. Lane one. No, it's. Only Emergency. Or else. Now, yes, she steps uplifted into the crowded up-lift and, yes, turn quickly as the. Doors close. Run, run. Through the bright video counters the books the scintillating bathrooms the churning Saturday crowds, pushing past to the escalator, leap on. Fearlessly. Down into Hades they don't go up. As Virgil said. Leap off. And another one. And another, damned slow. Through the gloves. The ladies' hats. The men's shirts, the ties. The scents and cosmetics. To the faint dreaming of a white . . . Christmas. Into the cold cold air and the freedom of more milling humanity.

Sunday. A dead day. At least in this area. Nice toy kitchen. Snow all over Queen Square, everything's thickly cushioned in white. And presumably all over London. White parks, a few early footsteps trail along white paths. And sloshy streets. No, not yet. Everyone cosily at home, reading their Sunday tabloids and preparing the Sunday roast, playing with the kids. Or queueing for the football match. But Paki shops open in Paki areas, and Indian. They seem to serve all round the clock, except those in Post Offices. Strange how naturally mercantile they are, like us, compared to West Indians and Africans. Though those must run shops back there musn't they? Still, never entered a shop here run by them. But then, shops became foreign territory. Except for fags. Hence Supermarkets also open now, didn't like the competition. Good. Must buy a decent jacket on Monday. Or wintercoat? No. Not enough. Be careful with that money, it wasn't all that much.

Coffee. Delicious. And toast and marmalade. No more of those sausages.

No telly. No books. Well, it's a foot-on-earth. Could go out in the snow and get nikes wet just to buy a few Sundays and more fags, that won't break the bank. This came just in time; bless her little heart. Cos little it is, her heart. Wonder how Tek's doing. He never did like the hostels. But sleeping in the snow's no great shakes. In a doorway though, not much difference, the wet's as wet, and snow usually means it's less cold than just before snow. Can't bring him here anyway. And wouldn't want to, hardly fit yet to be a continual anti-depressant.

What did that inspector mean, when he said that if it wasn't the man on the bench, and presumably he didn't know about Tek, then it could be anybody? Is that why he wanted a statement? And a sperm-test, very un-pleasant, that. What with a mugged face, could imagine a struggle? Said to put Caledonian as temp address. Well, he'll never find this one will he?

There's a tweed jacket in the cupboard. It fits! More or less. Pa-in-law's not big either. Well well. Usable for interviews maybe. If any. Okay off, stop fantasising. Where's the key? Here. Chrissake don't lose it. String round neck? No string. Must buy some.

And out, woa, don't shut the door, where's the key? Right, in pocket. Going nuts. Try it in lock first. Okay. Click shut. Down in the lift. Out into the snow-carpet. Old nikes already soaked but they'll dry later. Pale sun trying hard. Into the alley and Southampton Row towards Russell Square and its bare black snow-edged trees. Past the Russell Hotel, grand old brown mansion type in Victorian Gothic, lights in the high windows of the elevated ground floor, heads of people into newspapers in the lounge, heads and torsoes in breakfast-room, so many slices of humanity living at different levels. Round the corner to tube station for fags and papers.

And there's the grated carrot. Dark tall and handsome in that shabby sepia outfit. Olly.

Oh, hello Quentin, what are you doing here?

And you?

I slept at the YMCA round the corner. Well, further up there. Paying, but quiet.

He points vaguely along the street.

Where are the others then?

The? Oh, away.

Away? How? Where?

She landed a job. In Selfridges. Just asked at the cosmetics counter, imagine that, and was sent up to the top floor. She certainly got on her bike, didn't she, or on her high horse. And I, well, I escaped.

The stammer is gone, the manner is changed. This is fascinating. Invite him to pad? Breaking promise so soon? But only for a coffee. No. Might get around among the drop-outs. Or the Russell Hotel? No. Don't be rash with that bread. And it might arouse suspicion. There's a shabby little place near the station. Closed.

Olly, well, I'd rather call you Oliver, may I?

Please do.

Cos you seeym so transformed. Morphed back into a truer self isn' tha' sao?

Possibly. Would you like a coffee?

Let me invite you Oliver. Listen, can you keeyp a seycret?

Yes indeed.

Ex-wife lent me a tiny flat, her parents in fact, not far from here. To help me in the job-market you knaow. On condition I daon't contact her and daon't invite other drop-aouts. But you're different. And it must be aonely for coffee. Besides, I daon' want it to get araound. D'you understand? Will you come?

Ebsolyutely. I do understand. Mum's the word as they say.

The bed isn't made, but he helps me cover it. We take sneakers and socks off and put them on the radiator, walking bare-foot on the pale green carpet and even in the kitchen. He talks while I make more coffee, he takes the tray and we sit in the two small armchairs round a mini-table covered with glass. He tells me how he escaped, in detail. The coffee soon becomes lunch, scrambled eggs on toast and an apple, at the equally mini kitchentable. How he loved her. But she crushed me out of existence.

I knaow, Oliver, I could see that. But give it time, love dies aout you knaow.

In a way, Quentin, it's already gone. Simply from that sudden courage, running away. Though it aches at times.

And will, on and off, Oliver, but that act of courage was the important thing. You don't even stammer any more.

No. I think I'm cured. But she wasn't the first cause of that, don't you know, even if the act killed it. I was always frightened.

Haow come? Heavy father?

Heavy mother. But you see, I was given every advantage, sent to Eton and Oxford and all that, and got a degree. Then I ruined it all.

Haow? Why?

Oh, why, that's unanswerable. How is easier. Through computers.

You meeyn, carpal tunnel syndraome?

No. That I believe comes from too much typing, you know, muscles get inflamed and pinch the nerves in the fingers and wrists. Like tennis-elbow in a way. But it's physical. This is delicious.

Thanks. I'm not much of a cook but I can do scrambled eggs. Often did for the kids.

So you're a father?

Two boys. But they're not kids any more I keep forgetting. Sao, what went wrong?

It's called MUD, isn't it strange? Stands for multi-level dungeon, and that's even stranger, since one sits alone. But in touch with thousands.

But what does it meeyn?

Well, sort of, computer text-worlds from which many students never emerge. They plunge into internet relay-chat and popcul trivia instead of research-processing. It hits many undergraduates, at least in America where they're all computer-whizzkids. Oxford undergrads aren't too much into computers yet, but graduates are. Ultimately, it's a kind of infantilisation.

I see. But there must be a tendency to start with.

Ebsolyutely. I was infantilised from day one. By both parents. This just made it worse. It seemed to be an escape, and wasn't. I even became addicted to Pete and Pete on the Nickelodeon network.

Never heard of that. Haow come you knaow what was wrong with you? Did you get treeytment?

Yes. But I was made to feel — Oh well, Quentin, this must be boring for you, and it's over now. Two years of weening from computers. Except in that emporium yesterday. And that, in a way, is what spurred me. I feel terrific.

I'm glad. And I feel terrific too, Oliver. And you'll land a job naow, well, if anyone can, I meeyn, you didn't stand a chance, did you, with that stutter?

N-n-n-n-no. Indeed.

Christ the mere mention of it's starting you off, I'm sorry.

It's quite all right. I was just remembering that interview we both went to.

Sao you were there too?

Yes. I came later, after Ricky, and saw you leave. It was catastrophic.

And I thought I did sao well! But I wasn' chaosen. Yuppy was.

Yes, Yuppy. Do you want to know why?

Haow dyer meeyn?

It's a rogue firm.

I daon' understand.

They buy stolen components and sell pseudo-new software. Ridiculous really, all software should be inter-accessible, all computers intercompatible. And are anyway, to the computer-savvies. What with the Free Software Foundation.

The what?

We're washing up, I wash, he dries, though I tell him it can drip.

Well, it was a hacker ethic, as give-away, with copyright agreements that forbid restrictions on further use. Called copy-left. They aim, or at any rate aimed, I may be out of touch, to clone the AT&T Unix opsys that grids the Internet, or most of it. They were already exchanging software at the beginning of Internet anyway, with packet-switching, no one node dependent on any other, a sort of acephalic structure that made it impossible for anyone to control what people said to each other. But what Internet aims at is power over people's minds.

I can't understand a word you're saying.

It doesn't matter. Nobody plays the game anyway, every make of computer wants to sell its own inviolable software, oh, you know, it's still like TV at first, each country insisting on its own colour system, but of course with satellites it couldn't last. And this won't last either. It creates chaos, customer-confusion and cyber-pirates. It's like the manic obsession about sovereignty and the last bit of it left, the right to mint one's own currency, and that makes for rogue spec, insider-dealing and all the rest. Sovereignty is an illusion. As is the sovereignty of the people. Imagine, three quarters of the population of Bolivia is Indian, but has been kept out of all decision-making for five centuries. But that's only an extreme and more obvious version of popular franchise everywhere.

Let's go and sit down, I want a fag.

At least I never took that up. Or drugs. Except MUD. The young seem unable to provide their own stimulus nowadays. As knowledge used to in old novels. Well anyway, a group of young computer geeks broke into a store in Kilburn yesterday, stole components. Not for this firm perhaps. But it goes on all the time. Two were caught, but a policeman was killed.

Jesus. Sao? Where's the link?

It's only a guess, Quentin. Smalltime crime anyway. I noticed a component on a desk, which didn't seem to belong to the computer next to it. Of course I couldn't check. But the fact that they chose Yuppy makes me feel that this is what it was.

Why?

I knew Yuppy quite well. Better than Pavlova thought. Oh yes, he took Ecstasy tablets and Ketamine now and then, and sometimes worse, but he was bright enough to keep control, except once or twice. Yes, he was bright. But not scrupulously honest. That's how he crashed.

Did he tell you that?

Not in so many words. But I knew enough about it to guess. From dad you know, he was a stockbroker and hoped I'd be one too. He taught me a lot. And they probably guessed too. That slight element of unscrupulousness was probably just what they were looking for. As a feature in itself of course but also as a hold. I imagine.

Whereas I was stupidly honest giving them ideas on improvements. Oh ballocks. But why then did they give it to Elsie?

Elsie? Oh, yes. Well, maybe they thought she was bright enough to manage but girl enough to be managed. As I say, Quentin, it's only a hypothesis. But you'll find something, I'm sure. Now that you'll be less tired, and can give an address. And all that.

Whao knaows? There aren't any jobs. They keep talking about thousands of jobs created, but that's just statistics, it looks different from the streeyt. And I'm thirty-eight. And this flat isn't for keeyps, Oliver, it's aonly till Eayster.

It's all in the mind, Quentin, look at me.

Yes, you're a different person. You'll find something too, what with degrees and all.

Only one. In English of all useless things. And not even a good degree. Because I plunged into economics on the side, you can't do English *and* Economics for some reason, though it would teach economists to write clearer English. Shall I give you a nugget lecture on why we're all in this mess?

If you think I'll understand it.

Well, nuggeted mind you, from someone or other: first phase, an existing inadequate technology applied to natural resources, brings about scarcity and rising prices. And full employment. That's inflation. Second phase, that scarcity stimulates new technologies, and though prices are still rising the stimulus continues, with unemployment, but low. Third phase, the new technologies applied to resources cause abundance and falling prices, that's deflation. It's where we are now, with high unemployment. In a hypothetical fourth phase the demand would rise owing to economic growth, that's why politicians keep saying the solution is growth and demand. Eventually leading back to phase one. But full employment causes inflation. Vicious circle. You notice too that those in favour of the present system keep pointing to the hitech giants as job-creat-ors, but of course they aren't, they destroy thousands of clerical and ad-min and minor mechanical jobs and take on very few. So we're left with central bankism. One example only: it was the IMF, with its savage unre-payable loans, that ruined the Yugoslav economy and slowly revived long dormant ethnic rivalries, into that lunatic war. I mean it wasn't ethnicity as such. War is always the solution to economic chaos. And, more gener-ally, the globalisation of trade without the globalisation of reasonable controls, and of course we can't now degloabalise the globe, not to men-tion two opposing trends, worldwide, with each a deep inner contradic-tion: the right preaching both unchanged family values and dynamic eco-nomic change, the left both social assistance and dynamic economic change. But it takes two generations for mentalities to change on any one item, the old must die and somehow not transmit. Nor do the employed want more taxes on their threatened incomes to assist those who don't work and to feed the inefficient bureaucracies that deal with them. But it's worldwide. We can't marginalise four fifths of the planet's population and get away with it.

I see. More or less. I pounce on the one bit I understood: I always said the rush into hitec was wrong-headed, since hitec economises people.

Bang on, Quentin. Rubbish to educate all the young in hitec, as some suggest. The way they talk about the inforev as new power to the indi-vidual and not to a new elite or to yet another ideology! One example they give: on Internet anyone can redirect an item of info, say on incompetent lawyers or doctors, to millions, but effacing all trace of its origin. In the-ory that gives power to the victims but does it? And the danger's huge. Already journalists can zigzag between swallowing hand-outs as news like in the Gulf War, and irresponsible slander. Even historians can base a book on released KGB files fed by fake informers. And the same people say the weapons of future wars will be information. Fine, if information could really replace weapons but will it?

Nao, I seey. Well —

In any case, even the most perfect technology's no proof against human frailty, you know, stupidity, inefficiency, laziness, corruption, greed. D'you know the myth of Prometheus?

Nao. Something to do with fire isn't it?

Yes. He stole fire from the gods. Let that represent technology. But he forgot to steal the art of governing men. That bit usually gets left out. I'd say fifty percent of those in jobs work at undoing the harm done by the other half to humanity and to themselves, now or earlier. There's a nugget of truth in all myths, but they get corrupted and disintegrate through bad art, you know, verbose epics and dreadful paintings and the sloppy language of all religions and constant reinterpretation.

You lose me there, Oliver. But I can't seey why you're unemployed, with all that omnish knowledge, and an Oxford degreey.

Well, I told you, I fucked it up. Besides, that no longer means what it used to. They all want bright Estuarians now. Well, even Oxford and Cambridge are full of bright Estuarians. And Geordies and Taffies and Paddies and Macs and postcols. That's an excellent thing. Dissolves barriers. For instance I'm sure that now prison-psychologists all talk like the prisoners they'll be less resented and perhaps more helpful. But now it's this toffee-nosed accent that stands against me. It's still accepted in the elderly, because they can't help it and they're on the way out, but not in the young. I belong to a dying species. However, some things one can't change.

You've changed in all that matters, Oliver, and I like you for it. And the family . . . ? I meeyn, do you seey them?

No. I don't like going there. But I see a sister occasionally in London. To keep in remote touch if you know what I mean. But in fact we're all out of touch aren't we? We never talk family, do we? You're the first rough sleeper who's questioning me. Ricky, Pavlova, I spent months with them and know nothing about them. We all plunge into the present. Aggressivities and problems are no longer related to Oedipus and Electra and all that. The family romance is buried. Deeply perhaps but dead, disintegrating. Personal history's dead. I must go.

Oh, not yet, Oliver. If you're tired of talking let's just sit and leaf through the Sundays. You'll be warm.

No, I should be going, Quentin. Erm, she said you weren't to contact her, but I'm pretty sure she never undertook not to barge in on you here.

Jesus! I never . . . But she wouldn't.

Oh no? Double standard don't you know. Men are always accused of it, and that's traditionally true in sexual freedom, but in power-struggles it's not male, it's human. You don't want to push the old luck.

Right. Haow nice of you, Oliver. Naow I knaow I can trust you, not a word to anyone you meeyt, remember?

And especially not Pavlova eh? Of course not. Now she'd come barging in without a moment's hesitation. But I won't meet her now. Or Ricky. He was nice though. And he escaped too, or so it seemed. Thanks Quentin, you're a real brick.

I say Olly, look at that. Unemployment figures shot down to almaost nothing last month! Yet nothing's changed down here on the terrain, what did I tell you? I wonder if they counted us in.

Oh well you know, that's just the latest model in promises, political up-lift, seasonal feelgood factor. The latest buzz-phrase, we're coming out of it and so forth, they must produce statistics to back it. I once saw two different channels give a completely different graphic for the same statistics. It's not that they lie, but it all depends on how and when you apply this or that different parameter, and so on. Well, good luck Quentin. And don't worry, I won't come again. I'm very good at disappearing, at least, so I just learnt.

Don't say that Oliver, if ever you feel you want a chat, well, you knaow what I meeyn.

Disappearing. That's what the government wants after all. Bye.

And he disappears.

What ever happened to Croaky? Seems to be staying at that awful place in Caledonian these days. Never comes here for breakfast anyway. Last time was when he brought that paper. Then he disappeared.

Stay with us. Says the telly.

But the nation doesn't. The gap gets wider and wider.

There's a fat man waffling sausages and gulping tea opposite. Painful to watch. Straight brown wisps that won't stay down. Untalkative fortunately.

And now the snow. Started at five this morning. Woke up half-buried and trudged here through it. Stopped now.

Lahk another cuppa?

The fat man's standing there with the empty mug, hand stretched out. Could but won't.

No thank you. I'm just leaving.

In fact, to get things from the dryer. Risked changing into the jeans just while the corduroys dried, otherwise they remain in the plastic bag. One never knows. That man they got was released. Still, main i.d. was the red balaclava, and this jacket isn't black. Sunday today. They're dry. Change back into them now, there's a woman taking out clothes but she won't mind. Oh well, better change in the loo.

Back into the canteen. Stop in tracks.

At the last table near the wash-and-dry room sits a young man in a red woolly hat, black leatherette jacket and yes, blue jeans. He wears glasses and a freckled face, hair ginger under the red woolly hat. The murderer. No, the other me they're looking for. But it can't be. The man seen on the bench was me.

He's sitting alone at the bottom of the table, surrounded by mugs and dirty plates people left instead of taking them back to the counter. There's a group of men at the top of the table but the benches are otherwise free.

Excuse-me. Do you mind if I sit with you?

Pleeyse yerself. Sa freey countrey.

So they say. I'm called Tek, short for Wojtek.

Aow. Foreign are yer?

No. The family was, long ago. Polish.

Where's that then?

Sorry, forget it. Just call me Tek.

Bu' iss foreign is i?

Not now. But why so national? They used to say, when the Common Market began, that nationalism was now as dead as the religious wars. And look where we are now, religious wars and all. Scholars try to preserve a nugget of cultural difference and presto, it becomes separatism.

Aow yeah?

Not very communicative are you?

Nao.

Do you realise you're dressed exactly like a murderer they're looking for?

Yeah.

You do? You're a strange young man. If you were him you'd change at least the hat. And if not then you should change it anyway, to avoid confusion.

Oo are yoow? Aow d'yer knaow bou' i'?

I read the papers. Nothing much else to do in this life.

Thy arrested mey on Pu'ney 'Eath on Thursdie.

Oh, so you're the one.

Bu' thy releeysed mey. On a gen, gen . . . a jeans test. An friends give me a wa'er-tah' alibah.

Ah. You're lucky with friends.

Thy's no' friends any mooar.

Why? They did you a good turn didn't they?

Yeah. Bu' Pavlaova, weuw er nime's Pauwla bu' shey useter bey a dancer, shey eld a tah' grip on as, I meeyn, mey an Olley, thass the other friend, ee was okie, bu' wey go' fed ap an eskiped. A'leeys' Ah did. Ca' loowse from er in Seufridges. Ee wanted ter bu' mybey ee didn' manage i'.

And now you feel bereft?

Breft? Whass tha'?

Abandoned, lonely.

Ah bandoned er.

But it's tough afterwards eh? What do they call you?

Rickey.

And you can't find a job either?

Ah wiuw termorrer. Wiv the Chrissmus rash an auw. Bu' no' in Seufridges, thass where shey landed erself wahn.

Right. I never saw you here before.

Nao. Wey usuauwy stiyed a' Caledaonian Raoad.

Oh, that one.

An after thy kime wiv the poleeyce to freey mey thy took as to Scrabs Line. Bu' Ah didn' wanter gao there ahther in kise shey turn ap there. An Endon's toow far sao Ah slept aou'. Fackin caol', in the snaow.

I know. I do it all the time. I detest hostels. And we oldies aren't too welcome there.

Aow aold are yer then?

Thirty-four. I know I look older. With the fatigue of this life and this scumblond hair looking grey. Yesterday a young man on a scooter nearly knocked me down as I was about to cross a street, and he shouted Shove over granpa! Gives one a shock. The message apart from the manners.

Yeah, mussdoow.

Anyway the hostels are chiefly for young home-leavers now, except the emergency ones, when it's really cold and they drive round and pick us up.

Thy didn' pick mey ap.

Perhaps they didn't see you. Were you visible?

Dunnao. Deeyp in a dooarwie in Marylebone Igh Streey'. Sao Ah kime ere ter eey'.

Listen Ricky, it's less cold now after the snow, you should take off that red woolly hat, or some other over-zealous fuzz might arrest you again.

Cor, never though o tha'. Ah soomed Ah'd be reecorded lahk, as innocen.

You show a touching faith in police computer-coordination. But if that happened, the no-longer friends couldn't help, could they?

Yeah, yer rah' onlahn.

And tomorrow, buy another woolly hat in a different colour. If you can afford it.

Yeah. Bi' of mintenance left. Ah never though' o that', cheers mister. Ah meeyn Tek. Tek. Fanny nime.

Only half a name. I'm only half a person.

Ain' wey auw.

Like to walk a bit? We can't stay here you know, it's half past nine and they close and clean up between meals. Take that woolly hat off. Shove it away in a pocket.

Yeah, aokie. I' was wauwkin on Pu'ney 'Eath wiv tha' cauwsed auw the trabuw.

And out we go into the snow, pinky with the sodium street lights still on although it's day.

Where toow?

Well, not Hyde Park, too far and that's where that man they're looking for was sitting. D'you know Gladstone Park?

Nao.

There's nowhere much to go to on Sundays is there. Everything's closed. Except these Indian shops. Hey, I'll buy us a couple of nans for el-evenses. D'you know nans?

Nao. Iss foreign staff is i'?

Indian. Very good.

Sie, look a' thaose baldeys in raobes.

Three white and orange bonzes are walking together under the now pale orangey lights.

They're buddhist monks, Ricky, in harmony with the lights and don't they know it.

The monks stop at the same colourful shop, buy some poppadam and walk off.

Thy mass bey freeyzin in them raobes.

I expect thy're wearing British winter woollies underneath.

The snow is thick and soon seeps through into the worn-out combat boots. In fact they're not buddhist bonzes but Western corruptions. The sun-cult.

I like the snow like this don't you, Ricky? All crunchy and scintillating. Nobody around to turn it into sludge.

Yeah. Wiuw bey termorrer thaough, when the craowds turn ap. Where'-s this park then?

Oh, a long way yet, West of Cricklewood Broadway.

Weuw.

He stops.

What is it?

Weuw. Ah daon' wanter wauwk toow far ou' o' the wie.

What way, Ricky? Do we follow a way?

Ah dunnao. Bu' Ah lahk familiah lahk. Then Ah daon ge' los', Ah meeyn Ah can think o' ather thinks.

Such as what?

Ah dunnao. Daon arsk sao many queschuns.

I'm sorry. Look, we're still in Maida Vale, why don't we walk back a bit and cut East across St John's Wood Road to Regent's Park?

Thass posh inni'?

There might be a few posh people later, taking their Sunday walk. But it's very pretty. And it's only in parks one can sit down. And there's a coffee place. If it's open.

We turn.

Ain' the zoow there?

It was. They were talking of closing it down. Several years ago, but perhaps there were all the usual protests and appeals and fund-raising, I don't know what happened.

Yeah. Naobody gaoes ter zoows any mooar. Toow mach lahk as inni'? Animuws, thass as.

How old are you Ricky?

Nahnteeyn. An wasn' Ah ever in work, tha'uw bey yer next wahn waon'i'? Weuw yeah Ah was, after schoow. In a soowpermarke'.

At the cashdesk?

Nao, thass fer wimin. Trandlin a lectric trolley to the sheuves afore aopenin tahm. Bu' then Ah los' i'. Re-engineered, thass wha' Pauwla lahked ter cauwl

You mean the electric trolley now drives itself?

Nao. Ah dunnao, jes feuwa Ah spaose. Bu' Ah'uw fahnd samthink. Termorrer. Wha' wiv Chrissmus camin ap an auw.

So you said. I hope you do. Here's Regent's Park.

There's a roundabout, trafficless, and we cross over into Prince Albert Road, all tall elegant blocks of flats overlooking the park. After a while of silence we turn right onto a bridge over the canal and cross the outer circle road into the park.

I think that's a college on the left. Zoological maybe. Bedford College is further South.

Aow yeah?

Clearly he's not interested in higher education. Clumps of bushes are cushioned in clumps of snow, bare trees branch black and white. The shy morning sun vanishes behind a sudden grey cloud, pale but thick and huge, with a darker one looming, and the snow becomes duller, still dazzling in its sheer whiteness but no longer achingly scintillating. Just white, untrodden over a large expanse, and even the lanes are hardly visible except as lower snow, sunk into the higher surfaces on either side. Steps don't even reveal the black macadam below. We're treading virgin soil. It's a pleasurable experience. We reach the lake. And the tea-chalet, with snow-drifted wooden tables and benches outside. Whitely closed.

Oh well, I expect it only opens in the afternoons.

An Ah ain' stiyin araoun' tiuw then Ah can teuw yer.

No, of course not.

The conversation lags, as if switched off with the pale sun. Why did I pick him up? A murderer lookalike, I thought. An elderly couple passes us slowly on an early morning constitutional. A brisk young man with a push-seat and a child asleep. Otherwise posh London isn't awake yet. Eerie in this snow. And now I'll never get rid of him, no excuses on Sunday, no job-or-girocentres. Though in fact he seems to be regretting it too. Let him think up an excuse, he's young, with a lying imagination still active. But then I felt much the same about that old man, Ulysses. I let him down. Never turned up at Scrubs Lane as I promised. Well, said. Saying isn't a performative.

Ricky stops. I stop, raising eyebrows at him, probably like a schoolmaster.

Ah think Ah'uw bey orf naow. Cheers.

But I gaze at him, visibly waiting for the excuse. He hesitates. There isn't one so I ask why.

Fuckin generaishun gap.

Silent lunge where heart is.

Congratulations Ricky.

The chin drops in surprise.

For frankness. I was expecting some lame excuse. That's the nicest way of saying you were bored. Here, take the other nan for elevenses.

Yeah, cheers, weuw, tara.

He turns and walks back the way we came, following the footsteps we made and the tracks of the push-seat in the lane. There are few enough, but he'll find the way back to Maida Vale all right. A very alienating second self. Those congratulations were uncontrollably acid. Probably he didn't notice. The black jacket, blue jeans and ginger head are getting smaller and smaller. But he takes out the red woolly hat from a pocket and puts it on again. As a gesture. Tara.

On towards the inner circle road

and Queen Mary's Gardens.

not a ghost of a soul around

cross the curving road

No cars parked yet.

Open Air Theatre

for summer, used to be fun

Ariel among trees on a mound

vanishing in a dying spotlight.

With mum and dad.

The gardens are smaller, artificial, built up in hillocks and daleocks and tiny bridges

under the snow.

And the rose-gardens.

Dead white.

Benches eiderdowned.

Nowhere to sit.

Bad idea. Only point of parks is benches.

Eat the nan now,

too greasy to carry.

Another long day to get through

and then another short night.

That nan and chicken korla story.

Poor Ulysses. Let him down.

He was okay, trusting.

Trouble is inside.

In the brain

neuro-unplasticity

in the grey white day

piezo-electric

piezo meaning pressure

brain-cells swarming like people

brown grey white

but there's no-one around.

All asleep still

or late-breakfasting over their Sunday wads.

Better get out of this dead benchless park

back towards the familiah lahk

dixit Ricky

to think of other things.

Such as? Dunnao, daon arsk sao many queschuns.

How true.

Why ask why?

They must be happier that way.

Yet questions,

from the few of us who can still think a bit,

if it can be called thinking,

are all that's left to us

the only capital

so soon eroded

from whys to whines

of lowpercentile interest

      as we loaf the streets

    in this wornout supposed serial-killer chic.

Here's a bin.

    Take out Montaigne and dump, too heavy to lug.

Parce que c'estoit luy; parce que c'estoit moy.

        So what?

    Farewell, friendship.

        Disbelieving modern myths.

Those who believe in their myths providing they know them to

be untrue, that's one definition of culture.

    And culture-shock is only a clash of the rules people live by.

    Like moving to a different country called Streetland

where faces are like cerebral images from a scanner

    grubgrey ovals with say a yellow blob

    or green and yellow markers

marking what?

    A disturbance.

      Coming up next,

      Allah is great but first

      we'll take a break

    to learn how not to kill those whose existence we

    refuse to recognize.

Peace Prize winners seldom bring peace

the recognition being insufficient

    merely political.

    Et nous, les petits, les obscurs, les sans grade

taking permanent breaks

  into rehab units

   detox programmes

    Jobcentres

     foodcentres

      emergency shelters

doorways: thresholds of poverty.

        That nan lies greasily on the duodenum

        a switch-packet of misinfo

        packed with viruses.

Here's the Church Street Market. Pullulating with

people and stalls, took a wrong turn somewhere, too

far South of Maida Vale, damn, now a long walk up.

Foodcentre far away and long ago

         but necessary sometime.

And a sitdown would be welcome.

  Diogenes in his barrel

   his only possession a coat, a stick and a bag of bread.

    Here it's a bag for dry rags to change into.

        and a packaged plastic raincoat to sleep on.

    Did he change his clothes?

  But the barrel wouldn't come amiss

   at night. Against the snow.

         Wouldn't find a carton anyway,

     useless besides,

      not even the stick and the spot remaining dry.

       The dry man outside the soaked one.

Grosvenor Victoria Casino. Dead now.

Marks and Spencer's. A betting-shop.

The repetitive Exchange shops why?

Indian need to change prosperous pounds into

rupees to send home hidden in parcels?

Or the other way round, corrupt rupees into piteous pounds?

Not much traffic, no trucks.

Beginning Maida Vale, haphazard red brick

blocks with still lit up doorways.

Drop-Out at last, re-opened. It's nearly one after all.

Though not hungry after that nan. Still, better eat while it's
available.

Crowded of course.

Croaky's disappeared. Never see him here.

Only strangers.

Where do they all incarnate from?

The doorways seem empty of bundles

round here, compared to the

West End. Yet here they all turn up

Claiming the right to survive.

Telly on as usual, high on the washroom wall.

Nobody watching

or listening in the clamour.

Food a more interesting soap

and each other

at least tempwise.

Stay with us. But they weren't with you in the first place.

TV mag on the bench though. How's Derica doing? Who cares?

Fat woman opposite in a pink woolly hat over grey wisps. Tries to en-gage me in meaningful conversation. Meaningful to her.
About a phonebooth she sleeps in
Smooth and couth I don't think.
Don't you get cramps?
Yes o cauwse. But Ah doow mahraobics in the morning an it soown wears orf. Wha' with all the walking Ah doow.
We all do.
Must stop making these cheer-quenching remarks. Yet I approached Ricky; I approached Ulysses. I approached Elsie.
It can't be a real rest, really.
Wha' is? But at leeyst it's drah.
And what about the glaring white light?
Ah put the aold ead daown on kneeys.
I'm too tall. Couldn't fold myself in three.
Yoow should trah it Mister you'd bey surprised. In this caold it's nahce to bey insand, and awl alaone, not in thaose ostels with all them yang raf-fians.
I agree with you on that.
She seems to be reciting a lesson, as if it were her one topic of conversa-tion, all said many times before. So she uses the phone-booth closed to be alone and as an opening not to be alone.
Ah wonder where Craoakey is. Hey's a friend ah met ere the ather die.
Is he?
For some reason I keep mum. So he came here. For some reason I don't want her to talk about Croaky, to find out I know Croaky, to link me with Croaky at all. He probably talked to her about me. I hate small worlds. If she asks
Whass yer nime?
John.
Ah'm Ivey.
Nice to talk with you Ivy. But I must go.
Whass the arry? It's Sundie.
It's difficult to talk in all this clamour.

Well, wey can wauwk can' wey?
I'm like you Ivy, I like to walk alone.
She can't, after all, live it both ways, lone phone and pattering natter.
She wouldn't keep up with me anyway. Ulysses was slow enough, but at
least interesting as an oldworld well-meaning liberal . . .
Bye then.
Bah bah John, seeyer.

This is how street violence begins. And civil wars.

Great gulfs between people

and hurtful remarks

thoughtlessness

selfishness

Anyone else but a baggy old woman would slug me.

All cumulating through gossip and hearsay he was ever so rude

multiplying among small communities

the more you multiply the more you divide

until resentments pile up, flame out

in small riots, tiny atrocities

manipulated by local chiefs for power

into invasions

massacres

for years to exhaustion

then peace processes

and unquenchable memories

to be sublimated in war memorials, parades,

flags, medals, badges, dead rituals countless

thousands are willing to die for,

ceremonial swords

even nuclear missiles paraded as ceremonial swords

   out of date weapons

   out of date passions

a new superstructure emerging as infrastructures crumble

into hunger and homelessness

                all costing

        billions to repair

                all parties smothering their passions to get

                the billions, warped away into private

                pockets, from the rich countries

        who pay out,

        at the expense of their own welfare, their own poor,

                For prestige and new markets.

        Never mind human rights.

Kant said war is a contribution to culture.

                But we're like the new virtual communities now

                Existing only in some noossphere.

                As nootropics.

        A noo commodity for Wall Street et al

        That transformed citizens into consumers.

                Never mind those who can't consume.

                Yet. They will.

If progress means the disappearance of whole trades

and professions,

        as Elsie recalled,

                then the ultimate answer is fewer polluting

                people on the planet, everywhere, yet there are

more and more,

a plague of humans upon virgin forests,

needed, of course, as future consumers.

But if I think that, I should be the first to take myself off it.

On and on up Kilburn High

with its small shops closed.

Sainsbury.

NatWest Bank.

Bank of Ireland.

Headline says unemployment down to almost nothing.

Crude pixelated graphics

great coloured towers of pure info

blue red yellow

like those highrise tenements on the left.

Safeway on the right.

Granada.

State Kilburn Bingo

All lit up garish

waiting for the Sunday addicts.

McGovern's Free House.

How free? How safe?

Fish and chips. Closed.

Fringewear store.

Railway bridge

Sunrise Foodmart. Open. Empty. Elf.

and the black round arch of Kilburn Station

into Shoot Up Hill.

Burger King.

McDonald's. Open.

People still eating meat-fed herbivores.

Industrial products more and more pretending to be natural.

Scientists spending over a century

mimicking and replacing human muscles.

Result, mass unemployment

and exercise clubs for those still in work.

U for Unemployment

Underclass

Uganda

Ulster.

V for Vukovar

Verdun

Vietnam

Vorkuta

St Vitus dance. Volta.

W for quits

Her parting words.

Waltz

Towards Cricklewood Broadway

Council Estates

Cricklewood Lodge Hotel.

and now the low houses again, black, dirty yellow.

The Wishing Well.

Françoise and her suncult.

With its robes and croziers, banners, sceptres

and other hankerings,

masquerading as seminars.

run by a bald man and a woman with green hair.

In the days when withiting professors

professed withit hallucination.

Oh she was affirmative all right, made me positive all right,

Sero.

Then the dégringolade.

Estate agents. More Indian shops. Open.

The Beacon Bingo Hall

in blue and red lights.

Discount House.

Off-licence.

What licence? No pub-hours now.

Computer firm. Glass door broken and stickyplastered.

Blockbuster Video.

Courts Furniture on the right below the bridge.

Streetlights switched on already. They were hardly off six hours.

Towards the shortest day.

R for Rwanda, rumba.

S for Sabra and Shatila, squaredance, samba.

sectarians, Sarajevo, slowstep

Somme

Sudan

Somalia

Sarabande, sardane,

Smyrna.

Soweto.

Srebrenica.

T for Treblinka

Tienanmen

Tuzla

Tibet

Terrorism

tango, twist, tarantella.

The most murderous century

not that others weren't but there were fewer people.

so that murders and massacres could become

legends and romances

instead of forgettable footage,

since there'll always be idiot adventurers and plunderers

to follow calls for Crusades by the least urban of the Ur bans,

and Jihads, and Ethnic Cleansings.

And fools enough to follow mad leaders and hail and shout

slogans and mime their rituals.

The century, besides,

of the death of God.

In his own image man created him

then felt distaste. Not the other way round,

man couldn't admit the other way round.

The withering of the state,

the collapse of communism,

the corruption of capitalism,

the end of meritocracy, after other ocracies,

the cancerous growth of burocracy, eurocracy;

the end of the nation-state, of ideology, so they say,

though it still misleads

millions.

The end of meganarratives, of all the fictions we live under,

from the divine right of kings to presidents by universal

suffrage with half the nation not voting, from trial

by water to an eye for an eye.

The end of Europe, a fifty-year old child,

brain-damaged from birth,

paralysed,

though disintegrating nations are clamouring

helplessly at its doors.

as if it were adult.

The stifling, the poisoning, the depleting of the planet

though we are the planet.

The end of wars to end wars.

But what if all these end-stories were themselves meganarratives?

Fictions, words? People always want an End, without wanting it.

Stop this millenary declinism

declines usually crumble into creeping rebirths

elsewhere.

Aristotle on happiness

as development of potential

But where?

There seems no next, no story.

Except as Special Effects

on deepdish TV

new openings to the world with two hundred channels

in fact more of the same

ever downmarket

and we're out of it anyway except inside deepdish heads

perhaps it's the being out of it that's half-killing us,

as Ulysses said,

out of the millennium changes all around us, whatever they are,

out of

the reality shows reconstructing sub-judice murders

rapes and sexual molestations into

Hitchcock films. To help the judiciary.

Talk shows, fashion shows, travel shows, late

shows, rockshows, cyberspace shows,

extraterrestrials morphing

into terrestrials

or viceversa

bangbang busters bungees and beepers

or bourgeois tizzies

and sex,

sniggering schoolboy stuff

on and on to the motorway

might as well settle in early

it's nearly five

and quiet

before the trucks are allowed

to count Sunday night as weekday.

So. If the government states

in morphed stats

that we don't exist

Then we don't. Presto!

We disappear.

We're words, we're statistical curves and columns.

Under the straight parallel lines of pinky

orange lights

that lift ahead

into golden parabolic curves:

the motorway.

Arteries, nerves, lines of force,

ventricles of liquid cells.

The city as brain

as World Wide Web.

Here we are at last.

The square arch under the motorway like a huge city gate,

Watergate, Irangate, Surrogate.

Cross.

Climb over the wire fence

into the grass patch as was

now a thick white carpet

round the rectangular concrete tree

that supports the ascending branch

of the superstructure

and sit against it

watching the brain through the brain

activating the nitric oxyde
and later lie
　　dead to the brainworld.
　　　　It's snowing again.
　　　　　　But vertically.
　　　　　　So it should be all right here
　　　　　　Under the motorway.
While Special Effects bring out the millions
　　　　the billions
Les Misérables du monde entier,
　　　　the misled, les embrigadés,
　　　　　　every decade
joining hands
　　　　in a vast brown mass, like a growth, growing, enormous;
　　　　engulfing the globe
　　　　　　to the heavenly music of British Airways ads
　　　　　　with their red and blue hostesses smiling
　　　　　　and their black brown beige swirls of humanity
　　　　　　milling in every variety of native dress
　　　　forming the letters B A in some selected wilderness.
The tens of thousands of Rwandan refugees inundating the road.
　　The dwellers of shantytowns.
　　　　　　The fresques of fantoms on roads all over
pushing and pulling carts and permabulators full
of mattresses, cooking stoves, huge bundles,
　　suitcases,
　　　　infants and grandmothers,

the boat-people,

the prisoners of the Gulag

the Shoa skeletons

the Argentinian Disappeared,

the genocided Indians,

the victims of the long, criminal, careless poisoning

of Holy Mother Russia, her air, her fields and rivers

and arctic seas

after seven decades of unjudicial murders by the millions

the sold or stolen children weaving carpets for one

rupee

the street-kids of Bolivia, Rio,

the legless from landmines long after wars are over,

the uselessly war-dead from everywhere

every year.

FLAME-contorted faces or computer-generated rhinos galloping

through glass galleries

out of the Dream-Machines.

A for Angola. For Armaments Industry. Armenia, Afghanistan,

acid rain. Acid raves.

B for Biafra, Beirut, Bosnia. Burundi.

C for Chechnya, Chernobyl, Colonialism, Corruption.

D for Dachau. For Displaced Persons, deathcamp prisoners

freed by the Allies and kept

in half-life camps for years.

Deforestation. Disinformation.

Everyone displaced, in time, in space, in psyche.

F for Fohrenwald. For Fatwah. In whatever patois. Foxtrot.
K for Katyn, Kielce, Kolyma, Khmer Rouge.
Ku Klux Klan.
L for Lidice, Landsberg, Lop Nor, lambada.
M for Mururoa, Monrovia. Matthausen, Majdanek.
Mambo. Minuet
Morris dance. Mazurka.
Milk above quotas poured, not given away to the
starving in Latin America
or wherever
O for the Wings of a Dove. Oilslicks.
P for Polluting humanity,
Proxy wars like proxénétisme.
Passschendaele.
For polka, polonaise, pavane.
Politicians. The ultimate authors of all our woes.
But unlike authors they don't know us.
Though like authors they can kill us off with impunity,
as I am doing now:
A week's world, in one alphabet, but
QWERTYUIOP
Ten rough-sleepers.
Having accommodated five,
Two with jobs, one with death, another to die soon
perhaps, one with a foot-on-earth
That's about percentilely correct.
R for rocknroll

S for sarabande, sardane.

T for tarantella, tango, twist, twostep, tamouré.

V for volta. St Vitus Dance.

X for xenophobia. Y for Ypres. Z for Zaire.

Y no I?

Irradiation, frontierless.

Imperial mentality.

Ideology, blind as Injustice.

Inefficiency, blind as Ideology.

Z for zoos, thass us.

All the victims rising together as a plague of humans,

holding hands, massing together

invading the cities

the stock exchanges

the transnationals

the television centres

the parlotte parliaments

the cabinets, commissions, chancelleries, corporations,

till the cheating, gypping, fiddling, diddling stops, among

the mafias, the traffickers, the laundering banks.

They'll swarm all over them like braincells

piezoelectric, for pressure

brown, grey, white

for years, for months

for weeks

days

hours

(Is there a life before death?)

       under the lullaby of trucks

         as the snow, thickening fast, the now slanting snow,

                greypinkly eiderdowns him over,

          for hours,

       as he digests the nan and sausages,

until he is invisible, unpickupable, perhaps,

                 into a deep sleep

out of time,

         to be debriefed by eternity

                  but with no next.

We'll take a break now. Stay with them.